Upon a dais shroude[...]
a worm-eaten throne, a[...]
of armor. The plate ma[...]
once-bright metal was b[...]
fringed the purple cloak [...]
The tasseled helmet drooped forward. Only the faint lights flickering in the helmet's eye slits betrayed the fact that something lurked within that fire-blasted metal skin.

"On your knees," Azrael said, and the skeletal guard forced Gesmas to the dirty stones. The dwarf turned to the throne and bowed with overstated deference. "As you commanded, great lord, I have brought you the stranger."

The banshees ceased their keening and turned to the dais. Their faces grew even more horrible with anticipation. The skeletal warrior, Soth's loyal retainer of old, seemed to share their anxiety. Gesmas felt its bony fingers tighten on his shoulders.

Finally, Soth stirred upon his dilapidated throne. The twin flickers of orange light that were his eyes flared. Or perhaps the hall grew suddenly darker. All heat, all hope, drained from the room. It was as if those things flowed into Soth, fuel for his terrible gaze.

"Tell me my story," Soth said to the prisoner. "Tell me who I am and how I came to this place."

Ravenloft is a netherworld of evil, a place of darkness that can be reached from any world. Escape is a different matter entirely. The unlucky who stumble into the Dark Domains find themselves trapped in lands filled with vampires, werebeasts, and worse.

Each novel in this series is a complete story in itself, revealing the chilling tales of the beleaguered heroes and powerful evil lords who populate the Dark Domains.

Ravenloft

Vampire of the Mists
Christie Golden

Knight of the Black Rose
James Lowder

Dance of the Dead
Christie Golden

Heart of Midnight
J. Robert King

I, Strahd
P. N. Elrod

Tales of Ravenloft
Edited by Brian Thomsen

Lord of the Necropolis
Gene DeWeese

Shadowborn
William W. Connors
and Carrie A. Bebris

**I, Strahd:
The War Against Azalin**
P. N. Elrod

Ravenloft

Spectre of the Black Rose

JAMES LOWDER
& VORONICA WHITNEY-ROBINSON

SPECTRE OF THE BLACK ROSE

©1999 TSR, Inc.
All Rights Reserved.

All characters in this book are fictitious. Any resemblance to actual persons, living or dead, is purely coincidental.

This book is protected under the copyright laws of the United States of America. Any reproduction or other unauthorized use of the material or artwork contained herein is prohibited without the express written permission of TSR, Inc.

Distributed to the toy and hobby trade by regional distributors.

Distributed worldwide by Wizards of the Coast, Inc. and regional distributors.

Cover art by Kevin McAnn.
Ravenloft and the TSR logo are registered trademarks owned by TSR, Inc.
All TSR characters, character names, and the distinctive likenesses thereof are trademarks owned by TSR, Inc.

TSR, Inc. is a subsidiary of Wizards of the Coast, Inc.

Excerpt from "Little Gidding" in FOUR QUARTETS, Copyright 1943 by T. S. Eliot and renewed 1971 by Esme Valerie Eliot, reprinted by permission of Harcourt Brace & Company.

First Printing: March 1999
Printed in the United States of America.
Library of Congress Catalog Card Number: 98-85786

9 8 7 6 5 4 3 2 1

21333XXX1501

ISBN: 0-7869-1333-9

U. S., Canada, Asia,
Pacific & Latin America
Wizards of the Coast, Inc.
P.O. Box 707
Renton, WA 98057-0707
+1-800-324-6496

EUROPEAN HEADQUARTERS
Wizards of the Coast, Belgium
P.B. 2031
2600 Berchem
+32-70-23-32-77

Visit our website at **www.tsr.com**

To Sid and Dorie Davidson,
for support and encouragement
and Griffin-tending beyond the call of duty.

–JDL

To Jim, who dragged me into the darkling world.
And for Roderic, my husband and my own dark knight,
whom I love without measure.

–VWR

And last, the rending pain of re-enactment
    Of all that you have done, and been; the shame
    Of motives late revealed, and the awareness
Of things ill done and done to others' harm
    Which once you took for exercise of virtue.
    Then fools' approval stings, and honour stains.

                    T.S. Eliot, "Little Gidding"

ONE

The story of Lord Soth brought Gesmas Malaturno to Sithicus. Like most travelers who entered that spectre-haunted land, he became entangled in the tale of the thrice-cursed knight in ways more awful than even he could conceive. This was no mean claim, for Gesmas was a man of substantial imagination.

A talent for recognizing corners where others saw only solid walls had manifested early in Gesmas. Not long from the nursery, he envisioned a system of hillside terraces that tripled the output of his father's failing vineyard. His family considered such flashes of inspiration adequate compensation for the twisted leg with which the boy had been afflicted. Gesmas questioned neither the crippled limb nor the sudden, unexpected turns of thought that rendered the world so lucid. He understood neither, but recognized that both, in their own fashion, served him rather well.

The twisted leg saved him, some three years before he entered Lord Soth's domain, from conscription into Malocchio Aderre's forces as an infantryman. This often-terminal fate was one shared by many of Gesmas's fellow rustics. They bore the suffering wrought by his ambitious campaigns against both the rebellious factions within Invidia, led by his deposed mother, and the armies of the powerful lords that surrounded his thickly forested demesne. In this, if in nothing else, Aderre saw eye to eye with the grim and mysterious tyrants who ruled those neighboring states—Alfred Timothy of Verbrek and poison-lipped Ivana Boritsi of Borca, Count Strahd von Zarovich, butcher of Barovia, and, most enigmatic of all, Lord Soth of Sithicus. To them, peasants were nothing more than specie, coin to be spent in whatever fashion they saw fit.

The same inability to serve should have put a noose around Gesmas's neck and left him dangling as a warning for all who failed to embody Lord Aderre's spirit of vigorous conquest. The press gang who had declared him unworthy as a foot soldier got as far as readying a rope. When they scanned the crossroads where they had mustered the locals for review, they found not a single tree suitable for the display of a corpse. As the soldiers stupidly prodded the low scrub at the road's edge, as if that might uncover some tall and thick-limbed oak concealed there, Gesmas was graced with an insight that saved his life.

The solution came to him simply, but without any explanation as to why it was ideal. In those moments it was as if his mind observed the world on its own, processing details at improbable speed, then offered up an idea quite independent of Gesmas's conscious mind. Should Gesmas pause to examine it too carefully, to question its general logic, the answer would lose its clarity and he would be unable to put it into words. Only later, after he had presented the solution and the brilliance of it had become obvious, could Gesmas examine the weave and warp of its making. Such was the case with his escape from the hangman's noose.

It was obvious to all that the press gang's captain was impatient to conclude his business at the Malaturno Estate and reach the nearest town before nightfall. His nervousness had sound cause. Some growers whispered of werewolves hunting in the nearby Mantle Woods. The soldiers spoke of still more terrible creatures stalking the banks of the Gundar River after sunset. Gesmas suspected that both were correct. He knew with certainty that the gang would not enjoy the relative safety of the village of Valetta should they dawdle at the crossroads much longer.

"I have an idea," Gesmas said to the captain. "It will help you."

The captain, whose name was Dandret, gaped down from his saddle. It wasn't obvious in his expression if he were shocked at what Gesmas had said, or just startled that the doomed man had spoken at all, particularly to him. It didn't matter. His reaction would have been the same either way. He lashed out with his riding crop.

The blow spun Gesmas around. The young man turned back to the captain, a swiftly purpling welt running from his temple to the very tip of his chin. He could feel blood trickling from his split lip, but didn't wipe it away. Better to let the officer see that he was injured. He would seem defenseless.

"I can save your life," Gesmas noted calmly. He hobbled a step closer on his twisted leg. "Please listen, or you're not going to make it to the village tonight."

"That almost sounds like a threat. You're in no position to threaten, dead man," Captain Dandret said. A thick backwoods accent blunted every word, betraying the man's humble origins in the foothills of the Ghost Spires. "You can't take us all on, and that rabble certainly won't help you."

Dandret gestured over his shoulder at the two dozen spectators loitering nearby, his disdain for them demonstrated in the way he presented the crowd his unguarded back right along with another loudly voiced insult: "Gutless lowlife, the lot of them."

Gesmas knew everyone in the crowd: his evil-tempered older brother, a few breathless children who'd run all the way from the neighboring farm, a small mob of sun-addled pickers indentured to the family estate. One of his dogs was there, too, the only creature that seemed at all melancholy about the impending death. His parents hadn't even protested the execution beyond returning to work once sentence was pronounced. Neither had they denied the spectacle to the servants, who watched the proceedings with the not-so-secret joy of the downtrodden. They welcomed any strife that suggested the Fates frowned upon the wealthy as deeply as they frowned upon the poor.

Gesmas recognized their silent delight, but what he said to the captain was: "They fear you too much to raise a fist against you, against a soldier of your *reputation*."

Gesmas could almost hear the last word chime happily against Dandret's ego, and the sound of it roused the soldier's interest in the young man. Gesmas, of course, had never heard of Dandret before today. The leaders of these press gangs were only slightly longer-lived than the infantrymen they collected. But everything about this man declared his sense of self-importance, from the stiff and imperious way he sat on his horse to the careful patching of his hand-me-down uniform. A brighter fellow might have recognized Gesmas's words as an obvious prelude to flattery. A brighter fellow also would have realized that no amount of grooming will make a plow horse appear to be a destrier.

The captain yanked his reins sharply, trying to position himself between the young man and the setting sun. If they knew his reputation here, he intended to play it for full effect, blot out the light like a hero from one of the hill tales his father used to tell. But his nag wouldn't cooperate, couldn't make the turn in military fashion. By the time horse and rider slogged a circle back to Gesmas, the moment was lost. Dandret settled for a spot a few paces off his starting point. "Well," he said irritably. "Out with it."

"Drag me," Gesmas said.

That was the solution that had appeared to him, the one he presumed would extricate him from this grim situation. Gesmas did not know how, precisely, but he had faith that it would. Now that he had given it voice, he could only watch the crowd's reaction to that simple suggestion.

Captain Dandret stared for a moment, waiting for the young man to offer more details. Gesmas remained silent. For an instant it appeared that Dandret was going to lash out again, as was his wont when confused. Fortunately, the gang's sergeant deflected his attention by blurting out a question: "Uh, drag him where?"

"That's obvious. Drag him wherever it is we're going," one of the other soldiers supplied. "Instead of hanging him."

The press gang and the spectators had moved close, forming a rough semicircle around Gesmas and Dandret. The pickers nodded slowly as they discussed the proposal. "It's practical," one drawled. "They would be here all night throwing together a gallows, since they won't find a hanging tree anywhere near the road, not for a long ride in any direction."

"Why's that?" a soldier asked.

The worker deferentially cast his eyes down when answering. "Why, the growers cut down whatever's near the road, sir. The felled trees are easy to drag to their estates."

The sergeant rubbed his chin, a great block of bone and beard stubble. He had obviously finished mulling over the idea. "He's mad, frightened stupid at the thought of dying."

"So why suggest a worse way to go?" the captain said, more to himself than anyone else. He scowled a bit as he examined Gesmas's proposal, testing it for flaws or hidden hazards. Of course he could find none. That was the point: the offer was flawlessly simple, a perfect solution to the press gang's problem. More to the point, it was selfless, something Dandret couldn't comprehend.

The sergeant unslung the noose from his shoulder. "Why are you even listening to him, Captain? The law says it's gotta be death by rope for traitors."

"Use the rope to drag him," one of the neighbor children noted helpfully.

"Just kill him. He's trying to trick you," snapped Fayard, who Gesmas had the misfortune of calling brother. The sound of his hate-filled voice was enough to cause Gesmas's hound to growl and slink to a roadside ditch for safety. "Everyone thinks he's possessed, the way he comes up with those strange ideas." He shoved one of the pickers. "Go on, tell them."

The young woman mumbled something that could have been either a confirmation or a denial of Fayard's claim. The captain took it as the former. He could understand and accept possession far faster than he could an unselfish offer from a prisoner. "I've heard enough. We'll take him to the village tonight and pass him along to the Inquest. They'll figure out what's wrong with him and deal with the problem appropriately."

The sergeant groaned. "Kill him here. Drag him all the way to Karina, if that's what he wants. But keep us away from the Lord's Inquest. I don't like that lot even knowing my name, let alone having to see those awful faces when I testify."

The rest of the press gang proffered their opinions, as did Fayard and a few of the pickers. Gesmas maintained his silence. The suggestion had worked its magic, transfigured the scene as completely as an alchemist turning lead into gold. For the strange offer to continue to arouse Dandret's paranoia, though, Gesmas knew he had to hold his tongue. It was a wise move, as the scene at the crossroads had not yet played itself out.

The captain finally shouted the debate to a close. His sergeant, though, would not let the issue die. He shook the noose at Dandret and shouted, "These yokels are making a fool of you! If we don't do our duty and kill this dimwit, we'll be the butt of every barracks joke from now until the harvest."

Dandret didn't respond, only stared in utter bafflement at his underling. The sergeant misinterpreted that confused quiet as an abdication of command. Rope in hand and a murderous gleam in his eyes, he turned toward Gesmas. He took a step forward, gasped, then toppled face first into the dirt.

Captain Dandret motioned for one of the other soldiers to retrieve his throwing knife, which was planted almost to the hilt in the sergeant's back. "The prisoner will ride the free horse," Dandret said as he tucked the knife back into a boot sheath, taking exaggerated care not to nick the polished leather. "Tie the sergeant to the trailing horse. We'll test out this dragging idea on the way to Valetta."

So it was that Gesmas escaped the hangman's noose and left the Malaturno Estate. His hound followed at a run, dodging rocks hurled by Fayard, who didn't have the nerve to throw them at the riders. The faithful mongrel had nearly run itself to death by the time the press gang reached the little village of Valetta. It had opportunity to recover, camped dutifully outside the one-room jail where Gesmas awaited the arrival of the Inquest.

The four judges of the Inquest made an irregular circuit of Invidia, from the Vulpwood in the northwest to the Mantle Woods in the southeast and back again. They took testimony in cases involving treason, sorcery, and any incident pertaining to the wandering bands of thieves and fortunetellers known collectively as the Vistani. The Inquest arrived at midnight wherever it went. The quartet of wagons that made up the somber caravan were always gone before dawn. A month usually separated their visits to any particular village, though a pressing matter would draw them immediately. Gesmas obviously met whatever criteria the judges set for importance. The Inquest arrived that very same night to interrogate him.

The trial was brief. In nearly total darkness, Captain Dandret, a few of the soldiers, and finally Gesmas himself addressed the Inquest. The judges lingered in the jail's shadow-sealed corners, asking only a few questions, in voices that were strangely and disturbingly uniform. Only once, at the trial's conclusion, did Gesmas glimpse a face—eyeless, earless, its nose a small pair of gashes positioned over the larger, mobile gash of a mouth. "Service," that mouth said. The three other judges confirmed the sentence in exactly the same voice, the same grim tone, like echoes from the darkness.

It was one of only two sentences proscribed by the Inquest, and far more rare than the other: Death. The judges recognized Gesmas's talent for what it was, and recognized, too, its potential value to Lord Aderre. Captain Dandret was ordered to escort Gesmas to Loupet Castle, where the young man would become an advisor to Invidia's master.

So it came to pass that Gesmas cheated death and entered the service of Lord Aderre as a trusted envoy—the polite title for a spy. By year's end Gesmas had traveled more widely than anyone he knew and had seen wondrous and terrible things that plagued him only now and then as night terrors. He had wandered the decaying halls of Castle Tristenoira and gazed at the beast that dwells below that haunted keep in the Lake of Red Tears. His throat had been encircled by the mismatched hands of the flesh golem known only as Adam, and he had broken bread with the three hags of Tepest, whose guests often reposed *on* the weird women's table rather than at it.

Gesmas had been saved more than once by those flashes of insight, which Lord Aderre had taught him to read more carefully. He lacked any significant control over the timing of his visions, but quite often they revealed some scrap of truth about the strange lands and frightening individuals he encountered in the service of Invidia's master. So it was, until he entered Sithicus.

From the moment he crossed the border, Lord Soth's domain confounded Gesmas. In the few days he ranged the forest-choked land, searching for the origins of its mysterious lord, he made one wrong decision after another. His worst mistake occurred at a broken-down inn called the Iron Warden. The owner of that slouching two-story ruin came alarmingly close to tricking the spy into taking possession of the inn's deed—a virtual death sentence, as Lord Soth himself used the place to recruit unwitting generals for his skirmishes with the feral elves of the Iron Hills. Gesmas's instincts had encouraged him to trust the innkeep. Only the premature gloating of the man's mistress, deep in her cups, raving about the atrocities the elves would inflict upon "the new Iron Warden," saved him at the last instant from the trap.

Now, as he made his way back to Invidia through a deepening twilight, Gesmas wondered if he had finally exhausted his gift. At the very least, he had used up his interest in espionage. There was no more joy to be had in subverting Invidia's enemies. He thought about resigning his post, taking up the work for which he had long known himself to be best suited. But Lord Aderre would never allow Gesmas to become master of the hounds for Loupet Castle or any other estate. Aderre found the spy's tenderness for beasts amusing. He laughed aloud when Gesmas wept over the death of his faithful hound, which had lost its will to live during one of its master's long absences from the keep.

"Astounding," Aderre had said. "You've cut men's throats and cared only for the blood they spilled on your jacket, yet a dog's death makes you wail like an abandoned child. You're better suited to the work I've given you, Gesmas. Be glad for it."

No, Gesmas decided bitterly as he topped a rise in the narrow road, if Lord Aderre wants me to wear a spy's cloak, I'll never convince him to let me exchange it for another.

The rutted path wound down into a valley, meeting up with a rough stone bridge. Beyond the arch, which spanned a reed-choked offshoot of the Musarde called the Widow's Tears by the locals, lay the border. Gesmas cursed softly. Something was standing in the middle of the bridge.

The failing light made it difficult to see clearly, and Gesmas first mistook the thing for an animal—a small bear or a boar, perhaps. The beast would clear out of the way as the horse got closer, he guessed, but he drew his sword just in case. As he reached the bottom of the hill, he saw that the figure stood on two legs. At fifty yards, it was clear that the figure was too short to be a man or elf, too broad and bulky to be a child. A dwarf, then.

"Oh no," Gesmas whispered. "Azrael."

He reined in the horse sharply. It reared, nearly throwing him from the saddle. The elaborate brace forged for Gesmas by the smith of Loupet Castle made it easier for him to ride, but it couldn't completely compensate for his twisted leg. As he fought to bring the mount back under control, Gesmas lost his sword. He didn't pause to retrieve it. The blade would do him no good, not against Azrael.

"Give up," the dwarf shouted from the bridge. "There's nowhere to run."

The woods were too thick on either side for a mounted man to ride more than a stone's throw before being blinded or knocked senseless by a low branch. The best option, Gesmas thought, was to race back up the road, to put enough distance between himself and the dwarf to dismount, then to duck into the forest on foot. With a little luck he could later reach the border along the banks of the Musarde or some half-forgotten woodsman's path. Passing from Sithicus to Invidia would place him beyond the reach of the darkest magic employed by Lord Soth. The minions of that mysterious tyrant would hesitate as well before crossing in pursuit, for fear of drawing the personal attention of Malocchio Aderre.

Gesmas wheeled the horse about and spurred it to a gallop.

With the clomping of his mount's hooves, the clatter of his tack and his leg brace, and the near-deafening thunder of his own heart filling his ears, Gesmas shouldn't have been able to hear the other riders—but he did.

The approaching hoofbeats thudded across the valley like the slamming of coffin lids. Their terrible sound heralded the arrival of two horsemen, who appeared atop the rise just as Gesmas started up the hill. The world seemed to slow, time itself shuddering to a halt at the sight of the twin horrors. Fleshless hands curled around the reins of horses that shook off wormy clots of meat with each step. Armor that seemed more tarnish than metal clattered against bare ribs. Open-faced helmets framed visages of bone. Their mouths gaped wide in mirthless, rictus grins.

Gesmas did not need to turn his horse again to direct its retreat from the skeletal horsemen. The animal wheeled on its own. Eyes wide with terror, it barreled back toward the bridge. The riders followed. For all their preternatural slowness, they somehow gained ground on the spy quickly.

Given a choice, Gesmas would have faced the riders before Azrael. He had a particular dread of creatures like the dwarf—or the thing the dwarf was supposed to be, if the stories he'd heard were to be believed. Malocchio's generals, too, had warned him against tangling with Azrael. He was unpredictable, the sort who might turn a simple act of espionage into an excuse for open warfare.

Gesmas could only hope that the stories were exaggerations, for there was no stopping his horse now. It recognized the stench of the grave emitted by the dead riders.

"Fate favor me," Gesmas said, then kicked his mount into a full charge.

Azrael's iron-shod boots struck sparks from the stones underfoot as he ran to meet the assault. He balled his thick-fingered hands into fists in front of his face. Then his arms went slack, trailing loosely to his sides like broken wings. Claws burst from his fingertips. His heavy-footed gait became more certain, swifter. Fur sprouted in unpleasant gray-and-black tufts from his face and bare arms. A scream that was equal parts ecstasy and anguish blasted from his lips. The dwarf's entire frame convulsed, the bones of his skull grinding into a new configuration—a terrible mixture of dwarf and giant badger.

The transformation completed itself just as Azrael reached the near end of the bridge. An instant later, horse and rider were upon him.

Gesmas directed his mount's wild flight as best he could, hoping to drive Azrael aside or perhaps even trample him. For the briefest of instants, it appeared that he would escape.

Azrael fell to his back as the horse bore down on him. The mount leapt forward, and Gesmas gasped. The way stood open. The border and safety beckoned at the bridge's far end.

The elation that sight engendered was short-lived. Even as the spy turned his head, hoping to glimpse the battered form of the werebeast, his horse collapsed beneath him. The unfortunate animal screamed once, then crumpled. Gesmas pitched forward. The saddle, its straps somehow sheared, and the saddlebags flew with him. They landed in a snarl at the center of the bridge's span.

As he raised his head from the stones, Gesmas glanced back at his fallen horse. The animal had been split from breastbone to tail. The carcass lay atop Azrael, who struggled to free himself from the grisly tangle. The werebeast's claws were thick with gore, the fur on his monstrous face matted with blood. Azrael expelled a grunt of anger, a horrible sound matched only by the thunder of the approaching skeletal riders.

Gesmas started to crawl. From his wrist, he plucked a small locket. The filigreed silver gleamed softly, just as it had the day Malocchio Aderre had given it to the spy. Now, in his hour of greatest need, Gesmas pressed it to his lips and invoked the charm it carried. "Lord Aderre, aid me!" he called. "I have what you want. I have Soth's history."

He looked to the far end of the bridge. There, shrouded in the gathering gloom, stood Malocchio Aderre. Clad in black, he could have been cut from the darkness itself. He crossed thin arms over his chest impatiently. A breeze stirred his wild mop of black hair, uncovering his eyes for a moment. The dark orbs glittered brightly in a pale white face. "Give it to me," he cried. "Quickly."

Gesmas snatched up the saddlebags, stuffed to bursting with scraps of parchment and folios of notes about the Lord of Sithicus. As the spy raised the satchels above his head, the world went suddenly silent. Azrael's growls and the awful thunder of the dead riders, even the dull murmur of the river—all quieted at the same instant. A soft, unpleasant sound quickly filled the void. It was a voice, as deep and bleak as a bottomless chasm. It shook the soul and froze the blood. Gesmas found himself paralyzed.

"What do you hear?" shouted Malocchio Aderre, but his servant could not answer. The droning of the voice had become a song, a dirge of shattered faith and forsaken love. It was the tale of Lord Soth, sung by the thrice-cursed knight himself.

The words of that dire song gathered along the border, but would not pass beyond. They coalesced into thorny stems that reached high into the sky. With each new verse of Soth's lament, the stems stretched upward, swelling at the tops with tightly closed buds. Then the song grew discordant, the story confused. The orderly row of stems tangled. The thorns tore at each other, and the wounds they left wept thick, viscous tears.

Gesmas felt the song take root in his mind. The melody sent tendrils deep into his thoughts, seeking out memories the spy had carefully walled off. They tapped into his most ghastly deeds, the morbid and horrific reflections that surrounded them, and drank of their vileness.

The urge to expel that poison overwhelmed Gesmas, and he himself began to sing. His crimes—and those of every other soul within the spectre-haunted land—created a dreadful harmony that swelled the buds atop the tangled stems. Finally, when no more voices could be added to the chorus, the flowers opened.

Black roses. Their petals blotted out the sky and filled the world with the fragrance of corruption.

TWO

Countless pairs of hungry, hunting eyes followed the passage of Azrael's open-air carriage as it careened along the road to Nedragaard Keep. Nothing sprang from the night-cloaked forest or slithered up from the noxious mires that bordered the way. The creatures that stalked the Sithican wilds knew the distinctive sound of the dwarf's trap. The two-wheeled carriage was armored in the teeth of Azrael's fallen enemies. Tusks and fangs and molars chattered nervously at every bump in the road, warning away anyone or anything that might mistake Azrael for a common wayfarer.

Not that many travelers frequented the byways of Sithicus. The land's three main cities—Mal-Erek, Hroth, and Har-Thelen—were largely self-sufficient. The elves who inhabited those gray, joyless places shunned trade, even with their own kind. A plague known as the White Fever, which had swept back and forth across the land like a reaper's scythe for more than two decades, only made the cities more insular. That didn't slow the sickness. It ravaged town and farm alike, sometimes carrying off a single soul, sometimes an entire village.

As Azrael's trap hurtled through a crossroads, it encountered one of the more visible signs of the White Fever's presence in Sithicus. The horse's hooves and the studded wheels shattered bones and sent up a cloud of pale, choking dust. The crossroads were white with the sun-bleached remains of plague victims. Even isolated intersections such as this held the scavenger-picked leftovers from a dozen or more corpses. During major outbreaks, so many bodies choked the larger crossroads that their moaning, writhing mass halted all but the heaviest wagons. The ways remained blocked until scrounging animals picked the carcasses down to more easily trampled heaps.

Not long after the plague's arrival in Sithicus, superstitious farmers had initiated the practice of tying the sick and dying at the meeting of two roads. The bodies were staked out with each of their four limbs pointing down a different path, in hopes of confusing the plague spirits that supposedly carried the disease. The more sophisticated townsfolk labeled this practice sheer foolishness. They believed that the White Fever spread by sight, since the victim's eyes bulged grotesquely in the hours before death. The townsfolk, too, left bodies at the crossroads, but they didn't stake them out. They beheaded the afflicted, then bundled the head in a burlap sack and placed it atop the corpse's chest. In recent months, the two groups had adopted each others' safeguards, so that now the dying were beheaded and their remains splayed in four directions.

"I'm the only one to survive it," Azrael said as the trap lurched over a skull. He turned back to grin triumphantly at his captive. Over the grim chattering of the trap, he added, "I fought the White Fever for three years. It finally gave up back in 'thirty-six. The plague has slaughtered hundreds, thousands, but it couldn't kill me."

Gesmas only nodded. Scars on the dwarf's face matched those left by the pustules characteristic of the Fever's second stage. A prolonged battle with the Fever might also explain why Azrael had been described as stooped with age in some of the older stories Gesmas had heard. The disease leeched the color from the flesh and the hair, making the victim look ancient before his time. Two decades ago, when the plague was still obscure, its effects might have been confused with old age.

But Azrael had not told Gesmas about his triumph over the White Fever to clarify his understanding of Sithican history. The story was intended to underscore the hopelessness of his situation. The dwarf was really saying: *If Death itself couldn't best me, what chance does a spy with a twisted leg have?*

The reminder was unnecessary. From the moment Gesmas had come to his senses, he'd recognized the dire nature of his plight. Rust-rimed iron shackles clamped his hands behind his back. A rope looped through a metal ring on the carriage floor bound his feet. He could not stand, could maintain his balance enough to sit up only when Azrael slowed the horse—which had occurred only twice in their dash along the lonely road. When Gesmas managed to survey his surroundings, he found the two dead riders trailing at just the right distance to intercept him should he manage to get free of his shackles and the carriage.

The spy's instincts offered no clever vision of escape. The place had blinded his extra-sight, veiled it like the black moon Nuitari veiled certain stars as it made its way across the night sky. The utterly corrupt could view Nuitari's face. For the rest, the only way to "see" the ebon orb was to seek out what it concealed.

Gesmas stared hard into the velvet dome of the night. The constellations were all strange to him, but after a time he perceived a void where it seemed there should be stars. "Is the moon full tonight?" he asked, knowing that his captor would offer some sort of answer, even if it had nothing to do with his question. Azrael seemed to dislike silence.

"From the things you confessed in the song," the dwarf replied, "you should be able to see for yourself."

Gesmas could still taste the dirge's poison in his mouth, though he couldn't recall anything clearly from the time the song started to the moment he realized he was a prisoner, already miles from the border. "I don't know what you're talking about," he said. "I told you before, I'm no one. Just a bard collecting local stories."

Azrael whipped the horse furiously, though the beast could not have traveled any faster had it been graced with wings. "You'd be better served by a different tale than that," he said. "No bard I've ever met believed himself to be 'no one.' Besides, what storyteller is important enough to make Malocchio Aderre appear with a single shriek for help? I don't really care about that. But what I can't tolerate—" Without warning, the dwarf kicked backward with one foot. The iron-soled boot struck Gesmas in the chest. "I can't tolerate modesty."

Azrael's voice lacked the faintest trace of anger, which unsettled his prisoner even more than the attack. "You confessed to some pretty gruesome deeds," the dwarf continued, as if the conversation were occurring across a cozy dinner table. "There aren't many with your tolerance for bloodshed. I could have used you. Why, I'll wager you've never lost a night's sleep over any of it—the assassinations, the torture . . ."

"I've done nothing I'm ashamed of."

"Who mentioned anything about shame? Pay attention," Azrael said flatly, then kicked Gesmas again. "Shame is even more useless than modesty."

Gesmas groaned and shrank back as far as his shackles would allow. The burning ache in his side told him that the last blow had cracked a rib.

"You should realize that you've put yourself in this sorry position. Calling on Aderre got Soth's attention, which is no small feat these days. What really grabbed his interest is this." Azrael used the butt of his whip to rap the worn saddlebags at his side. The leather satchels still bulged with the notes Gesmas had gathered.

"They're only stories," Gesmas said, wheezing softly from the pain.

"*Only* stories—ha! That's all that matters in Sithicus! Soth has barely moved his armored ass off his throne for fifteen years. All he does is brood about the turns his story has taken. And the more he broods, the more marvelous this place becomes."

Gesmas could hardly agree with Azrael's choice of adjectives to describe the current state of Sithicus. As Soth retreated into his own mind, the domain and its inhabitants suffered greater and greater torments. The White Fever was only the first, most persistent trouble. Within a year of the plague's arrival, the wild elves of the Iron Hills began to stage raids against their civilized kin, sowing chaos for its own sake. Even now, the horizon to the east flickered red from a huge fire; yet another farm on the outskirts of Har-Thelen had fallen to the feral elves.

If the tavern talk Gesmas had heard in his travels was to be believed, a leader had gathered together the Iron Hills bands into an army set on driving Soth from Sithicus. This warlord was known only by a symbol: the White Rose. Some within the domain saw the White Rose as a savior. Most understood that commoners would little concern a warrior powerful enough to threaten Lord

Soth. These wise folk kept to their own business and hoped any war that broke out would be a brief one. Each new day of Soth's neglect undermined those hopes a little more.

The mere presence of Azrael's escort, dead men astride decaying mounts, marked Sithicus as different from all the places Gesmas had explored on his missions for Lord Aderre. Necromancy and creatures that cheated the grave were factors to be countered in all those places. There were wild, disreputable yarns in some of the kingdoms hereabouts that identified a particular nobleman or general, or even the domain's ruler, as a monster— a vampire, werebeast, or sorcerer of the most vile sort. The world, at least according to these macabre tales, was full of malevolent powers and corrupt souls.

Some of these legends were true, though few who knew their veracity lived for long. Enough were obviously false—drunken inventions or misinformation spread by the tyrants themselves—to allow the peasants in most domains to delude themselves about their strange and sinister environs. In Sithicus, though, the unnatural was so conspicuous, so brazen in announcing its existence, that Gesmas wondered how anyone slept at night.

If Azrael were to be believed, the only thing Sithicans truly feared was him. "I'm their only nightmare," he said whenever the conversation touched upon the horrors of the place.

The third time the dwarf offered up that bit of braggadocio, Gesmas couldn't hold his tongue.

"What about the Whispering Beast?" he asked. "Or the Bloody Shoemaker?"

"Cobbler," Azrael corrected with a snarl. "The Bloody Cobbler. They're both bogeymen, children's stories."

Gesmas almost repeated Azrael's own comment about the importance of stories in Sithicus, but thought better of it. It was foolish and unnecessary to provoke a response. The tension in the dwarf's shoulders, his white-knuckled grip on the reins, told the spy that his captor was lying. It was the same sort of fearful reaction the names had provoked in all but the most reckless locals, and even they would not offer much about the creatures beyond a line or two of fractured verse. That the Beast and the Cobbler frightened a thing like Azrael, a bogeyman in his own right, was reason enough for Gesmas to wonder at their power.

Before the prisoner could summon the courage to ask again about the two horrors, Azrael slowed the carriage to a relatively sane speed. Gesmas levered himself to a sitting position. Groaning at the pain from his ribs, he peered out of the trap.

The road here skirted the Great Chasm, so close that the wheels kicked stones into the rift. The vast scar ran for nearly one hundred miles, north to south, through the heart of Sithicus. It gaped as wide as five miles across in some places, narrowing to less than a mile only at its ends. Light wouldn't penetrate the chasm, even when the sun shone directly overhead. Only sickly, leafless trees grew along its perimeter. They thrust up from the earth like sorry scarecrows to warn travelers away from the rift. With good reason.

The darkness of the Great Chasm quivered with excitement at the approach of the trap and the dead riders trailing it. Each hoofbeat sent a ripple across the gloom. The rattle of tusk and fang from Azrael's carriage was answered deep within the murk by a famished gnashing of teeth.

Gesmas noticed none of this, though he was an observant man. His attention had been drawn to a more astonishing sight: Nedragaard Keep.

A peninsula like the cupped hand of a giant turned to stone held aloft Soth's ruined castle. Granite crags rose up on three sides, fingers picketing the keep from the chasm's greedy darkness. The marvel sheltered within that stony grasp resembled a massive stone rose. The domed central tower had been designed to approximate a tightly closed bud. On all sides, lattice-work bridges led from the main keep to landings opened like leaves. But the rose that housed Lord Soth was blighted. The crimson-tinged stones had been blackened by some ancient blaze. The walls had been breached, the bridges and landings shattered.

The longer Gesmas studied the keep, the harder it became to focus on details. A flickering light drew his attention to a window high up in the tower. One moment, the window appeared intact—a huge circle of stained glass lit from within. The next, it was simply gone. Gesmas blinked and rubbed his eyes. He scanned the tower's face. Nothing. It wasn't that the light had gone out in the room, abandoning the window to darkness. The tower itself had changed somehow. He tried to recall the window's exact location, but the castle blurred in his thoughts until he could no longer remember what he'd been trying to do.

The road swept away from the chasm's brink, passing through an elaborate garden and a large graveyard. Time and neglect had obliterated the boundaries between the two. Weeds covered the graves. Climbing roses, their blooms as black as the unseen moon overhead, entangled memorial statues and stormed the walls of crypts long ago robbed of their dead. The wind hissed through trees of overripe fruit. The gusts mixed the tang of a harvest gone to rot with the smothering fume of grave mold.

"Last chance to come up with a better lie about your mission here," Azrael shouted as the carriage passed through a crumbling gatehouse and onto the isthmus that led to the castle. "Soth finds spies annoying, but bards make him angry."

The wind picked up suddenly, shifted to the west. It howled now like an enraged animal—no, carried the howls of something unhinged with fury from within the keep itself.

"Th—that sound," Gesmas stammered. "Is it Soth?"

"You'd better hope not."

An extensive section of the castle's outer curtain and the ground beneath it had slid into the chasm, leaving a break in the isthmus that was now spanned by a wooden bridge. The carriage rattled across the planks and into the bailey. On platforms overlooking the courtyard, a trio of armored dead men kept ceaseless, senseless watch. Gesmas could not imagine what purpose their patrol served. A general would have to be mad to lead an army against Nedragaard.

The sound Gesmas had taken for the howl of a single creature fragmented into several distinct voices. Each member of the unseen chorus proclaimed its outrage in shrieks that echoed in the night:

"He hears us still!"

"He attends us not!"

"The fire-blasted rose has turned inward, away from us, away from his damnation."

"But he will stir, sisters. The first dark in the light's hollow will wake. Once more will he feel our song's lash upon his unbeating heart."

An apparition manifested in the open doorway. The ghostly figure was slim and clad in a flowing gown. Her face was that of an elven maiden, composed with sharp angles that would have been unattractive on a human. On elves, though, the features hinted at a sort of geometric perfection. Gesmas felt a weight on his heart that had nothing to do with his injuries.

"He is here," the apparition announced in a soft voice, so unlike the piercing shrieks that rang through the hall behind her. "It is time."

"It's time when I say so," Azrael snapped. The dwarf walked through the phantom as if it were nothing more than an errant patch of mist.

The face that had been so lovely a moment before was now a mask of fury. The gentle curves and perfect angles were gone, replaced by a riot of sharp teeth. "Eater of dirt!" the banshee wailed. "We will make you suffer!"

"How many of you are there in 'we' today?" asked the dwarf lightly. "Three? Thirteen? Three hundred?" He turned and gestured to Gesmas. "Come on. She, and however many sisters she has at the moment, can't hurt you. They used to be banshees. Soth's inattention has reduced 'em to harmless spooks. There's supposed to be a certain number of 'em, but they can't even decide on how many that should be."

One of the dead riders lay skeletal hands on Gesmas and shoved him through the apparition. The banshee howled her impotent rage at the violation. The sound shook the spy as he passed through. Her chill form clutched at him, trying to seize his living warmth even as it shrank from his coarse physicality. He emerged, breathless and shivering, in an immense entry hall.

Twin stairways climbed the walls of the vast circular room, leading to a balcony opposite the main doors. The balcony might once have been a musicians' gallery. Now the only music in the hall came from the banshees' keening song. The unquiet spirits hovered in midair or wove frenzied patterns through the chandelier suspended from the ceiling's center. All the candles in those triple rings of iron were lit. Their radiance diluted the gloom that choked the hall, but could not vanquish it.

Upon a dais shrouded in the hall's deepest shadows sat a worm-eaten throne, and upon that throne hunched a suit of armor. The plate mail appeared empty, deserted. The once-bright metal was blackened with soot and age. Tatters fringed the purple cloak draped over the armor's shoulders. The tasseled helmet drooped forward. Only the faint lights flickering in the helmet's eye slits betrayed the fact that something lurked within that fire-blasted metal skin.

"On your knees," Azrael said, and the skeletal guard forced Gesmas to the dirty stones. The dwarf turned to the throne and bowed with overstated deference. "As you commanded, mighty lord, I have brought you the stranger."

The banshees ceased their keening and turned to the dais. Their faces grew even more horrible with anticipation. The skeletal warrior, Soth's loyal retainer of old, seemed to share their anxiety. Gesmas felt its bony fingers tighten on his shoulders.

Finally, Soth stirred upon his dilapidated throne. The twin flickers of orange light that were his eyes flared. Or perhaps the hall grew suddenly darker. All heat, all hope, drained from the room. It was as if those things flowed into Soth, fuel for his terrible gaze.

"Speak."

The voice was hollow, deep beyond imagining. Gesmas felt the word more than heard it. He opened his mouth to reply, but only croaked something incomprehensible. The breath had vanished from his lungs. Fear had consumed it.

"Speak!"

Azrael elbowed Gesmas in the side, causing him to cry out. Only the skeletal hands on his shoulders prevented the prisoner from falling forward. "Mighty lord," he wheezed, "I don't know what—"

"Your name," said Soth. "Your mission."

Gesmas could almost feel the sharp corner of Azrael's smirk jabbing him. He knew that the dwarf was waiting for him to trip up, to anger Soth by some misstep he could never avoid. Perhaps Azrael had lied to him about Soth's hatred of bards. The dwarf was, after all, commonly described in Sithicus as an unrivaled liar.

Gesmas had nothing to fall back upon, no secret knowledge or flash of insight to guide him. So he told the truth.

"I am a spy."

A sound echoed from Soth's helmet, a soft exclamation equal parts surprise and mirth. "What have you tried to steal from me, honest thief?"

The second of the skeletal warriors came forward. It held up the spy's worn saddlebags. Azrael tore away the buckles and leather straps holding them closed. Paper cascaded onto the floor. "Mighty lord, he—"

"I did not ask you, seneschal," Soth interrupted.

The banshees sniggered at the rebuke. There were only four now. The rest had disappeared.

"He has returned," said one.

"Returned to his duty," added the second, hovering close by Azrael's side.

"Returned to his torment," a third hissed.

The hideous quartet chorused, "Returned to us."

Soth ignored the unquiet spirits, if he heard them at all. He had focused on Gesmas. "What did you try to steal?" he prompted.

"Your story."

"Who is your master?"

"Malocchio Aderre."

Slowly Soth raised one hand. A thick lace of cobwebs fell away from the gauntlet it had draped for so long. Fingers that had not moved in years gestured stiffly for the prisoner to approach the throne.

Gesmas rose, reclaimed the saddlebags, then gathered up the pages Azrael had scattered. The combination of the pain from his ribs and his fear of Lord Soth swelled into waves of dizziness that washed over the spy every few halting steps. When he came upon a section of floor that appeared translucent, insubstantial, he mistook it for an hallucination born of his lightheadedness. But Azrael grabbed his arm and steered him around it. Gesmas looked questioningly at the dwarf, whose only reply was the same oily smirk he'd worn since arriving at the keep.

As he continued across the hall, Gesmas noted more bits of his surroundings that did not appear entirely corporeal. A large piece of the stone stairs to the right was missing—not crumbled or fallen, simply not there. Other small sections of floor fluctuated between opacity and translucence. Poised over the center of the circular room, the ponderous iron chandelier fluttered like a mirage. The ceiling where the massive metal rings should have been anchored gaped black and vacant. The chains reached up to nothing.

Gesmas gave up trying to understand the strangeness around him. He took in the details of his odd surroundings with an uncharacteristic indifference. It was almost as if he were watching the events unfold from a distance, like one of the inconstant phantoms floating over the hall. That detachment, and little else, made it possible for Gesmas to approach Soth's throne, to stand so close to the death knight that he could discern the original decoration on his fire-blackened armor.

An intricate pattern of roses and kingfishers laced the blasted metal. Dust, soot, and age had obscured some of the blooms, annihilated some of the finer detail on the birds' wings. Still, the design retained enough of its old beauty to suggest the knight so feared, so fearsome, had once known peace and honor.

"Tell me my story," Soth said to the prisoner. "Tell me who I am and how I came to this place."

Gesmas climbed the three broad steps one at a time and set the saddlebags down on the dais. Fragments of broken glass littered the stone, winking like earthbound stars. Only now did the spy note the six iron ovals gaping on the walls behind the throne. Malocchio Aderre himself had warned him about the mirrors once cradled in those frames, enchanted glass that allowed Soth to venture into his own memories and follow his life down the myriad paths it might have followed.

Obviously, the lord of Sithicus no longer needed such things to sustain his reveries.

As he retrieved the first pages from the saddlebags, Gesmas wondered vaguely if Soth's daydreams were any more bizarre than the stories he'd collected. He doubted it.

"I learned this tale from the elves of Hroth," Gesmas said. He squinted at his own scribbled notes and began to read: " 'The thing known as Soth first appeared some thirty-two years ago, in the land of Barovia. As such a powerful being could not have escaped the notice of the bards that wander these haunted realms, he could not have existed before that time. Strahd von Zarovich, lord of Barovia, must have created Soth, conjured him with dark sorcery. This would explain why Soth is never seen but when he is fully armored. In truth, the metal skin is empty, cursed mail that turned against the sorcerer who first brought it to life.' "

"Untrue," the banshees hissed. "Untrue!" There was no conviction in their exclamations, though. Like Soth, they seemed uncertain of the truth.

For a moment Soth considered the claims. "I recall this Strahd von Zarovich," he said, "and know that my way to this cursed realm passed through his demesne. As to the rest, it is easy enough to prove or disprove. . . ."

Soth slipped his gauntlet forward, exposing the slightest sliver of his wrist. Gesmas did not get a clear look, though the little he saw of the strangely corroded flesh told him that the lord of Nedragaard could be no living thing.

"Ah," said Soth. "There can be no question that I am more than just a hollow metal skin. What other tales do my people tell of me?"

For several hours Gesmas related all that he had learned. Most of the stories were obviously false, easily disproved in Soth's grim presence. The banshees both supported and refuted the very same claims. Sometimes the phantoms contradicted each other, sometimes even themselves. Azrael remained silent, though Gesmas could not help but notice the dwarf squirming uncomfortably whenever his master displayed any interest in the tales.

A few similar reports drew the most attentive responses from Soth. These stories claimed the lord of Nedragaard Keep had come from a land far from Barovia or Sithicus, a place called Krynn. In that kingdom of light and hope Soth had perpetrated some terrible crime—the slaughter of his brother and sister, the assassination of a saintly cleric, even the destruction of the gods themselves. The tales could not agree upon which acts were true, which merely fiction, but all seemed to conclude that Soth's infamous deeds had cursed him with an eternity of unlife.

From time to time as Gesmas spoke, banshees would vanish and appear, their sum as changeable as their ghostly frames. During the stories of Soth's supposed past in Krynn, however, the banshees always numbered thirteen.

His voice little more than a hoarse whisper, Gesmas came to the last of the tales he had collected. It told of Soth's passion for an elf maid named Isolde, a passion so intense that it inspired the once-noble knight to betray both his marriage vows and the chivalric order to which he had dedicated his life. Disaster and disgrace followed, with the murder of Soth's wife and expulsion from the knighthood he so loved. As was so often the case in tales of unbridled appetite, the ending proved tragic.

" 'Lord Soth confronted fair Isolde in the main hall,' " Gesmas read wearily. " 'That he would come to accuse her of infidelity should have been little surprise, for surely no man can trust once he himself has broken sacred vows. At the same moment as he gave voice to his jealous fury, a tremor rocked the castle and the triple-ringed chandelier crashed to the floor. Fire swept the hall, trapping—' "

A thunderous clatter rang out. Gesmas gasped and dropped the tattered parchment. He turned to find that the chandelier had fallen. It lay twisted upon the cold stone flags. Above the debris hovered thirteen silent banshees. Thirteen skeletal warriors stood at attention around the fallen iron rings. Their grinning faces seemed to flicker crimson, illumined by some blaze all out of proportion with the few guttering candles scattered about.

"Trapping Isolde and the infant she clutched in her milk-white hands," said a sepulchral voice. Slowly Soth rose to his feet. The cobwebs fell from him like a rotted winding sheet. The lord of Sithicus was not reading the spy's report, but speaking an uncorrupted memory.

"The gods, ever merciful, left the once-famed knight a chance to prove his heart held something more than hatred," Soth continued. "From the flames, the elf maid begged for him to save their son. But his anger and his pride would not allow him to act. He turned away and let them perish."

As Soth completed his recitation, the banshees began a song yet again. Only now their terrible voices sang as one

"And in the climate of dreams
When you recall her, when the world of the dream expands, wavers in light,
when you stand at the edge of blessedness and sun,

Then we shall make you remember,
shall make you live again
through the long denial of body."

Azrael grabbed Gesmas roughly by the arm. "Who gave you this tale?"

The banshees' song, which continued to catalogue Soth's crimes, made it hard for Gesmas to think. "I—I can't remember." He fell to one knee, his twisted leg jutting painfully to one side. Frantically he rifled through the fallen pages in search of the one that held the final tale. "There were so many stories . . ."

"The Wanderers," Soth said. "Only they know my true history."

Azrael's smirk was gone. He licked his lips nervously, then said, "Do not tax yourself, mighty lord.

If you suspect Magda's thieves of betraying you, I can deal—"

"No. I have slumbered too long, forgotten too much of myself." Soth flexed his gauntleted fingers, then tightened them into fists. "It is time I take back the reins of my fate."

The death knight descended the stone steps. He surveyed the hall's disorder—the missing stairs, the oddly insubstantial sections of floor. "I will call upon Magda and her tribe come sunrise," Soth announced over the banshees' keening.

"And I will dispose of the prisoner," Azrael offered. "There is still some room in the dungeons for—"

"No," Soth snapped. "He will be put to work in the mines." He turned his glowing eyes on the spy. "Consider that a reward, honest thief. You may yet live a while there. My thanks for delivering these . . . entertainments."

Two of the skeletal soldiers approached the dais and took hold of Gesmas. "Have the dungeons emptied, as well," the spy heard Soth order. "Ransom any nobles or merchants. Put the rest to work until they can buy their own freedom. That is how a knight treats his prisoners, Azrael. Take note."

Gesmas felt Lord Soth's unblinking gaze follow him across the hall. "No ransom for you, though, honest thief," Soth noted as the spy passed close. "I have not forgotten who you serve."

In the rubble-strewn bailey of Nedragaard Keep, Gesmas watched the night dwindle.

Exhausted, numb with fear and pain, he stared at the horizon and waited for dawn to break. But the darkness was reluctant to lose its grip on the land. By the time the skeletal warriors had carried out Soth's orders to empty the prisoners from the dungeon, Gesmas had begun to wonder if the light would ever return to Sithicus.

A heavy wagon arrived just as the last of the filthy wretches was herded into the bailey. A trio of gruff, well-armed soldiers took command of the prisoners without a word being spoken, an order given. Whatever arcane means Soth had used to summon the transport must have conveyed his wishes to the drivers, as well.

Gesmas was the first into the wagon. Those prisoners able to walk crowded in after him, forcing him to the back of the box, as far as possible from the single barred window in the door. The invalids were stacked onto the floor like cord wood. The stink of excrement from these ragged men made the gorge rise in the spy's throat. Their weeping, festering wounds—the obvious result of lash and rack and other, more exotic devices— made Gesmas glad that Azrael's plans for him had been undone.

One of the three soldiers entered the wagon and closed the door behind him. There was no threat of revolt; the prisoners either stared at the armed man with wild, unfocused eyes or averted their faces whenever he looked their way. No one spoke as the wagon lurched into motion. Gesmas wondered if they had all lost their tongues—until he realized that most were likely deaf from months or years of exposure to the banshees' shrieking.

Once the bedlam of Nedragaard receded, the steady tread of the horses began to sooth Gesmas. It seemed that his truthfulness had saved him after all. He was out of Azrael's grasp, going to a place where he would have a chance to keep himself alive. Work in the mines would be hard, maybe fatal, but he might live long enough to escape. His leg would disqualify him from the most treacherous digging. He might even get the opportunity to care for the ponies and other animals that hauled the carts. That had always been his true calling, anyway.

Gesmas shook his head. His duty was to free himself, cross back to Invidia and make his report. Even without the notes, he now knew enough about Soth to satisfy Lord Aderre.

A thud against the wagon's thick side startled Gesmas out of his musings. A second and a third drew the guard's attention. He turned to peer out the door's barred window. An instant later he slumped backward, onto the heap of wounded. A white-fletched arrow protruded from his eye socket.

Prisoners retreated from the arrow as if it might pull itself from the gory wound and fly at them. Their incoherent shouts were drowned out by the sudden screaming of the horses and the pained groan of wood as the wagon struck something. It careened wildly for a moment, then flipped onto its side.

Gesmas reacted quickly enough to brace himself for the impact. It didn't help much. He lay stunned within a bleeding, moaning tangle of limbs. Dazedly he heard the splintering of wood, felt the pile shift as bodies were removed. He kept still, knowing it was better to play dead, to gather his wits and his strength, until he knew what was happening.

The prisoners, both the living and the dead, were removed one by one. Gesmas heard a few words of Elvish spoken, instructions mostly. The dialect was one he'd not heard before. It was thick with gutturals, far removed from the musical language of the city-dwelling elves. The Iron Hills wildlings, he realized with a shudder.

The sun was finally rising, the dawn reaching into the wagon through the breach. Gesmas tracked the play of shadow and light across his closed eyelids. There was no telling how many wild elves moved in and out, leading or dragging away the prisoners. He listened intently. Men were weeping outside, and a large fire had begun to crackle. There were no screams, but soon the weeping and the growled Elvish commands dwindled, until only the sounds of the fire were left.

Then he smelled it: the awful stench of burning flesh.

Gesmas opened his eyes and found himself alone in the shattered wagon. The light of the Sithican dawn streamed in through the ragged hole where the door had been. He rolled onto his stomach and crawled slowly toward the breach. Each carefully considered movement seemed to take an hour. Every creak or scrape made his teeth clench until his ears rang from the pressure.

"The fire's for the dead," said a voice at the spy's shoulder.

Gesmas shouted in surprise and spun around. In the shadows at the very back of the wagon, where Gesmas himself had lain but a moment before, stood a tall, masked figure. His form was mostly obscured by a cloak and a wide-brimmed hat. They, like his mask, his shoes, and his finely tailored breeches and coat, were all of a uniform hue. It was not a color so much as the ashen remnant left when all color had been leeched away.

The stranger held out his gloved hands, empty palms toward the spy. "Don't be afraid, Gesmas. I didn't intend to startle you."

"Who the hell are you?"

He reached for his mask. Gesmas had seen its like before—padded cloth, the large hooked nose hollowed to hold flowers or herbs or whatever else the wearer thought might ward off plague. "You don't know me," the stranger said. His voice was melodious, the accent cultured. "I'm a tradesman hereabouts."

As the mask came away, Gesmas thought for the briefest of instants that no face lay beneath, only smooth flesh the same pale color as the stranger's clothes. He blinked and saw that he'd been mistaken.

The man would have been considered handsome in any land Gesmas had traveled, and more besides. His fair hair framed proud features. Deep-set eyes returned the spy's nervous gaze with a twinkle of good humor. "I knew the fire, or rather what the elves have sizzling upon it, had frightened you. I wanted you to know that the flames weren't your fate."

"I'd rather you tell me how to get home from here," Gesmas said. "Actually, I can find my own way."

He turned back toward the door, but found the way blocked. The stranger stood framed by the gaping hole, haloed by the rising sun at his back. In the light, his pale clothes proved not so uniform; everything he wore was spattered lightly with crimson, from the tip of his hat to the little case he now held in his gloved hands. Carefully he opened the pale leather like a book. Inside, displayed in several neat rows, were a shoemaker's tools. The tacks, the snips, the small hammer, even the needles and thread had been wrought from pure silver. They, too, were flecked with gore.

"The Bloody Cobbler," Gesmas whispered.

The Cobbler nodded and removed a knife from the case. The blade glinted in the sunlight. "I want you to know that I'm sorry about this."

It was pointless to run, useless to fight. Gesmas knew that. But he had so taken on the mantle set upon him by Lord Aderre, the role of spy and relentless seeker of facts, that not even his fear could prevent him from asking, "What are you?"

"Actually, I'm a *who*, not a *what*." The Cobbler leaned close and whispered his name into the spy's ear.

A grim smile spread across Gesmas's face. "Of course."

"I wish there were another way," the Cobbler said as he raised the blade. "But you only get so many chances to walk your intended path."

Later that day, when a group of huntsmen discovered the ruined prison rig, the white-fletched arrows told them most of the tale. Elves allied to the White Rose had attacked the wagon. As was their way, the Iron Hills wildlings took whatever prisoners remained alive and burned the dead, so that the corpses could not be raised through necromancy to serve Lord Soth. The horses were butchered for food. Anything of value from the hitch was stolen.

They found the body of Gesmas Malaturno within the shattered wagon. His arms had been folded gently over his chest. A look of peace graced his haggard face. Even his twisted leg lay straight, as if death had released him from that lifelong scourge and blessing. The white-fletched arrows did not explain this death; the only wounds upon the spy's body did.

Cleanly, carefully, the bottoms of Gesmas's feet had been cut off.

THREE

White roses filled the chapel. They framed the windows and doors, dangled from the rafters on ribbons, floated in glass globes upon the altar. Their fragrance drifted through the room, soothing even the most troubled heart.

White roses were rare in Sithicus. No gardener could cultivate them. They grew wild only in the most isolated reaches of the Iron Hills, deep within the territory controlled by the feral elves. Ganelon didn't know how his friends had gathered together so many for the ceremony, but their unlikely presence didn't surprise him. Ambrose, Kern, and the rest of the miners had performed even more miraculous feats in his name. Ganelon did not doubt they would stand against Lord Soth himself in the name of friendship. If his bride wanted white roses for their wedding, his friends would make certain they brought her every bloom in the land.

Helain had reserved one particular flower for her hair. It was neither the largest nor the most perfect, but something about the rose had captured her eye. With her usual impulsiveness, Helain decided it would be the only flower she wore. The white petals contrasted sharply with her red tresses, a snow sculpture floating upon a cascade of liquid flame.

The ceremony was brief and elegant. Ganelon wound a simple silken cord around one wrist as he spoke his vows. Gently he took Helain's hand and waited for her to bind herself to him.

Her fingers trembled as she wrapped the cord around her own wrist. Ganelon looked into Helain's blue eyes to reassure her. He found confusion there and the shadow of something dark and fleeting, something he did not recognize. She hesitated a moment before opening her mouth to speak her vows. What emerged from those tender lips was a scream.

Ganelon reached for Helain but pulled back in sudden pain. The cord around their wrists had become a rope of bloody thorns. Ganelon called out for Ambrose, for Kern and Ogier, but they did not reply. His friends had fled the chapel, leaving only their shadows behind. The dark forms lingered, surrounded by roses that had all turned black.

Helain was still screaming when Ganelon awoke. Sleep fogged his thoughts. Dazedly he wondered if he might still be dreaming. He'd had them before, horrible dreams within dreams in which he thought he was awake, but wasn't.

No. Ambrose was at Helain's door, speaking soothing words to her. "We're here to protect you," the shopkeep said in his soft wheeze of a voice.

"Needle and thread," Helain shrieked. "The spy's path. Don't you understand? The spy's path!"

Stiffly Ganelon rolled off the hard wooden bench. He found himself standing upon a blanket, which Ambrose must have covered him with some time during the night, only to have it kicked off onto the floor. Ganelon wished he'd kept himself wrapped up; his feet and legs ached with cold.

"Helain, are you all right?" Ganelon called. He knew she might not answer, but to ask Ambrose instead of her would be to admit that she was truly lost to him.

The shopkeep held up a hand, a halfhearted warning to keep Ganelon back. The young man came to the door anyway. It wasn't that he lacked respect for Ambrose; his heart would not allow him to abandon Helain to her pain. "What is it, dear heart?" he asked through the small barred window.

Like a wary animal, Helain slowly backed away from the door. Her red hair all but covered her eyes. She cautiously swept aside matted bangs and stared at Ganelon. "Who are you?"

The question cut him like a blade. Even in the worst of her delusions she had recognized him, if only as a fond acquaintance. Before Ganelon could respond, Helain's features softened and she laughed. The sound was bright and clear. "You're looking very handsome this morning," she said, "even if you do need a shave."

Ganelon glanced at Ambrose and found his own astonishment mirrored on the older man's face. The question was far more lucid than any Helain had posed in the last few weeks. Her laughter was more amazing still. Neither man had heard that sweet sound for almost a year, since she'd shown the first signs of incipient madness.

Smiling broadly, Ganelon turned back to the little window. "You never did like it when I skipped a day with the razor."

"You're mistaken," she noted flatly. "We've never met before."

As swiftly as his spirits had been raised, they plummeted. "Don't you know me?"

"Ambrose said that you were here to protect me," Helain replied, "but I've never seen you before. Do you work the mines?"

The young man stifled a sob. "I'm Ganelon. We were to be married—and will be, just as soon as you get well again."

Helain clamped her hands over her ears. "I will not hear talk of love," she said. "I cannot."

"But you must, because I love you."

She screamed, not so much in fear as in grief. Ganelon thought briefly of the banshees that haunted Nedragaard Keep. He could almost hear an echo of their keening in Helain's cry. Had he not been so overwhelmed by his own sorrow and concern, he would have wondered at that insight, since he had never been near the keep and had heard of the unquiet spirits only in stories.

Ganelon felt Ambrose's hands upon his arm and let himself be steered away from the door. "You should not have told her that," the shopkeep said. "You know how it upsets her."

"Why?" said the young man piteously. "What have I done to her that she cannot bear to hear those words?"

There was no answer to this question, at least none that Ambrose or Ganelon or any of the other people who cared about Helain had been able to discover. A few days before she was to marry Ganelon, Helain had fallen ill. At first Ambrose had dismissed it as a fever brought on by all the excitement. As her guardian, he saw to it that she rested. Everyone expected her to recover in time for the ceremony.

The subsequent weeks and months saw Helain's condition worsen. For a time Ambrose feared she had contracted the plague, though he never let the possibility that he might catch the fatal sickness keep him from her side. With the help of Ganelon and a few of the more courageous miners' wives, he attended to her physical symptoms, which eventually abated. It was not the White Fever that had Helain in its grips, but some malady of the mind. For a full turning of the calendar the madness tormented her with paranoid delusions, kept her sleepless for days then plunged her into such profound slumber that she could not be roused by any means.

Through it all, Ganelon had proved constant. It had never been his nature to commit to anything unreservedly. He'd held a dozen jobs at the mine, none for very long. Only the support and tolerance of friends like Ambrose kept him fed. He missed shifts, slighted his duties, and disappeared for days, carried along by whatever "adventure" caught his attention. It was no easy task for Ambrose to keep the impulsive young man from the notice of Azrael's pit bosses. Somehow, though, he managed.

Ganelon's devotion to Helain, to their mutual happiness, was the only repayment Ambrose needed. Even after she fell ill, the youth never wavered, never let his wanderlust draw him far from the mine. In fact, Ganelon dedicated himself to the stricken Helain with such fervor that Ambrose feared he, too, had been possessed by a sort of madness, but it was nothing less than the frenzy of passion.

"Best we leave her to herself," Ambrose said after he and Ganelon had sat together in silence for a time. He drummed stubby fingers on the bench. "We should get to work. The sun's up, and so are our customers."

Ganelon nodded but didn't follow the shopkeep down the stairs from the balcony to the store. He sat with his head bowed, listening to Helain's screams and to the mundane sounds of Ambrose readying his shop for another day. Soon her shrieks dwindled to sobs, then whimpers. All the while, Ambrose went about his work, opening barrels and shifting crates. He was moving the wooden chairs used for the previous night's prayer meeting when Ganelon finally pulled on his boots, walked to the rail, and looked out over the ordered chaos below.

The large, dimly lit two-story room served as store, warehouse, meeting hall, and gathering spot for the people who worked the Veidrava salt mine. The miners and their families thought of the store as belonging to Ambrose, though he only ran the place. Like everything else of value in Sithicus, the shop really belonged to Lord Soth. The master of Nedragaard Keep had never seen the store or the mine, but his stunted seneschal visited often enough to keep that fact fresh in their minds.

"With the new stock of cloth from Borca, it should be a busy day," Ambrose called up to Ganelon. The shout brought on a fit of coughing, a reminder of the weakness in the older man's lungs from years of working in the mines. Still wheezing, the shopkeep unbarred and opened the front door. He expected to find customers queued impatiently.

He found his stoop deserted.

Ambrose stepped outside. As was his habit, he kept close to the door, within the confines of the building's early morning shadow. His years below ground had left him unaccustomed to sunlight. Unlike the other men who'd survived their time in the pit, he had never reacquainted himself with it. As eccentricities went, this was unusual, even for a place of back-breaking, soul-deadening toil like Veidrava. But the shopkeep's kindness had long ago eclipsed this quirk in the locals' minds.

Squinting against even the weak light of dawn, Ambrose looked around. A group of miners' wives, dressed in coarse clothes of a uniformly drab style, milled together on the opposite side of the wide gravel road. They met the shopkeep's eyes but did not return his waved greeting. "What's the matter now?" he wondered aloud.

"Sheep do not traffic with wolves," answered a soft voice.

Ambrose turned to find himself facing a petite, gray-haired woman dressed in the brightly hued clothing of her tribe. "Magda Kulchevich," he said. "As always, I am pleased to see you."

Ambrose did not wonder how the woman had got behind him without making a sound, or why the miners' wives kept their distance. Madame Magda was *raunie* of the Wanderers, the small Vistani tribe that roamed the wilds of Sithicus. They were fortune tellers and traders and thieves. The locals shunned them, until they needed some shady work done. Then they were glad to pay the Vistani's fees, whether the price was reckoned in silver or blood.

Ambrose limited his dealings with the Wanderers to barter of the more mundane sort. "What have you for me today?" he asked, gesturing for the matriarch to enter his store. "Blankets? Some jewelry?"

"Would you accept anything more esoteric?" she asked. Before he could reply, she laughed in the way a mother laughs at a child's silliness. "Of course not! You wouldn't even take a charm to help the mad girl."

"You can help her?" Ganelon called out. He bolted down the stairs four at a time. "Ambrose, why haven't you told me about this?"

"There are few creatures beyond the help of the Vistani," Magda said.

The shopkeep grabbed Ganelon by the arm. "Their aid comes at the peril of her soul," he whispered. "Leave it be."

Magda shook her head. "No need to hiss, Ambrose. I know what you think of my people. Who knows, you may be right."

She turned to Ganelon. Her green eyes called to him as the sea beckons a mariner; they were full of mystery and adventure and even peace—but it was the peace of death. "You think that love will save her. Sometimes love makes things worse."

"Or maybe the boy doesn't know what love is," offered a burly Vistana. The man strode into the store and dumped the huge roll of carpet he'd been carrying. The roll thudded on the wooden floor, raising up a cloud of dust. "He doesn't look the sort who's had much practice." He smirked. "It's all right, boy. I will stand in for you with your ladylove if your saber's not up to the duel."

Magda spat her disgust. "We speak of the heart, Bratu. In a duel of hearts you would be unarmed."

Bratu replied gruffly, in the patchwork language of the Vistani known as Patterna. He was obviously upset at being insulted in front of a *giorgio*, someone outside the tribe. Magda let him speak, but when his words took on an angry edge, she silenced him with a single, subtle flick of her hand. "You've had your say," she declared, then gestured at the carpet. "Unroll it. We do not offer a friend like Ambrose a pig in a poke."

Ganelon stared at the burly Vistana with undisguised hatred on his face. Bratu returned the angry look in kind, a sneer curling his lips. The gypsy was twice the size of the younger man. His arms were nearly as muscled as Ganelon's legs. However, Ganelon had never walked away from a fight in his life, particularly over an insult even remotely connected to Helain.

Ambrose had tended Ganelon's bruises and cuts enough times to know that a scuffle was imminent. Moreover, he'd seen the younger man pounded unconscious enough times to know that he stood little chance against Bratu. So he redirected Ganelon's attention to the carpet with a simple comment: "None of the miners' families would pay for this, but I think Helain would like it in her room."

"The carpet was looted from Duke Gundar's castle on the night he was murdered," Magda noted. She lifted a corner and ran her slender fingers over the abstract pattern. "Or so claimed the man who traded it to me. I don't believe that, though. Gundar would not have owned anything so beautiful, even if only to tread upon."

She mouthed a silent word and chased it from her lips with her fingers, an old Vistani curse upon the memory of the slain nobleman. Magda had traveled for more than a decade in that tyrant's domain before assassins cut him down and his territory was divided up between his equally monstrous neighbors. Long ago she had vowed to curse his name once for every hour of sorrow he had inflicted upon her and her small tribe, which she had cobbled together from the few Vistani left alive in his domain. Gundar had been dead for sixteen years and would be dead a dozen more before Magda fulfilled that vow.

Ambrose began haggling over the carpet's fair price, which would be paid to the Wanderers in salt. Hard currency was difficult to come by at the mine, even for Ambrose, but that was no problem to the Vistani. Few sources for salt existed in the lands hereabouts, and they could trade the stuff again at the border for an additional profit.

Bratu did the bargaining for the tribe, as such activity was below Magda's station. Instead, the older woman saw to it that the other items the Vistani wished to trade were brought in and laid out for Ambrose's consideration. Ganelon watched as a girl carried in an array of more mundane wares: pots and pans, clothing, a large wooden chest. She carted even the heaviest items with ease, a bored look on her pretty face.

"Careful with that, Inza," Magda said, as the girl let the wooden chest drop to the floor.

"Of course," she replied sweetly. "Though I would surely care for it better if it were my own."

Magda sighed her disapproval. "Have you not given up on it yet?" She went to the girl's side and laid a hand on her shoulder. "What do you own that deserves such a thing to hold it?"

"Nothing yet." Inza ran her delicate fingers across the top of the chest, upon which was carved a lone wayfarer encircled by a riot of greenery. "But some day I will."

Seeing the two side by side, Ganelon realized that Inza must be the *raunie*'s daughter. The resemblance was so strong that they might have been the same person distorted through a lens of thirty-five years, one that restored the mother's gray hair to raven black, her care-worn face to its youthful beauty. Only their eyes shattered the illusion. Inza's green eyes did not bring to mind the sea's fathomless depths. In them Ganelon glimpsed the verdure of the deepest forest, a sunless labyrinth of creeper and vine. The effect was mesmerizing.

Ganelon didn't realize he'd been staring until he found both mother and daughter looking at him with something close to revulsion on their faces.

"Sorry," he murmured, abruptly turning his attention to the tops of his boots.

But the women didn't react. Ganelon had only just begun to wonder why when he heard the scrape of iron-shod boots behind him. He spun about and saw the real object of their loathing.

Azrael, Lord Soth's seneschal, emerged from the darkness of a shadow-draped corner. How he'd got there Ganelon couldn't imagine, though he accepted the dwarf's presence without hesitation. Such weirdness was becoming all too common around Veidrava, from sightings of dead riders to rumors of what lay hidden within the mine's gigantic Engine House.

The dwarf was grinning, an expression so exaggerated that it made his bone-white mustache and muttonchop sideburns bristle like an animal's whiskers. Cheerful malice glinted in his brown eyes. "I've had dreams about this day," he said in a throaty whisper. "How long's it been, eh, Magda? Twenty years? Twenty-five?"

"Thirty-two," the *raunie* replied. "Still not enough for my taste." She held her right hand before her, fingers loosely curled. Suddenly she was holding a club. The cudgel was as long as her forearm, its wood dark and knotted. Bratu was at her side now. Both he and Inza brandished silver-bladed knives.

Azrael laid one meaty hand on Ganelon and tossed him aside. The young man crashed into a crate of apples. He lay there for a moment, stunned.

"Enough."

Two tiny orbs of orange flame—eyes, Ganelon realized numbly—flickered like marsh lights in the same gloom-locked corner from which Azrael had appeared. A wave of unearthly cold rolled out from the shadows, harbinger of a figure armored in seared and ruined plate. His single word of command had been enough to halt both the seneschal and the Vistani. His presence was enough to compel Ambrose to his knees. Though he had never seen Lord Soth before, Ganelon realized it could only be the master of Nedragaard Keep and joined the shopkeep in that show of subservience as quickly as he could manage. "Great lord," he murmured.

Soth ignored the merchants. He focused instead on the Vistani. Bratu and Inza lowered their knives and averted their eyes as a sign of respect. Magda, however, kept her club raised. She met Soth's gaze evenly, without the slightest hint of surprise or alarm. "Greetings," she said. "What is it you wish from me?"

"Your skull," Azrael growled. "I need something to throw at the rats that keep getting into my pantry."

Magda sighed, but did not look away from Soth. "Your time alone in your almost-home has made you forget about courtesy," she said. "Even we thieves without title know to leave our animals outside."

"I'll eat your heart!" Azrael snapped.

"Then, at least you would possess one," she replied.

Azrael took a step toward the *raunie*, but she drove him back with a feigned swipe of her club. Azrael had felt the touch of that enchanted wood once, not long after Magda had first gained the weapon. The single blow had knocked him unconscious. He had no desire now to see what worse damage she could do after three decades of practicing with the thing.

Soth gestured toward the open door, beyond which a number of other Vistani from Magda's tribe had gathered. There was a hound there, too, a large, snarling thing that was only restrained by the strong arms of three men. "Outside, seneschal," he said. "What I have to say to the gypsies does not concern you."

Azrael paused, mulling over some reply, but never gave it voice. Muttering a curse under his breath against all Vistani, he slowly exited the store. Both Inza and Bratu followed the dwarf outside, as did Ganelon. Only Ambrose hesitated. He stood in the doorway, staring at the sunlit world beyond, and trembled.

Finally he turned, head bowed and hands clasped before him. "Pardon me, great lord, but there is a sick woman upstairs. I do not want to leave her alone. She is asleep now, but when she awakens she might rant and—"

"She is his ward," Magda interrupted, "and he takes his responsibility toward her quite seriously."

"I vowed to care for her as my own," added the shopkeep nervously.

Soth dismissed the topic, and the man, with a wave of his gauntleted hand. "Go to her, then. You could scarcely comprehend what will be said here. Before you depart, though, swear an oath to me upon the woman's soul, that you will not repeat anything you overhear."

Ambrose spoke the oath, then scurried up the stairs, wheezing and huffing all the way.

"What a world this might be if everyone's vows were as inviolable," mused the master of Nedragaard.

"Had you honored your pledges as a Knight of Solamnia, Lord Soth, this world would not exist."

The fallen knight turned sharply. "We are speaking of you now, lady, of promises to me that you have broken."

"Then we have nothing to discuss." Magda finally released her grip on the cudgel, and it vanished. "Seven years ago I vowed that my Wanderers would no longer repeat what we know of your infamous past, even to you. In return, you promised to keep us safe from the assassins Malocchio Aderre dispatches across the border to slaughter us."

She pinched the sunburned flesh on one arm. "I am still alive, eh? So I assume that you've kept your end of the bargain. That you can no longer recall the details of your existence before you came to this gods-forsaken place—well, that should be proof enough that we have kept our word."

"I captured one of Aderre's spies," Soth replied. "He had been ferreting out my history, and someone provided him with some bits of truth."

Magda nodded. "I do not question that. Only the truth could have roused you from your waking slumber upon the throne. But there are others beside my tribe who claim to know your origin."

"Others?"

"The Thorns of the White Rose. It's said they know even more about your life before unlife than I do."

"Who are they?" Soth rumbled.

"Bandits and warriors, mostly drawn from the Iron Hills elves," Magda said. "They serve a reclusive general called the White Rose."

"To what end?"

"The general's name should be explanation enough, Knight of the Black Rose. They wish to see you defeated, perhaps destroyed. I don't know how they learned of your history. I've never met their leader. But even the most insignificant thief in their ranks knows the story of your life. Perhaps their general is an old adversary of yours, eh?"

"Perhaps." Soth paced for a time, hands clasped behind his back. From outside came the sounds of an argument and a dog's frantic barking. Neither Soth nor Magda reacted. Both had confidence that their followers could handle themselves.

Finally the death knight spoke again. "This White Rose might indeed be funneling information to Aderre, but I am not convinced your people are without blame in this. I will require proof of your loyalty."

"Loyalty has never bound me to you," Magda said coldly. "From the moment you entered my family's camp in Barovia and forced me to be your guide, we have been linked only by necessity and self interest."

"And fear," Soth added.

"Once," Magda agreed. "But I am no longer the girl you abducted from her grandmother's *vardo*. I have seen darker things than you, done more terrible things than you might suspect. Self interest is all that binds us now."

Soth bowed his head in acknowledgment. "Of course. Then we need to be clear on this fact alone: it is in your best interest to side with me in this fight, Magda Ilyanova Kulchevich. Do not mistake my patience with an old ally's sharp tongue for weakness."

That last comment took Magda by surprise. "Ally," she repeated, and the hard lines of her face softened just a little. She slipped her blouse off her right shoulder, exposing three long scars. Time had paled the marks, but not erased them. "The gargoyle's slash," she said. "From the battle in Strahd's castle. It still aches when the weather changes."

"I wish I could remember the fight more clearly," Soth said.

As the tale was beyond the scope of her promised silence, the *raunie* told him of their escape from Castle Ravenloft, how she battled one of the vampire's living gargoyles while he defeated the red dragon guarding the castle's exit. As Magda related the tale, she paced around the room in a slow but deliberate pattern. Her movements elaborated some of the story's more subtle descriptions, until words and gestures had been woven into a single voice chronicling the battle.

Soth noticed that the candles lighting the room were dancing with her. Figures formed in the tiny flames: a young girl, a twining dragon. Soth even recognized himself, a knight of fire cloaked in smoke wisps. Magda had used the same magic to tell the story of her ancestor, the Vistani hero Kulchek, on the first night Soth had met her. Shadow play. That was what her grandmother, Madame Girani, had called it.

Before he murdered her.

Before she cursed him with her dying breath.

It was Madame Girani's face the death knight saw in the candle flames now, her voice he heard from Magda's lips. " 'You will never return to Krynn again, though your home will always be in view.' "

"I tire of this," Soth said, breaking the spell of the dance and the memories it had revived. "You will attend a meeting with Aderre, to demonstrate to him that our alliance is intact."

"I am nothing to him," Magda said. "Just another gypsy to be butchered."

"Then he is a fool. Did not your grandmother trap me in this wretched place with her curse? Do you not have the same powers?"

Soth didn't wait for an answer, but strode to the door and called for Azrael. To his surprise, the dwarf was laughing as he entered the store. "Hey, Magda," he said between chuckles. "Your mutt tried to bite that miner's feet off. Pulled off the sole of his boot trying to get at him."

"I will be meeting with Malocchio Aderre three days from now," Soth informed the dwarf as he directed him toward the shadowy corner. "You will arrange it."

"Are we going to kill him?" the dwarf asked eagerly.

"*You* are not attending," Soth replied. "Your time will be better spent discovering the identity of the White Rose." He grasped Azrael's shoulder, and the two disappeared into the darkness.

Inza and Bratu came in a moment later, Ganelon between them. The young man was limping heavily. His left boot had been torn apart.

"That beast went crazy again," Inza began. "It attacked him and wouldn't stop. You really should destroy that thing before it kills someone."

Magda came to Ganelon and knelt before him. She examined his foot, wiping away the blood with the hem of her dress. The sole of his foot was gray. Odd scratches crisscrossed the heel and arch.

"There is nothing I can do to help this," she said, backing away quickly. "I am truly sorry."

"That's all right. I'll be fine," Ganelon said, then started up the stairs. A small splash of blood marked the fall of his left foot on each step.

Bratu scratched his head. "You've healed dog bites before. Why can't—" Magda silenced him with a look.

"Those wounds are not the mark of any hound," the *raunie* said softly, once Ganelon had reached the balcony. "Besides, we have other matters to tend to." She turned to her daughter. "Call a meeting of the tribe."

"For what purpose?" Inza asked.

"To strengthen the oath you swore to keep Lord Soth's history secret."

A scowl crossed Bratu's face. "There is no need for that, is there?" He absently ran his hand across the top of a crate. His fingers came away coated with the dust that settled over everything near the mine. "And these people call *us* unkempt, eh?"

From across the room, Magda was studying the man. He feigned an ease he clearly did not feel. The muscles at the back of his neck were tight enough to break boards over. "How much did he pay you?" she asked.

To his credit, Bratu did not lie or try to hide his crime. In fact, he puffed out his chest as if he had actually accomplished something noteworthy. "The money was more than enough for the little I gave him," he said. "Some of that wasn't even true."

"You broke your word," Magda said.

Bratu glanced at Inza. He hoped to find support in her eyes, but the *raunie*'s daughter kept her attention focused on the wooden chest. The man's confusion quickly became defiance. "An oath to a dead man is not an oath," he said. When he saw that he was making no headway on that tack, he swiftly took another. "We owe nothing to Soth!"

Magda turned her back on her tribesman. "The oath you swore was to me," she said. All emotion had fled her voice. She stood as still as a statue. "To all who wish to hear, to man and—"

"Magda, no!" Bratu shouted.

"And to beast—"

The burly Vistana rushed toward her. "In mercy's name!"

"I declare you Oathbreaker."

On the upper floor, Helain screamed herself awake. Ganelon and Ambrose tried to comfort her, but to no avail. Her shrieks drowned out their gentle words and underscored Bratu's pleading.

"Inza," he cried. "Make her take it back. Help me."

The girl looked up from the carvings on the chest. "There is nothing I can do," she said, fingers lightly tracing the twining vines and leaves.

"It is done," said Magda. "It cannot be undone." She told her daughter to leave Ambrose a note about the trade, then left the store.

Inza set to work on the note, ordering the shopkeep to use the chest as a container for the salt owed them for the carpet and other items. "They wouldn't appreciate it anyway," she said brightly. "I know now what I'll store in it, too."

Tears streaming down his cheeks, Bratu fell to his knees at Inza's feet. He clutched at her skirts. "Make her take it back," he begged. "If you don't, I'll tell her there were others."

"No, you won't," Inza said. There was a sudden edge to her voice, a viciousness that stopped Bratu's blubbering. He looked up into her green eyes and found them empty of everything except anger. "There are worse things than the Beast, you know."

"What will I do?" he whimpered. "What will I do?"

Inza walked into the store's shelving, strolling up and down the aisles until she found what she was looking for. She returned to Bratu and dropped a knitting needle into his hands. "The Beast may just be a myth, of course. But if it isn't, this may help."

She did not turn away as Bratu raised the needle to his ear and drove it in, first the right, then the left. Howling, he dropped the bloody spike to the floor. He rocked back and forth, hands clasped to the sides of his head. After a time, he looked up at her with fear-wide eyes and rasped, "The Beast! Oh, Inza, I can hear it whispering!"

FOUR

Azrael trusted the dark.

It had spoken to him many times over the years, in many different places, and while the dark always told the truth, it never used the same voice twice. Sometimes its voice was masculine, sometimes feminine. Occasionally it was strident, more often sonorous and vibrant. The dark told Azrael things he should know and, more importantly, things he should do.

The first time he listened to the dark was in far-off Brigalaure, on the day he caved in his father's skull with a hammer. Azrael's mother had banished him from her workshop for shattering a priceless lava opal, just as his father had dismissed him from the family forge a month earlier for causing a fire. He had no chance of landing an apprenticeship after those disasters, but his father still insisted that he pay for both the gem's replacement and the forge's restoration.

In the midst of the resulting argument, the old dwarf shouted at his wastrel son, "What's wrong with you?" for what very well could have been the thousandth time. Bored beyond belief, Azrael decided to do something he'd never done before: He attempted to answer the question.

The priests had always said the quickest path to solving such unsolvable questions was "soul searching," so the young dwarf did just that. He turned his vision inward, to hunt for what he imagined his soul to be. If there were something wrong with him, as his father seemed so convinced, surely the flaw could be found here. But Azrael didn't find his soul. He found only the dark.

It whispered to him in a voice that sounded very much like his own, only without the edge of anger and resentment he'd grown so accustomed to hearing from himself. He'd long ago forgotten exactly what the dark said to him. He knew, though, that the words had made more sense than anything his parents or the clan priests or anyone else had ever told him. So he acted upon them.

Azrael liked to think the blow came as a particular surprise to his father, since the old man always said his son was never any good with tools.

The dark didn't tell him to complete the slaughter of his family. It didn't have to. Azrael understood the instant his father's corpse finally stopped jerking and twitching that he had found his calling. The blunt fingers his mother had always disparaged as useless for any sort of delicate craft work proved more than adequate to snap her neck. He might not be strong enough to work a bellows for hours on end, but his kin were too slow and muscle-bound to catch him when he fled into the narrow tunnels that channeled waste from the vast underground city.

The dark spoke to him again in the lightless labyrinths outside the city, as he hid from the Politskara, those much-feared police who were hunting him for the murders of his family and anyone else he'd managed to ambush in the months since his father's demise. In return for a promise to destroy beautiful Brigalaure and all who dwelled within her jeweled walls, the dark gifted Azrael with lycanthropy. He'd heard of werebeasts before, but the stories told about them always referred to their powers as a curse. Azrael couldn't imagine why. The transformation was agonizing at first, but he'd grown accustomed to the pain. At times he even enjoyed it—and the abilities he gained were well worth the discomfort.

Only once did Azrael wonder if the dark had betrayed him. After a year or more of hunting the hapless inhabitants of Brigalaure, the werebadger grew bored. He fought the boredom, for it seemed to him a sign of ingratitude, but couldn't banish the taint from his thoughts. The dark, he knew, could most certainly read his mind.

It was at a moment when the boredom was strongest that the dark transported Azrael from Brigalaure to the cursed domains through which he had roamed ever since. At first he bemoaned his fate, certain his boredom had earned the dark's wrath. It had offered him no choice in the matter of his relocation. One moment he crouched in a cavern outside Brigalaure, wondering about the mist that suddenly surrounded him. The next instant he stood in a dreary land called, appropriately enough, Forlorn.

He loathed that land, which lacked Brigalaure's beauty and its happy population—not that he valued either thing for itself. Without beauty, he had nothing to defile. To a people who know little of joy, fear and pain are merely a slight degradation of their usual monotonous melancholy.

His subsequent home in Gundarak proved to be no improvement at all. The vampire lord who ruled that place practiced the sort of sweeping, unsophisticated butchery that left Azrael little to do. The careless carnage also offended his nascent aesthetic sensibilities. If murder were an art, Duke Gundar was a hack of the lowest order. Being surrounded by the duke's clumsy slaughter day after day, Azrael was so profoundly unhappy that he even considered ending his own life.

It was then that the dark, silent for so long, spoke to him once more.

Half-heard whispers, voices from the moon-shadow of a corpse-dangled tree, led him from Gundar's domain into the realm of Barovia. Joy and terror mingled there in startling ways. The master of that place, Count Strahd von Zarovich, painted both emotions across his land with broad, bold strokes. When the sun shone, the happiness of the Barovians was almost palpable. When night descended, fear washed across the land and replaced the day's bright colors with a thousand somber hues. This, the dark told Azrael, was the sort of world he could fashion.

Finally, the dark provided the dwarf with the means to that end. The dark gave him Lord Soth.

Azrael hadn't recognized their meeting's true purpose, not at first anyway. He only recognized Soth's raw power and quickly cast himself in the role of servant. It was a natural mistake.

In his homeland, the Knight of the Black Rose had been a murderer on a scale Azrael could scarcely imagine. Given the chance to prevent a world-rattling cataclysm, Soth refused. He let his anger and his jealously turn him from his gods-given mission. As a result, thousands upon thousands perished. This was a crime worthy of infamy, one that made Azrael's few dozen murders seem paltry.

Or so it had seemed at the time.

Now, after years of watching the death knight loiter on the throne like so much discarded scrap metal, Azrael thought differently. Soth was weak, incapable of ruling his domain. Even his crimes betrayed his deficiencies. He had not murdered those countless victims of Krynn's Cataclysm. Rather, he merely allowed them to die. He could no more claim credit for those lives than Azrael could add the victims of the White Fever to his tally.

With that recognition of his master's weakness Azrael came to an even more profound realization: Soth was a pawn. The dark was using him to provide its true heir a kingdom, a suitable canvas upon which Azrael could paint his masterpiece of terror. The domain of Sithicus might have formed around Soth, but it was intended for him. All he needed to do was usurp control of the kingdom from its inattentive lord. That was just what he planned to do.

First, though, he would deal with a stone that had been rattling about in his boot for decades.

"No one is to open this," the dwarf said. He patted the lid of the chest that lay in the middle of Ambrose's shop. "Someone does and I'll chop 'em up for Nabon's dinner, right?"

Ambrose nodded glumly. "I wish you'd find another way. Involving me in a double cross of the Vistani—"

"I've watched over you since the accident, haven't I?" the dwarf replied. He reached up to pinch one of Ambrose's fat cheeks. "No fear, shopkeep. They won't blame you for the tainted goods. 'Sides, I've got too much time invested in you to let a troupe of half-wit pickpockets and whores slit your throat."

Ambrose turned away, shoulders slouched. "I wish they would," he muttered.

"Wouldn't do a bit of good," Azrael said flatly as he climbed onto the chest. He laid a rough hand on Ambrose's shoulder and spun him around. With one fat-fingered hand he grabbed the man's face and drew it close to his own. "You're not thinking of doing anything stupid, are you?"

The reply Ambrose managed to spit out was garbled, but it satisfied Azrael. The dwarf pushed the shopkeep away.

"Smart man," Azrael rumbled. "That girl up there is counting on you, shopkeep. You cross me and I've got no reason to stop the pit bosses from putting her to work." A leer split his ugly face. "I'm certain they could find something for her to do. Her mind may be shot, but she ain't half bad looking—for a human."

The reference to Helain silenced Ambrose. With a snort of laughter, Azrael leapt down from the trunk. His iron-shod boots had blighted the intricately carved foliage on the lid with scratches. "Just tend to your business, shopkeep, and know that you're on the right side in this little game."

"I still don't know what you're trying to win," Ambrose said.

"The only stakes that matter," Azrael replied. "Everything."

The dwarf left Ambrose to await Inza's arrival. As he headed for the door and the chill afternoon beyond, he snatched a fistful of salted meat strips from a jar on the counter. The stuff was wretchedly tough, with a taste like mummified dog flesh. Azrael loved it.

Humming through a mouthful of the unappealing stuff, he surveyed the locus of suffering that was the Veidrava Salt Mine. Down the road from Ambrose's store squatted the miners' hovels. The buildings huddled together on the broken hillside. They were situated far from the tree line, ostensibly to make them easier to defend. The miners knew, however, that the isolation simply made the buildings easier to police. Even now, the armed and armored riders circled the shanty town like wolves around a stranded flock. The soldiers' eyes, and their crossbows, were turned toward the buildings, not the forest.

The steady thud of the rock crusher and the other, more erratic sounds from the mine itself drowned out any noise coming from the squalid camp. Azrael couldn't hear the screaming infants or the drunken brawls, but he could smell them. He breathed in the stench of piss and blood and despair as someone else might enjoy a wine's bouquet. He held the foulness in his lungs and savored it as he did everything about the mine.

There was something about Azrael that thrived at Veidrava. It was more than a vague inclination for the place, more than some mental sympathy. A spiritual sort might have attributed the feeling to a resonance of the locale with his soul. But Azrael knew with certainty—and more than a little relief—that he lacked any sort of spiritual essence.

Still, Azrael could almost feel something inside him writhing blissfully with each bleak sunset, fattening itself on the strife and misery and chaos that preyed upon the land and, in particular, his mine. It was the dark, he supposed, some little piece of it he carried with him. Usually, though, any such metaphysical musings were swept away by the awful rapture Azrael leeched from the suffering around him.

In search of just such agony, Azrael turned his back on the workers' homes and headed up the hillside to the mine. The lowering sun made the place look unearthly, full of twisted shadows. Towers and buildings reared up from the broken earth. Ropes hung between their roofs, while wooden sluices crawled between them closer to the ground. A thick saline dust covered everything—the towers, the tin-roofed warehouse, even the watchmen making their slow circuit of the grounds.

Azrael nodded a greeting to one of the pit bosses as he headed for the building closest to the main shaft. It was a hulking block with walls constructed of seamless, windowless slabs of wood. The miners called the building the Engine House. No one but Azrael and his most trusted pit bosses ever went inside. The workers who had built the place in only three days lay in a mass grave not far away. Most of the miners assumed it sheltered some wondrous mechanical works that powered the elevator and the water screw and the rock grinder. The assumption was both correct and mistaken.

The Engine House did indeed contain the mine's primary source of power, but that source was not mechanical. Machines do not weep.

The din of clanking chains and thundering hammers usually masked that sound to anyone passing the Engine House. But Azrael could hear it clearly enough after he clambered through the short earthen tunnel that served as the Engine House's only entrance. There, in the foul and cacophonous half-light, sat a giant. He'd sat in that spot for five years, since the Engine House was first constructed around him. Iron bars pinned his legs to the ground at angles that were painful even to see. Even without the restraints, those filth-caked limbs were clearly useless to him.

"Nabon! Stop blubbering," the dwarf shouted. "You'll rust up the works."

The giant continued to sob, even as he cranked a massive wheel with one hand and reeled in a chain with the other. Thinking the brute might not have heard him, Azrael grabbed a whip that hung conveniently by the tunnel. It took three lashes to draw Nabon's attention and two more to get him to cease his work.

"But the lift," the giant began. Nabon glanced at a pillar marked with various cryptic symbols; a rusty arrow waved between two of those marks. "They're stuck between tunnels."

"Don't talk back," growled Azrael. He snapped the whip as close to the goliath's face as it would reach, which was the center of his chest. "You do *what* I tell you, *when* I tell you."

"Yes, great Sorrow."

The dwarf grinned at the honorific. It was one Nabon himself had coined for Azrael—the Sorrow of Sithicus. The dwarf had liked it so much that he'd ordered his pit bosses to use it. The title had since spread to the elves, and even the Vistani. Only the humans seemed reluctant to use it; they couldn't understand how someone would consider the label an honorific at all.

"I'm going down to the chapel," the dwarf announced.

Nabon stopped reeling in the chain. Somewhere close by, a massive hammer silenced.

"What are you doing?" Azrael shrieked. "Keep the crusher going. Let go of the lift."

Nabon hesitated. Azrael waited three heartbeats, then tossed his whip aside. From the shadows he retrieved a huge maul. The mallet's head was studded with metal, its wood blotched with gore. He wielded the thing exclusively against the giant's legs, though the blows did more to crush his soul than his already mangled limbs.

Once, Nabon had been a wayfarer, a traveler with no particular destination. The journey's pleasure had been his only desire, and he indulged that pleasure for weeks and months and years on end. He kept to the secret trails and hidden paths that wound through all the dark domains, ways so desolate that even a giant could walk them unseen. He harmed no one. He asked for nothing but the freedom to travel.

Azrael wished that he could take credit for capturing the brute, but that distinction belonged to another. The dwarf had to be content with reaping the benefits of that treacherous act. He had also discovered that the quickest way to break the giant's spirit was to break his legs. Nabon hoped to take to the road again someday. That hope, more than any chain or threat of violence, bent his kind heart to Azrael's twisted whims, for the dwarf promised to heal those shattered legs, but only if Nabon followed his commands.

Advancing upon the giant, Azrael raised the maul. "I'll mash your shins to paste, Nabon. Let the lift fall."

The giant closed his eyes, as if that might somehow mute the horror of what he was about to do. It didn't. He opened his hand and let the wheel spin, faster and faster, until it stopped with a sickening abruptness. The lift had struck the bottom of the shaft. Anyone inside was surely dead.

When Nabon finally opened his eyes once more the tears were gone. Those blue orbs might have been stone for all the life they displayed. Mechanically he hauled the crusher chain with one callused hand. He held out the other, palm up, and said flatly. "What would you have me do now, my Sorrow?"

"Much better," the dwarf said. "You can stop the crusher. I'm going down to the chapel."

He waited for Nabon to ready the special lift, a gate-fronted black box that only Azrael used. The dwarf stepped inside, slid the wrought-iron gate closed, and took a seat on the padded bench. Nabon slid back the trap door that opened to the main shaft. Sound welled up from the pit like water from a tainted spring. Cries and clatter from the resting place of the ruined lift mingled with the more mundane clamor—the thud of countless picks and hammers, the braying of mules, the shouts and curses of the miners as they went about their backbreaking labor.

Azrael luxuriated in the noise and the darkness as the lift began its descent. He had no fear that Nabon would drop him. The possibility was as remote to him as the miners rising up in revolt or Ambrose turning against him. They feared him too much for that. More importantly, he left them enough hope to stave off total despair. They'd be dangerous if they thought they had nothing left to lose, but he had no intention of letting them realize that.

The lift came to a smooth stop at a cross shaft. The landing was dark, strewn with debris. Neither proved any obstacle to the dwarf, who trod through the rubble as easily as someone else might cross an open field lit by the noon sun. The landing quickly narrowed to a tunnel even more choked with rotting beams and broken tools.

Niches had been carved into the walls every few yards. They were carefully wrought from the salt-thick walls, with sconces chiseled to resemble flowers and other sun-loving things that had no place so far below ground. The sconces held no candles. Darkness had claimed this tunnel since the last human miner passed this way almost a decade ago.

After a time, the tunnel opened into a broad hallway. Here the rubble of shattered wood and crumbled stone had been swept away. The walls and floor became smooth and level. The simple sconces were now elaborate statuary of hounds and harts and more exotic creatures, all hewn from salt. Carvings covered the entire ceiling—scudding clouds and high-flying hawks intended to lend the illusion of open sky. In torchlight, the effect was overwhelming; a quirk in the composition of the salt dome here made the rock glow blue.

Azrael scarcely glanced around him as he stomped down the hallway toward the arched portal at its far end. He hadn't yet found the time to renovate the statues and the ceiling. Too much of the place's original intent lingered; its identity as an island of beauty within the bleakness of Veidrava made the dwarf distinctly uncomfortable.

Not so with the chamber that lay beyond. Azrael felt at home there.

As the dwarf entered the room, braziers sparked to life. The feeble flames they contained were not his doing, but the remnant of some ancient magic that had long outlived its maker. Even the dim light cast by the magical fires was enough to make Azrael's eyes smart after so long in the lightless tunnel.

The vast, vaulted room had once been a chapel. An observant visitor might still recognize the detritus of its sanctified past. In the room's center stood a scarred and stained block that once served as an altar. Like everything else in the chapel, it had been carved from salt. Half-melted forms that had once been benches were arrayed everywhere in neat little rows; the rounded masses seemed like supplicants bent before the blighted sacrificial table. Repulsive human forms, the vestiges of statues, lined both walls. The once-beatific heroes of the faith were reduced to grotesqueries that even the most debased human god would banish from its temple.

The wavering light sent shadows slithering up the walls and shooting across the floor. The sinuous shapes appeared to follow Azrael, to trail him across the room in ways no earthly shadow could.

They seemed detached somehow from the objects that had formed them.

"I don't have time for you now," the dwarf said. The silent chapel offered a response, a susurrus that someone unfamiliar with the cursed place might have mistaken for a cold breeze. Azrael, however, knew this place and its denizens quite well.

"Soon enough you'll all be free of here," he announced. "By year's end, you'll all have your own forms."

He exited the chapel through a rough-hewn tunnel opposite from where he'd entered. In his wake, the shadows danced obscenely across the forsaken altar and the deformed statues. Even after the magical fires dimmed and sputtered out, shapes darker than the chapel's lightless murk moved through the darkness and schemed in voices few sane men had ever heard.

Beyond the chapel, a narrow tunnel wound deeper and deeper into the earth. Something large had burrowed here, with claws that cut through salt and stone like garden soil. The work impressed even Azrael, and he was pleased to make use of the tunnel system and the network of chambers it connected.

The chambers made ideal storage for the seneschal's hoard. Boxes, chests, bags, even a few small coffins intended for child victims of the plague were lodged in the hollows, each crammed full of gold and silver. It had taken Azrael two decades to pilfer this loot from the peasants and skim it from the mine's profits. But he did not cast a loving eye over the gold as he strolled along the tunnel; the dwarf had long prided himself on a disinterest in precious metals atypical for his kind. No, he valued the currencies only for what they would buy—and these coins were earmarked for a purchase few could imagine.

Azrael knew the sight of all that money, more than enough for his purposes, should have made him happy. He knew, too, that the Vistani would soon be out of his way—the only one that mattered, anyway. He had made Ambrose squirm, Nabon suffer, and he was on his way to his favorite spot in all of Sithicus, a site that usually filled his heart with glee. All that wasn't enough to make him forget that Soth had risen from his throne.

"Damn him," the dwarf muttered. A scowl stole across his features as soon as he realized what he'd said. The grim expression quickly became a smile. "Heh. Too late."

A weird purple glow at the end of the tunnel let Azrael know that he had reached his final destination. The air grew thick with the smell of brine, more overpowering here than in the rest of the mine. A chill dampness suffused the air. It wrapped itself around the dwarf like wet cerements.

Azrael emerged from the tunnel on the shore of a vast underground lake. High overhead, stalactites glowed with a violet light. The radiance was born of a moss that clung to the rock. The sickly plant seemed to thrive nowhere else in the mine, making it useless as a light source. Azrael had found it brewed down to a serviceable poison, though, one that caused a hysteria in its victims that was quite amusing to watch.

The water was black and still, a dark sheet of glass stretching to the horizon. Azrael cupped a hand and dipped it into the lake. The water looked black even in his palm. It had a strange feel to it, too. The liquid was heavier and more solid than water should be. Still, he did not hesitate as he lowered his face and slurped up the awful stuff.

Each swallow made his teeth ache and his temples throb with pain. The water burned like molten tar as it coursed down his throat. That awful heat had barely filled his gut when he heard the first voices. He sat down before they overwhelmed him.

The fragments were unconnected, a swarm of words that filled Azrael's mind. Questions without answers, cries of joy, agonized screams, the keening of the banshees at Nedragaard Keep—from all across the domain these sounds came to him. He focused and began to filter out the dull stuff of everyday life. The dwarf didn't care about the drivel people spouted over the breakfast table or lovers' inane pillow talk. He wanted to hear fear—

"Quick, Tomas, hide! They've got swords!"

Or sorrow—

"I can't face another day like this."

Or, better still, words edged with madness—

"Dead, eh? No bother. We've still got a use for your corpse, my dear."

Azrael listened for a time, letting the grief and pain of Sithicus fill his mind. He'd stumbled across this place a decade ago, not long after the Great Rift opened on the surface. The tremors that accompanied that event collapsed the chapel's back wall and revealed the tunnel that led him here. He assumed that this Lake of Sounds, as he had come to call it, was somehow linked to the rift, that the gaping rent gathered up the cries and whispers and funneled them here.

The cacophony had threatened to overwhelm his mind that first day, but he mastered it. And from that chaos he had forged a clarity of mind that left him immune to the confusion plaguing the domain. He alone could remember his past with crystal clarity—and the pasts of anyone else he cared to remember, too. For when Soth and the rest of the land raised their voices in confession to close the domain's borders, Azrael could hear and recall later the sins they proclaimed.

Why the lake's voices were only audible after its fetid water had been sipped didn't concern him. Azrael only knew that the place was more useful than any network of spies. One gulp and he could listen in on anyone he wished—well, not quite anyone. For some reason the White Rose, the Bloody Cobbler, and the Whispering Beast all remained beyond the reach of this magic.

Like everything else concerning that trio, this was a matter for concern, but one he assumed would be rectified soon enough. The dark resided in the vast, black expanse of the Lake of Sounds, and Azrael always trusted the dark. It was a voice in the dark that had prompted him to taste the waters on the day he discovered this lifeless shore. Just as it had given him Soth, it had given him access to all those voices, all that information.

And the dark used that cacophony now to pass along a message to Azrael, a message he had been expecting. The voice of the dark did not cut through the babble. It rode upon the mundane utterances, touching individual words, juxtaposing phrases that had already been spoken.

"*They're* not going to like this at the mine."

"Pay attention when I'm *talking* to you, young man."

"Why does it always have to be *about you*, Ginnie?"

"We're supposed to meet them *on the border* at noon. You coming?"

"Are they now?" Azrael said. He focused his thoughts, winnowing away all but two familiar voices.

"He's a beast," Magda said. "Below your notice."

He could hear a slight breathlessness in her voice. It wasn't prompted by a fear of the meeting about to take place, but by the cold. The dwarf smiled. She really is getting old, he thought, when a chill as mild as today's makes her shiver.

Soth's response was a low rumble of impatience, but Magda pressed her point anyway. "Azrael should not be trusted, *cannot* be trusted."

The dwarf's smile broadened into a grin at the irony of the situation, and his coarse laughter filled the purple twilight hanging over the Lake of Sounds. In the reverberations the dark was laughing, too, but Azrael was too caught up in his own mirth to hear that laughter's mocking tone.

FIVE

The wind whispered around Magda's deceptively slight frame and tugged at strands of her graying hair. It was no more than a breeze, the chill breath of a dying day, but she shivered nonetheless. The cold reminded her body of old battles, skirmishes long since fought and wounds not quite healed. At home she would have cloaked herself in her favorite shawl, but she'd left the wrap back at her *vardo*. It wouldn't do to meet Lord Aderre swaddled like some feeble old grandmother—though Magda had to admit she felt at least twice her fifty-one years tonight.

Soth's presence did not help matters. He radiated the unrelenting cold of the grave. Magda kept a discreet distance from the death knight, but it helped little.

She glanced at her silent companion. How much worse for him? she wondered. The ache of five hundred years wracks his bones, and no hope of death to free him from it.

The Vistana shook her head. It was a trap to pity the dead man. He'd brought his fate upon himself, was even proud of that fact. That self-destructive urge ran strong in Soth. It colored every decision he made, right down to his choice of Azrael as seneschal to his domain.

"He's a beast," Magda said without preamble. "Below your notice."

Soth's only reply was a low rumble of impatience.

That was not enough to make the Vistana let the matter drop. Pulling a few errant lengths of hair away from her mouth, she continued.

"Azrael should not be trusted, *cannot* be trusted." A measure of aggravation crept into her voice. "You must know, after all these years, just what manner of beast he is. Yet you continue to keep him by your side."

Magda had tried to break their vigil's silence many times in the past hour. She was cold and weary, and the quiet only let her focus on those discomforts. She was also unnerved by the situation. Any Vistana would have been.

Magda and Soth stood at the center of a stone bridge that spanned an offshoot of the Musarde, the feeble little waterway known as the Widow's Tears. At the far end of that bridge lay Malocchio Aderre's domain, a land that was death to all Vistani. Despite her powers, despite her years of battling the terrifying creatures that roamed the Sithican night, Magda would not have come here had Soth not requested her presence.

Requested? Magda frowned. It was no request that brought her to the perilous place, but a demand. She could have refused, of course, could have made the master of Nedragaard pay dearly for the impertinence. But Soth had been correct in noting a show of solidarity was important now. It might keep Malocchio at bay, at least for a little while.

Restless, Magda paced a little on the rough-hewn stones that comprised the bridge between the two lands. She paused to see what it was that had captured her hound's attention. Sabak snuffled intently at a dark blotch. Bloodstains. They were too fresh to have been washed away by storms or licked clean by scavengers.

Magda did not know of the battle that had occurred on that spot, how a gallant animal had tried to carry its master across the bridge to safety, but the bloodstains told that tale to Sabak, and more. The hound lapped at the gore, sniffed furiously at the tiny bits of horseflesh that remained on the bridge. In that admixture of fear and blood and sweat, he recognized the scent of the one animal his hound's heart was able to hate: Azrael.

A low, deadly growl issued from Sabak's throat, echoed off the bridge and across the valley. The angry rumble seemed to be endless. Not even the dense forest could contain it.

Her nerves on edge already, Magda had no patience for whatever nonsense Sabak was up to. She made the shortest of whistles. The dog's ears pricked up instantly. After only a moment's hesitation, which was a moment longer than he normally took to answer her summons, the giant hound padded silently to stand at Magda's right side.

She rested her hand at his shoulders and unconsciously traced patterns in his coarse, gray-white fur with her fingertips. This motion soothed both woman and beast.

Lord Soth's dead voice broke that momentary respite. "I might ask the same question of you, Magda Ilyanova Kulchevich."

At Magda's puzzled expression, he continued: "You asked why I allow a beast such as Azrael to serve me. Yet you keep a creature as fierce and unpredictable by your side." He pointed to Sabak, who regarded the death knight without the slightest hint of fear. "Your own child wishes the hound dead. Is there any other member of your troupe who does not walk in fear of the creature?"

"No."

"Surely your daughter has warned you that the hound might turn its teeth on you."

"She has."

"Yet you keep the beast with you, and demand your people accept him—despite their fear."

Magda nodded, but she had lost the thread of the discussion. Her attention was focused instead on Soth himself. The topic seemed to have fanned some spark in him. His words held a passion she had last heard in him years ago, on their trek through Strahd's domain.

"Azrael is the same to me," Soth continued. "He is my beast, and useful—despite his need of housebreaking."

Sabak snorted at a fly buzzing around his snout. For all the world, it sounded like a huff of laughter.

Finally, the death knight leaned close to Magda and said, "We both know too well that we would slay our beasts in a moment, should they turn against us."

Soth seemed willing to continue the conversation, but a distant thunder shook the forest to the north. Birds burst up from the tree line and raced across the red-gold sky. Through her boot heels, Magda felt the rolling tread of a group of large creatures. She glanced at her companions. Both Soth and Sabak remained utterly still, as if they'd been carved from the bridge's stone. Magda was not so calm; her pulse quickened and a flush suffused her cheeks.

Malocchio Aderre had arrived.

Thirteen ogres served as the procession's vanguard. The lumbering brutes marched along the verge of the narrow road, stomping the undergrowth and shoving aside trees. Like most of their kind, these were large, hulking giants, with little intelligence lighting their purple eyes. Some stood partially erect, but most crouched in an apelike fashion. Their orders must have been to clear away any flora that impeded their movements, so their posture saved them some work.

Magda studied the ogres as twelve of the thirteen arrayed themselves into a semicircle to either side of the road, sealing off the Invidian end of the bridge. At first glance, they weren't particularly impressive, even for ogres. A few wore rusted, poorly fitting chain mail, while most sported ratty furs or other lice-ridden bits of clothing. A closer look at their weapons told another story, though. Their clubs were notched from countless battles and darkly stained with the blood of fallen adversaries.

The thirteenth ogre, Onkar by name, stood out from his kin. He was neither dirtier nor coarser than the others, of average height and build. What set Onkar apart was an unusual feature, or rather, a lack of one. When this ogre approached the bridge, he squatted down in profile fashion and balanced on the balls of his feet. Because of this angle, Magda could see he was quite clearly missing his nose.

Before the Vistana could wonder what became of the ogre's snout, and what price his foe had paid for taking it, the semicircle opened at its center to admit a single rider: Malocchio Aderre.

He rode a black stallion large enough to carry one of his monstrous soldiers with ease. A cloak the color of midnight flowed out behind him like the wings of some immense predatory bird. His breeches, boots, shirt, gloves, everything he wore was of the same ebon hue. Only his face, as white and smooth as bleached bone, presented a contrast. That was all that there was to him: black and white. He was all extremes and nothing else.

He brought his mount to a stop with a casual tug of the reins. Behind him, a score of armed riders and another dozen ogres clattered to a stop. Malocchio kept his gaze locked upon Lord Soth as this rearguard arrayed itself along the banks of the river. A slight frown creased his pallid mask of a face when the death knight offered no reaction to this obviously superior force.

In one easy motion, Malocchio swooped down from his mount, cape aflutter, black spurs jangling. Just as he alighted, a pair of neatly attired soldiers approached. They were identical twins, half-elves, Magda guessed. Such crossbreeds were common enough in Sithicus but not so in Malocchio's domain. Malocchio has trotted them out for some reason, Magda mused. But what?

Lord Aderre strode purposefully to the bridge's terminus, the very brink of Invidia's southern border. Even had he wished it, he could have gone no farther. Within their domains the dark lords ruled supreme, but those same domains were prisons, too.

The half-breeds took up positions flanking Malocchio, but a few respectful paces behind him. They kept their gazes turned down, their slender-fingered hands clasped before them like monks at prayer. The rest of Aderre's forces moved restlessly among the horses and trees, clearly ill at ease. The ogres and human soldiers didn't really appreciate the restraint required for this sort of politicking. Their style of negotiations involved clubs and burning brands.

For a few moments, neither Soth nor Malocchio spoke. It was as if some unwritten rule decreed the first exchange would be an admission of weakness. The stalemate might have continued until the sun set and long after had Magda not spoiled the game.

Whatever dread Malocchio had inspired in the Vistana was gone, banished by the man's appearance. Such was often the way with fear, she'd found; the half-hidden beast was always more frightening than the thing crouched in the open—not less dangerous, of course, but easier to cope with.

"How long do you two proud birds plan to perch in this spot?" she asked brusquely. "Winter's not far off, you know. If it's going to be a long wait, we should look for something warm to feather our nests with."

"Silence that refuse clinging to your cloak," Malocchio spat. When he realized he'd been baited into speaking first, he reflexively warded himself against Vistani magic. With a V formed by two fingers of his left hand, he bracketed his eye.

Magda smiled inwardly at the superstitious sign. She'd needed no magic to trip Aderre's tongue. For all his facade of composure, this butcher was not so certain of his footing here. That might explain the show of force, too. The louder the clatter of arms, the less noticeable the quaver in the general's voice.

Lord Soth, too, seemed to sense the young man's uneasiness, for his first words were as provoking as they were unexpected. "My ally is unskilled in the ways of nobility," the death knight began. "I will not ask you to forgive her, for it would be below one of your rank not to do so."

Malocchio swallowed whatever caustic reply leapt to his tongue. From the pained expression on his face, it burned like molten lead. He gestured to one of the half-elves, who stepped forward and unrolled a piece of parchment. In a voice that held far more confidence than it should have, he read:

" 'In the name of justice and honor, the citizens of Invidia demand the extradition of Magda Kulchevich and all Vistani traveling with her, be they formal members of the band of thieves known as the Wanderers or merely—' "

"Enough," Soth said.

The half-elf glanced up from the page. Whether he was supremely foolish or merely convinced of his safety because of his proximity to Lord Aderre, he dropped his gaze back to the edict and continued. " 'Or merely those citizens of Sithicus known to her as carrying the taint of Vistani blood. Her crimes are many, but include—' "

Lord Soth spoke again, this time a single word of magic. Only one person heard the word. As soon as it left Soth's lips, the half-elf who so boldly proclaimed the extradition edict dropped his parchment. A startled look crossed his face before he doubled over in pain. He sprawled on the road for a moment, twitching violently, as the word did its work. A thin ooze that had been his brains seeped from his ears and nose. He vomited up the tattered remnants of his guts. Still the word of power careened inside his increasingly hollow shell, slicing through everything in its way, until finally the half-elf's skin lay empty on the ground.

"I did not come here to listen to the demands of 'the people of Invidia,' " Soth noted. "But they have my answer anyway. Now, Lord Aderre, we have matters of state to discuss."

"He was under my protection," Malocchio said darkly.

"I understand," Soth replied, "but I told him to stop. His impudence is to blame for his death, not your failings as a protector."

Malocchio mocked a bow. "How kind of you to clear my name."

Soth acknowledged the remark with the barest tilt of his head.

As the lord of Invidia straightened, he produced a dagger. "I'll be certain to offer you the same courtesy after I've corrected that Vistani witch for her earlier impertinence."

"It would be amusing to see you try," Soth said calmly, "but I will do you the favor of preventing you from dishonoring yourself in front of your troops." He gestured to Aderre's dagger. "Unless you plan to raise that blade against me, I would suggest you sheathe it."

The Invidian troops stirred. The human soldiers were disciplined enough not to draw their swords, but the ogres raised their clubs and muttered threats. All were ready to charge, awaiting only the word of Lord Aderre.

"It's tempting," Malocchio said after a tense moment. He slipped the dagger back into his sleeve and continued, "You rested far too long upon your throne of dust. Things have changed while you slumbered, dead man. Powers have arisen that do not fear you."

"They should," Soth said. "The carcass flapping at your feet like a torn sail should be proof enough of that."

Malocchio shrugged. "They say your kingdom fares little better than this unfortunate soul. Travelers carry back reports of—"

"To the heart of the matter at last," Soth interrupted. "Call them travelers or agents or spies, I will have no more of your minions crossing into my domain."

"Your own people are more than happy to help me," Malocchio said snidely. "They'll tell me everything they know about you, about your land, about anything, so long as I don't send them back to Sithicus."

He pulled the remaining half-elf forward; the fellow was so shocked by the fate of his twin that he could only stare. Malocchio looked at him and laughed. "He doesn't seem too bright, but that's what you get with half-breeds, eh? Of course, you wouldn't know about that. Against your military code to sire bastards, I would think."

Magda gritted her teeth. Here, at last, she understood the reason Malocchio had trotted out these particular traitors. They were a test. One was meant to gauge the death knight's magic, the other to discern the state of his memory. Malocchio must have learned enough of Soth's history to know about the son he'd fathered with the elf maid.

The Vistana opened her mouth to respond, to say something that would spoil Malocchio's test.

She never got the chance. Lord Soth waved one gauntleted hand, as if to wipe the trembling half-elf from existence. "Enough of these games," the death knight rumbled. "You dally with the past, and I am here to discuss the future."

"Then we have nothing to discuss." Malocchio shoved the half-elf aside. The cracked facade of civility was gone, shattered finally by a towering rage. "The future belongs to me, and you forfeited any place in it by consorting with that Vistani trash. I mean to purge every last one of her kind from the world, dead man. Do not doubt that for one moment."

"I do not doubt your intent," Soth replied coolly, "and I care nothing for the fate of the gypsies within your lands. But know that Magda and her troupe are my subjects, my *allies*. This alliance is as my power: unquestionable, inviolate. I will not stand for any discourtesy shown to her troupe by you or your agents."

Discourtesy, Magda mused. An odd term for the slaughter Aderre has in mind for us. She regarded the death knight, standing stiffly by her side. It's as if he's speaking from rote, she thought, drawing half-remembered words from his order's ancient code.

"Furthermore," Soth continued, "you will cease any traffic with my subjects, particularly the elves of the Iron Hills. You would be ill-advised to offer support to them or their leader."

Malocchio could scarcely contain himself. He turned his back to Soth, as if to walk away, then whirled around and stabbed an accusing finger at him. "You have no right to lecture me like some, some . . . *child*. If the White Rose and her Thorns will bring me one step closer to seeing that whore dead, I will empty my treasury to fund their war with you."

The next few minutes of Malocchio's rant were lost to Lord Soth. A single word sounded through his mind again and again: *her*. The White Rose was a woman.

Since he had risen from the throne at Nedragaard Keep, the death knight had been tormented by myriad fractured memories. The strongest of these was a woman's face—a darkhaired beauty with a crooked smile. Her image flitted about the ruined castle of Soth's memories, always out of reach, just a turn of the corner away. Now, thanks to Malocchio's revelation, that phantom had a form and a name.

She was a warrior, a general in the Dark Queen's armies on Krynn. He had been dead for hundreds of years when he met her, but Soth instantly recognized the woman as his perfect foil, a dark gem with facets enough to keep him occupied for all eternity. The fractured memory had healed itself, and she was revealed before his mind's eye. She stood defiant, clad in the blue armor of a dragon highlord.

Kitiara!

She must be the White Rose.

In the hours before he'd been drawn into the netherworld, Lord Soth had attempted to capture

Kitiara's soul. He had planned to raise her as his undead consort. That plan would have succeeded, too, had it not been for the treacherous ghost who had served as his seneschal on Krynn—*Caradoc*, the death knight recalled bitterly. That whimpering cur had attempted to barter the captured soul for some reward so trifling Soth could not recall it now. The betrayal had cost Soth dearly. Before he could retrieve Kit's essence, he found himself transported far from Krynn, stranded in the domain of Strahd von Zarovich.

Kitiara's soul must have been taken, too, Soth decided. It had eluded him for all these years. Now, though, she had shown herself. Of course her army knew his true history; she had witnessed some of his dark deeds herself. Soth smiled grimly; it seemed Kit had not lost her will to fight. He was certain, though, that he would win her to his side in the end. It was their destiny.

The death knight's sudden preoccupation was lost on neither Magda nor Malocchio. The *raunie* watched the Invidian troops, alert to the possibility of attack. Though she tried not to betray her concern, she could not help but glance at Soth. The death knight's burning eyes were little more than faint sparks. His arms hung slack at his sides.

The lord of Invidia continued to catalogue his grievances against Soth and Sithicus, pausing now and then to voice his hatred for the Vistani and anyone who harbored their kind. Hidden within his rant were the words of a command. It was heard only by the poisonous serpents that lay coiled near the river. These creatures, by the lives they had stolen, had helped the waterway earn the name "Widow's Tears."

At Malocchio's subtle bidding, a trio of serpents crossed from the weed-choked bank on the Invidian side of the river and slithered onto Sithican soil. With the stealth only snakes possess, they crept along the rail. Hidden by the lengthening shadows of twilight, they crawled to within striking distance of Magda's legs.

With a savage snarl, Sabak whirled to meet them. In the blink of an eye, he had two of the snakes in his jaws. Green poison and limp pieces of reptilian flesh mingled with the hound's own frothy drool and hung like icicles from his chops.

Alerted by Sabak's snarl, Magda turned in time to kick the third serpent away, back toward Sithican soil. The hound took off after the retreating snake. As he bounded across the bridge, Sabak's paws burned smoking prints into the stones. Like his ancestor, the mythical hound of Kulchek the Wanderer, this beast did not hunt without leaving a clear trail for his master.

The last serpent was almost to the grass and relative safety when Sabak grabbed its tail and flung it from side to side. The serpent reared, hissing loudly and displaying its glistening fangs. Sabak paused for a moment; the potential threat this creature posed was clear even to his canine intelligence. He made a few quick feints at its head, trying to draw the serpent forward. Finally, the enraged snake lunged toward one of Sabak's front paws. The hound sidestepped the attack and snatched the creature by the tail. With a deliberate twist of his neck, Sabak snapped the serpent's head against the bridge. Sabak's tail swished happily as he sniffed the gory remains.

Magda breathed a sigh of relief as her faithful hound trotted back onto the bridge. She was so startled by the abrupt attack, so caught up in Sabak's skirmish, that she hadn't seen Soth draw his sword. The death knight leveled the blade at Malocchio in a manner that made it quite clear he intended to bury that ancient steel in the black-garbed man's skull.

For his part, Malocchio sighed raggedly. "In for a penny," he said and gave the signal for his troops to attack.

The vanguard clattered onto the bridge. Soth did not reposition his blade as the ogres thudded across the stones. He kept his arm stiff, the blade pointed at Malocchio, stoically watching the ogres rumble forward in a sweaty, swearing mass.

Magda cast Soth a frantic glance. The ogres were close enough that she could smell the stench they gave off, and still the death knight stood. Was he lost in another reverie?

Magda got her answer an instant later. The first of the ogres had reached the tip of Soth's outstretched sword, far enough onto the bridge that the entire vanguard had pressed in behind him. The ogre raised its club with both hands and shouted "Invidia!"

The ogre did not see Soth open his empty left hand. Neither did he see the small spark of orange flame erupt from the death knight's palm and speed toward him like a sling bullet. The ogre only realized his peril at the very instant his patriotic cry had left his lips. A fireball, his sluggish ogre mind noted. Uh oh—

The magical fire incinerated the ogre at the front of the charge, then swelled to fill the bridge. The rest of the brutes in the first two ranks met a similar fate. Those half-dozen ogres toward the back were less fortunate. The fire had diminished just enough to allow them to realize they were ablaze, then to shriek in agony before they died.

The burst of flame blinded Magda for a moment, and the horrible *whoosh* made by its passing left her ears ringing, so she didn't hear the clumsy splashing beneath the bridge, nor Sabak's warning barks. Before she knew she was in danger, her head snapped back with incredible force.

A brutish hand covered in rotting river weeds had grabbed her by the hair. As the stars of pain cleared from her eyes, she saw the ogre to which that much-crusted hand belonged. He was clinging to the rail. He and the remaining troops had used the vanguard's demise as a distraction.

At a thought, Gard was in her hand. Before the brute could drop back into the water, taking her— or at least her head—with him, Magda twisted around so that her stomach braced against the rail. The ogre's face was so close to hers that she could count the hairs on each wart dotting his pug nose.

The Vistana lashed out with her cudgel and

kicked away from the rail at the same time. That single blow from Gard caved in the left side of the ogre's face; his death cry was punctuated by the clatter of his broken teeth on the rail. But the ogre never relaxed his grip. As the corpse dropped from the bridge, it tore loose a bloody trophy. The ogre sank into the weedy mire still clutching that hank of hair and scalp.

Panting, Magda fell against the rail. She looked up to see Soth calmly assessing the situation. Ogres were scrambling up from the water on either side of the bridge. A dozen human soldiers held both ends. The troops on the Sithican side, still wet from their charge across the river, had swords. The soldiers standing with Malocchio had strung bows and were already nocking arrows.

The Invidian lord gestured to the archers. "They may not kill you, Soth, but they're almost certain to pierce *her* withered heart."

The death knight waved his gauntleted hand once, directing outward the awful, unearthly cold that wracked his body. Before the archers could loose a single arrow, they found themselves facing a wall of ice that sealed off the entire Invidian end of the bridge. Soth turned to the other human soldiers. "You are in my kingdom now," he said, and raised his sword.

Magda didn't see what happened next; two more ogres had pulled themselves up onto the bridge. She turned to face the first. The other had to contend with Sabak.

The Vistana sparred with the brute, testing him

for weaknesses. She knew better than to rush the duel. Impatience would only cause her to make a fatal mistake. But Magda was tiring much more quickly than she had expected. Each blow from the ogre's club made her arms shake just a little more, her guard drop a little lower. When she remembered that there were more ogres to fend off after this one, Magda felt an unprecedented despair sweep over her. Once I could have stood alone against such threats, she thought, but no longer.

That realization was underscored for Magda when the ogre's next blow knocked her from her feet. She kept her hold on Gard, countering with a strike that broke the brute's leg. Still she was vulnerable, if the ogre could only take advantage of the situation.

Fortunately, he couldn't.

Sabak entered the fray, having finished off his own adversary. As the wounded ogre hobbled forward, the hound sank his teeth into the brute's side. He came away with a mouthful of rusted chain mail and more than a little of the flesh beneath. When the ogre toppled, Sabak went for his throat.

A weird howl drew Magda's attention back to Lord Soth. The death knight stood at the bridge's center, arms raised over his head. The air behind him had split open. In full battle regalia, thirteen banshees thundered out of the torn sky. They rode chariots of bone drawn by wyverns. The dragon-winged beasts lifted them high over the bridge, but only long enough to choose a victim. The howling spirits descended upon the troops trapped on the Sithican side of the span.

Magda watched in horror as the banshees drew their weapons, swords and flails of ice, and attacked. The humans tried to run, but that only fueled the wyverns' battle lust. The beasts lashed out at the soldiers with talons, impaling them with barbed tails. Those few the wyverns spared were cut down by the banshees long before they reached safety.

The ogres fared no better. Soth slaughtered the few remaining on the bridge. The rest fell to Sabak or the banshees. The brutes who had yet to climb onto the bridge were the fortunate ones. Their awkwardness or their fear of Soth had left them some hope of escape. Using the bridge as cover, they stumbled back to the Invidian shore. Onkar, the ogre with the missing nose, led the retreat. They skirted the wall of ice, which had finally begun to show the effects of the archers' steel, and vanished into the woods.

For her part, Magda sat in the midst of the carnage and mourned—though for whom, she could not really tell. Herself, she supposed. Gore-spattered and aching, she watched Soth clean his blade on one of the fallen ogres. A wyvern waited patiently for the death knight to be done with the corpse before it began to tear apart the prize. Even Sabak joined in the feasting.

A chill that penetrated even her numbed soul told Magda that Soth was near. She looked up into the gathering darkness and found the death knight standing over her. He was staring at something near the Sithican end of the bridge. Without a word, Soth drew his blade again and walked off. Magda levered herself to her feet and followed.

As she neared the death knight, Magda was able to see what had drawn his attention. In the midst of several dismembered soldiers, so goresoaked that he had been discounted as a corpse himself, knelt the half-elf. How he had escaped the melee was anyone's guess.

"The battle is over," Soth said.

The half-elf held out empty hands. "I have no weapon," he said piteously. "Please."

Soth studied the half-elf for a moment. Then a flicker of recognition sparked in his eyes. "Tanis Half-Elven," he said venomously.

"No, my lord," replied the half-elf. "Stefan of Mal-Erek."

"Flee then, Stefan of Mal-Erek. You are unarmed, and I follow the Measure even now." Soth's voice chilled the blood-heated air. "Carry your disgrace with you as you leave this land."

The half-elf staggered across the bridge and over the chunks of ice from the felled wall. Magda could almost feel the death knight's disdain for the youth. She asked him about it, though his reply was cryptic.

"I knew one like him on Krynn," Soth said. "His kind was never suited to the sword."

From across the bridge, touched by the final, fading light of day, Malocchio Aderre called out. "This," he cried, indicating the carnage with a broad sweep of his arm, "this means nothing."

Without moving, Soth replied, "You are correct, child lord. I swept aside this attack as if it were nothing. So, too, with any other annoyances you send against me." He sheathed his sword. "We can agree to end this now, since I have no further time for such foolishness."

Malocchio ordered his remaining troops to mount. He lingered a moment longer, though, his black-clad form indistinguishable from the gathering gloom of night.

"You're correct, Soth," he said at last. "For now, you have more pressing problems than me, bogey men under your bed with prior claim. But you, Vistana—" again Malocchio Aderre warded himself "—I am your worst fear. I am your only fear."

With those words hanging in the air, Malocchio Aderre vanished. To their credit, the soldiers held their ground for almost ten seconds before fleeing headlong down the road.

"You are under my protection," was all Soth said as he turned and strode away from the bridge.

Magda Kulchevich found some comfort in those words, but not nearly enough.

SIX

There was a dank coolness to the *vardo* that comforted Inza. The wagon's high shutters were open, which Magda never tolerated so late in the year, and the curtains were drawn tight to keep out even the starlight. The ashes were cold in the stove.

Magda was not there to object. Not two days after her encounter with Lord Aderre, she'd taken to the road, only Sabak by her side. The sudden leave-taking had surprised her troupe; though Inza and the others sometimes traveled for weeks on their own, Magda rarely spent more than a few hours away from the Wanderers. This time, though, she had been gone for eight days. The troupe still had no idea what quest had prompted her to abandon them so soon after Malocchio's threats and a battle that had clearly left her shaken.

Inza didn't really care why her mother had gone, only hoped that her business kept her for a while longer. Not too long, of course, but time enough for the girl to enjoy some privacy.

Except for the time it had taken to handle one minor task she could trust to no one else, Inza hadn't left the *vardo* for more than a few moments in the past eight days. Much of her time had been spent admiring the intricately carved wooden chest she'd retrieved from Ambrose. The box still held salt, payment for the other goods they'd traded to the mine store. Soon enough, though, the troupe would journey to the border and turn the salt into gold or wine or some other commodity with more value in Sithicus. When they had done so, she would have the chest for her treasures.

There was something hypnotic about the patterns on the chest's lid. Now, as she had done each night since her mother's departure, Inza carefully withdrew the chest from beneath her cot. She ran her fingers over the tangled vines. Not even the deep scratches left by some clumsy oaf at Ambrose's shop could diminish their appeal.

She might have spent hours contemplating those twisting, twining vines, had not a shrill cry from the camp disturbed her meditation.

"By Nuitari's black glow, who has done this?"

It was her mother's voice. *Better that she's returned,* Inza noted silently. *Better that we get this unpleasantness over with.*

The girl sighed, pushed herself to her feet, and brushed the dust from her scarlet skirt. Carefully, so as not to disturb any of the junk her mother so prized, she made her way to the entrance. Flinging aside the jewel-spangled cloth that served as the *vardo*'s door, Inza stepped out into the night.

Magda stood beside the communal fire, her travel pack at her feet. Dust caked her boots and legs. Her cloak hung in tatters from her shoulders.

"Why, Mother," Inza said sweetly, "I'm glad you've come back to us. I was worried."

Inza danced down the wagon's steps and entangled her mother in a hug not all that dissimilar from the clinging embrace of the carved vines she so admired. "You must be exhausted," the girl said, still hanging from Magda's neck. "Rest by the fire and let me fix you something warm."

Magda was indeed tired, and a drink would have done much to improve her spirits, but she disentangled herself from her daughter's embrace and waved away her offers of hospitality. "I told you to look after him," she said. Her face flushed with anger.

Inza batted her lashes. "I don't know what you mean, Mother. Have I failed you somehow?"

"Don't play the cherub with me," Magda shouted, words hotter than the roaring fire. "You're too old for that role."

The *raunie* hefted her small travel pack and tossed it onto the *vardo*'s steps. She walked slowly to stand over a bald Vistana, who was rolling in the dirt nearby. It was Bratu. The burly man seemed oblivious to everything around him save his tightly bandaged hands.

From the instant Magda branded Bratu an Oathbreaker, his mind had begun to fray at the edges. He had punctured his eardrums in hopes of silencing the Whispering Beast. When that did not hush the mysterious creature's voice, he tore off his own ears. Still Bratu heard the mutterings of his unseen accuser. Slowly, the sporadic murmuring became a constant litany. Every lie, every broken promise and dark deed, was chanted over and over, a never-ending recital of every crime and trespass. Day and night the accusations continued, until the man's mind unraveled completely.

Such was the possible fate of any Sithican caught betraying an oath. Elf or Vistani, peasant or nobleman, breaking one's word might draw the most unwelcome attention of the Whispering Beast down upon you. He did not stalk every liar, which made some dismiss the "Whispering Madness" as nothing more than the ravings of guilt-racked consciences. It was true, too, that some who had never been caught at their deception were driven mad by fearful anticipation, wondering when the whispering would start.

Only the Wanderers knew that the Beast's ire was always drawn to those who broke an oath publicly sworn, their betrayal publicly revealed. Magda had realized full well what the brand of Oathbreaker had meant to Bratu. The burly gypsy, too, had known of the risks when he breached the communal vow he'd sworn to her.

Magda detested meting out such cruel punishments, but she knew they were necessary if the Wanderers were to survive in Sithicus. In the wake of her harsh verdict, though, she also insisted that the troupe continue to care for Bratu. His fate was now in the hands of the Beast; his fellows would do nothing to make his life any harder.

As she stared down at the man, it was clear to the *raunie* that someone had disobeyed her. Bratu's mouth was caked with blood. His tongue had been torn out at the roots. Only one of her tribe would be so bold.

Magda turned to her daughter. "You did this," she rumbled.

"No!" Inza gaped in shock. "He did it himself."

"Through these?" Magda knelt and gently took one of the man's hands in hers. Thick bandages bound the fingers together. After Bratu had injured his ears the second time, the *raunie* herself had ordered his hands swaddled so. "You are a poor liar."

When Magda stood, all the anger was gone from her face. Her voice had no more emotion than Soth's. "I want to know why, Inza. Sit with me. Speak to me of reasons."

The Wanderers had learned to fear that command. Magda used it only when she herself could see no reason to allow a Vistana to stay with the tribe.

Inza decided there was no point in maintaining the facade of innocence any longer, so she settled on one of the chairs that had been drawn to the fire. As her mother saw to it that Bratu was bathed and his wounds given fresh dressings, the girl surveyed the camp. The remaining fifteen Wanderers had suddenly heard the urgent call of tasks inside their *vardos* and fled to them. Inza thought them cowards, but secretly wished she might run off as well. Her mother had reacted all out of proportion to her crimes, and Inza really didn't have the patience to coddle the old woman tonight.

Inza didn't wait to be asked again for her reasons. "You've been gone," the girl said before her mother had even sat down opposite her. "You haven't had to listen to the awful things he's been saying. He rants night and day—about you, Mother, and the others. Even me. The things he says are terrible, obscene!"

"He is ill," Magda said simply. "Where is your compassion?"

Inza lowered her voice to a conspiratorial whisper. "The others were ready to kill him for what he said. What I did *was* compassionate compared to what they had planned."

"The others will have to answer to me, as well, one by one. First, child, I have your fate to decide."

Inza bristled at the word "child." Her mother caught the indignant flare in her eyes and corrected herself.

"You're right," Magda sighed, "you haven't been that for a long time."

"For which you should be thanking me," replied Inza. "We have no captain in this caravan. You wouldn't think of sharing that much of your power with any man. I'm left to be your second."

She was warming to the topic now, her passion fanned by her mother's silence. "The others know that you've trained me to use Gard, shown me the

secrets of the shadow play. So when you and that—
that *mutt* disappear for a week on some secret
journey, they trust me to keep the troupe together.
That is all I did."

"What you did was monstrous." Magda shook
her head. "There was a time not so long ago when
Bratu would have done anything for you. Don't try
to deny it. The camp's not so big that anyone could
miss the way he trailed after you."

Inza shot to her feet. "More reason for me to
hate the old letch," she snapped. "We'd be smart to
rig up a cage for him and show him off at Veidrava
as a lesson for any other lying sod who takes after
little girls."

"Enough," Magda said coldly. "The Wanderers
will never display their own as sideshow freaks."

Inza gawked in amazement. "Was calling the
Beast down upon Bratu not a show for Soth's benefit, a demonstration of our loyalty to him? At
least the *giorgios* at the mine would pay for such
a spectacle."

"If you think Soth offers us an empty hand, go to
the Widow's Bridge and count the corpses of our enemies. We need him, Daughter. Do not forget that."

"I will not forget that you value a dead man's opinion of you more than you value your own people."

The slap caught Inza completely by surprise. No
tears rose in her eyes, only a writhing, curling fury.
The girl grabbed for the dagger in her boot. The
blade had just cleared her boot top when Sabak's
jaws locked onto her hand. His warning growl sent
tremors all the way up to her shoulder.

"Let her go," Magda said, seizing the hound by the scruff of his neck. But Sabak held tight until Inza dropped the weapon into the dirt.

The dagger's thin blade reflected the firelight like a mirror. The radiance was almost blinding. Even the leather-wrapped handle seemed to glow.

"I don't remember giving you this," Magda said.

"Not everything I own came from you."

Ignoring her daughter's peevish reply, the *raunie* reached down for the dagger. She drew her hand back quickly when she nicked her finger on the blade's point. "Ai, that's sharp. Where did you get it?"

"A trade," Inza said sullenly. "A very good trade." Eyeing Sabak, she warily slipped the weapon back into the sheath she'd sewn into her boot. "In some things you taught me very well, Mother."

Inza turned her back on Magda and disappeared into the woods. She hadn't been dismissed, but the *raunie* knew it would be pointless to force the issue. At best, she might make her daughter acknowledge her power. At worst, she would be left shouting after the disobedient girl while the rest of the troupe listened from within their *vardos*.

Exhaustion settled over her like a shroud, and Magda sank back down before the fire. Sabak slipped his head under her arm. After a moment, he nudged it up a little.

"So," Magda said as she stroked his head, "even you make demands of me this evening, eh?" His tail thumped agreeably.

The *raunie* stoked the fire and sank into deep thought. She had no idea what she was going to do about Inza. The girl was impetuous, hot tempered, and willful. Very much like her mother at that age, Magda recalled ruefully.

But there was a viciousness in the girl that Magda could not comprehend. It was as if she'd taken in all the destructiveness of the storm that shook Gundarak on the night she was born. The unearthly tempest had followed hard upon Duke Gundar's death. Some said it was the land itself mourning his demise. If so, it was all the grieving Gundar would get; his subjects marked the occasion with more festive displays of emotion. Perhaps that storm had damaged the newborn's soul somehow.

Magda ran a hand through her hair and winced as she brushed against a raw patch of scalp. The wounds she'd received at the bridge had been slow in healing. Her hiss of pain made Sabak glance up at her, canine worry in his eyes.

"Don't mind me, boy," she soothed, scrubbing him behind one ear. "My mood will brighten with the sunrise."

Her smile drifted away, and she gazed into the fire. It had been some time since she had tried to use her powers of precognition. Up until the day Soth rose from his throne, events had been unfolding as they should, in ways she could predict even without resorting to foresight. Things were different now. She could scarcely imagine what the morning would bring, let alone the coming months.

The incidents at the bridge still preyed heavily upon her mind, but more unsettling still were the secrets she had uncovered on her journey.

One part of Malocchio's rant had been correct—forces more ancient, more relentless than the lord of Invidia were stalking Soth. Magda had seen their faces. Soth would, too, before long. But what horrors would that long-delayed reunion unleash upon the Wanderers, upon all of Sithicus?

Magda focused on the fire. She tried to open her mind to the future, looking for its pattern in the flames. Flashes of white and red, curls of black smoke, filled her vision. They expanded into roses that burst into bloom, then withered. None held the field for long. Each overpowered another, only to be overwhelmed itself a moment later.

The *raunie* tried to turn her sight to the tribe's future. As she did, the fire roared up and filled the night with crimson light. Gone were the roses, drowned in a red sea—a sea of blood.

Magda pulled back sharply, forcing herself from the trance. At her side, Sabak growled softly. Magda thought the hound had sensed her discomfort at the vision's grim theme until she realized his attention was focused on something lurking by the *vardos*.

Magda turned to the semicircle of barrel-topped wagons. Shadows swayed over the brightly painted side of her *vardo*. They warped into unbelievable shapes, slithered and flowed down along the spoked wheels and onto the ground. Magda rubbed her eyes. Shadows played across the other wagons, too, but they were faint, fleeting things compared to the dark silhouettes creeping across hers. Nothing lay between the fire and her wagon to cast such weird shapes there.

Magda was on her feet the instant that thought was complete, a moment before the telltale saline reek reached her. "Salt shadows!" she screamed.

At the cry of recognition, the shadows retreated a little. For all that they were deadly, they were cowardly things more used to ambush than battle.

Muffled shouts sounded from inside the *vardos*, and Magda's warning was echoed and re-echoed. " 'Ware," the others hollered. "Shadows! Shadows!" The Wanderers burst from their homes, armed with whatever weapons were at hand. The mundane swords and knives would do no good against the animate darkness, but the Vistani hoped that they might distract the things long enough for their *raunie* to deal with them.

As the gypsies surrounded the dozen or so shadows, Magda held out her hand and summoned Gard. The cudgel had been carved by her ancestor, Kulchek the Wanderer, from the tree at the top of the world. The enchantments upon the weapon were strong. Its wood was unbreakable, able to turn back steel or stone with ease. Normal weapons might not be able to touch the salt shadows, but Gard could surely do them harm.

Since she had first unlocked the weapon's secrets, Magda had only to think of Gard and the cudgel would appear in her hand. This time, though, she closed her fingers on empty air. She could feel the club's reassuring weight in her hand, but it had no substance.

Cursing, she sidestepped a salt shadow as it slithered toward her foot. Sabak lunged at the oozing darkness, and it turned. The hair between the dog's shoulder and along the ridge of his spine bristled as the black shape darted across the ground toward the hound's paws.

"Sabak, back," Magda shouted, and the hound leaped out of the way.

Vitorio, the first Vistana to join Magda's fledgling troupe in Gundarak, drove a spear into the shadow's center. The darkness paused, then flowed around the offending spearhead like water around a post.

"*Raunie*," he cried, "where have these come from? We're nowhere near the mine!"

Magda didn't reply, for she had no answer. Salt shadows were denizens of Veidrava. Dark rites performed deep within the mine, in a chapel once known as a haven for hope, had resurrected the souls of the pit's countless victims. Clothed in the mine's eternal darkness, the shadows hungered for new flesh. They could not leave the dark; sunlight was fatal to them. How these lost souls had got so far from Veidrava was a mystery, one the *raunie* had no time to solve.

The Wanderers had succeeded in drawing the shadows apart. The gypsies taunted the shades with the simple lure of their own warm flesh. Men and shadows turned in wary circles like dancers at some macabre ball.

Magda concentrated again on conjuring Gard. As she understood the workings of its magic, the weapon resided in some hidden pocket, intangible but close to hand. It seemed now, though, that someone else had taken hold of it. She could feel the resistance, cold hands countering her own.

"I am Kulchek's heir," Magda snarled. "Gard belongs to me!"

With that she wrenched the weapon free. No sooner did Gard appear in her hands that Magda lashed out with it.

Like a rock breaking the surface of a still pond, the blow from Gard sent ripples across the shadow's form. The thing screamed, a liquid hiss that made Magda tremble. Another blow and the shadow detonated. Globs of darkness splashed in all directions.

Where they struck flesh, the awful missiles burned. They withered grass, peeled paint from wood, and leeched dye from cloth. The fragments lacked the power of the sum. The disrupted shadow could not press its assault. The lumps and puddles only wriggled and oozed across the ground, slowly but steadily reforming into a lethal whole.

Sabak pawed at the assembling pieces, delaying their merger for as long as possible. In quick succession, Magda shattered two more of the shadows. Each time the cudgel fell, the things let out agonized screams that chilled the Vistana to the core. Still, she felt hopeful. The Wanderers were holding their own against the creatures.

"Mother, help me!"

The cry came from the forest's verge. There, at the very edge of the firelight's reach, stood Inza. Two salt shadows had somehow escaped the Wanderers' notice. They had the girl cornered, one on the ground, the second on a thick old oak. If she retreated back into the woods, it would be too dark to distinguish the salt shadows from the normal nighttime gloom. The shades would have her at their mercy.

Magda hesitated. The others were tiring. They needed her help, too. But this was her daughter. Of all the ragtag troupe, only she was the *raunie*'s blood. Magda dashed across the clearing.

She struck the shadow on the ground three times before it finally broke apart. The spattering ooze caught Inza full in the face, and the girl fell back against the tree. The shadow there slithered onto her hand. It wrapped itself around Inza's fingers, pulsing up to her forearm before Magda lashed out again with Gard. The blow fell upon the part of the shadow that still clung to the oak. That one strike blasted the thing apart. From the sharp *crack* that rang out, drowning out the creature's scream and Inza's shrieks for help, Magda thought that she had cleft the tree.

It was not the oak that had cracked, but Gard. Magda stared at the cudgel, tracing the hairline fracture that now ran the ancient weapon's length. "Unbreakable," she murmured, repeating a line from an old Vistani tale. " 'Only Kulchek's own blade could cut the wood of Gard.' "

Magda was so caught up in considering the remarkable damage to Gard, she didn't hear Vitorio's cry of warning. The shadow he'd been baiting had broken away suddenly and was rushing toward the *raunie*. Three more followed, as if they'd realized the significance of that resounding *crack*.

With a cry, Vitorio threw himself onto the shadow.

The thing shuddered at the impact, then curled back upon the old man. A dozen inky bands clamped around his arms, pinning them. The shadow slipped across his chest, his neck. Finally it swept onto the Vistana's head and formed a seamless mask. Vitorio didn't scream. He kept his teeth clamped shut against the shadow, to no avail. The ooze patiently seeped into his ears and his nose. When his lungs finally shrieked for air and his mouth flew open in a futile gasp, the rest of the shadow pulsed down his throat.

The old man staggered to his feet. He tried to take a step toward the fire, but the shadow would not let him. "For my soul's sake," he pleaded, "destroy me!"

From the steps of one of the *vardos*, a hulking figure emerged. Bandages held his fingers together and covered his ravaged ears. It was Bratu.

The madman loped through the chaos and scooped up Vitorio. Arms that had held the man in innumerable bear hugs over the years now hoisted him high off the ground. A look of fathomless sadness hung upon Bratu's face as he raised Vitorio up—and tossed the old man into the fire's heart.

Vitorio's body was alight in an instant. He rolled in the fire, caught between the shadow's urge to save itself and the Vistana's desire to see the thing destroyed. Now that it had taken flesh once more, the salt shadow was vulnerable to those things that consumed the flesh, particularly fire.

At last Vitorio collapsed into the coals. The man's sigh of satisfaction was mingled with the wail of the shadow, having found form after so many years, only to have it stripped away. Bratu lingered a moment. It was unclear if he were saying a silent farewell to his friend or merely making certain the corpse would not escape the blaze. Finally, though, he turned his back on the carnage and disappeared into the woods.

From her vantage at the edge of the fighting, Inza watched Bratu go. It was tempting to go after him, for the madman could have only one destination: the secret lair of the Whispering Beast. Once he set off on that journey he was lost to the tribe forever.

A piteous barking drew her attention back to the camp. Sabak had finally got too close to one of the shadows. The thing was wrapped around a forelimb. Though he bit at it furiously, the hound couldn't get a grip on the shadow. The darkness clung to his jaws, wrapped around his lolling tongue, then flowed down his throat.

A shudder rippled through Sabak's flesh, and a single yip of confusion escaped his muzzle. He turned circles—once, twice. On the third turn he stopped and faced the nearest Vistana. Lips pulled back in a snarl, he pounced. The woman managed a gulp of surprise before Sabak tore out her throat. The hound stood over her body in triumph. Blood dribbled from his jaws onto her white blouse.

Magda howled with anguish, but noble Sabak had not finished his grisly work. He leapt from the corpse and charged toward the edge of the woods, toward Inza.

Magda moved to block Sabak's charge. If there were any of his faithful hound's heart left untainted by the shadow, she might win him back. If not, she would be the one to end his suffering.

As the *raunie* stepped toward her daughter, something cold seized her foot and she stumbled. By the time she regained her balance, the shadow that had grabbed her was almost to her knee. Another squirmed across the ground to join it. With all the strength she could distill from her rage and sorrow, Magda struck this second attacker. The creature exploded, but the victory came at a terrible price. As Gard struck the ground, it snapped with the sickening sound of a bone breaking.

Magda clutched a fragment of the shattered cudgel as she fell to her knees, hacking at the shadow wrapped tight as a tourniquet around her right thigh. Each blow gouged another grisly runnel in her leg and sent a crimson haze of pain across her vision. "The sea of blood," she murmured. "The end so soon."

The fog before her eyes cleared just enough for Magda to see Sabak corner her daughter against a *vardo*. The hound lunged, but Inza didn't flinch. With the coolness of a trained assassin, she sidestepped the attack and plunged her dagger into the top of Sabak's head. The knife's handle still jutted from the dog's shattered skull when his corpse hit the ground.

Magda wept tears of relief and sorrow. She scarcely noticed as another shadow crawled onto her crippled leg, and another. Finally she toppled to the ground. She could feel the dank coolness of the shadows' touch as they crept across her back. The dark, liquid forms merged, forming a single band around her throat.

The shadows did not intend to possess her form. They meant to destroy her.

A single name escaped the *raunie*'s lips: "Soth."

The death knight emerged from the mundane shadows cast by the fire. He drew his sword, blade dark with the blood of a hundred slaughtered foes, and scattered the salt shadows before him. The damned souls cringed at his passing. They could not bear the touch of his dead flesh, and the unearthly cold that radiated from his form, the eternal ache of the grave, withered them like orchids in a blizzard.

The Knight of the Black Rose fell to one knee beside Magda. With his gauntleted fingers he tore away the shadows from her throat. They writhed in his grasp until he crushed them, leaving only a fine ebon dust that whispered through his fingers.

"I gave you my word," the death knight said. "I am here."

"Not soon enough," she rasped, "but that is my fault." Magda closed her eyes and held her hand to her savaged throat. The fingers came away bloody. "I am through."

Soth dropped his other knee and cradled Magda's head in a fashion that was almost tender. He raised her so that he might hear her swiftly fading voice.

"I go to my ancestors," she said, "or, rather, they come to claim me. Such is always the way, great lord. The past cannot be denied."

"Perhaps," he murmured.

"But it need not be a trap." The *raunie* looked up at the Wanderers, who stood in somber array behind Soth. Inza was there, too. The girl's green eyes were hard, her face an unreadable mask.

"My child will help you prove that," Magda continued. "Swear you will protect her as you vowed to protect me."

The death knight bowed his head. "As master of this cursed land, you have my word."

"In return, I lift the curse my grandmother laid upon you on the night you entered these dark domains," Magda said. A fit of coughing took hold of her, and it was a moment before she could speak again. "For killing my family, Madame Girani damned you never to return to your home, though it always be in view. For vowing to preserve my family, I remove that curse and wish you safe journey."

Had Soth's withered heart been able to beat, it would have thundered in his chest. "Can you grant me passage from this place?" he asked.

"No," Magda said. "But there are others . . ."

Her eyes fluttered closed, and she reached up a trembling hand to the death knight. In her bloody fingers she clutched a single white rose. "She comes for you."

With that, Magda Ilyanova Kulchevich died.

Lord Soth plucked the rose from the corpse's fingers. As he took that fragile bloom in his hand, something marvelous occurred. A white moon joined unseen Nuitari in the nighttime sky. Its lovely light shone down on Sithicus, bathing the land in a radiance that made everything seem at peace, if only for a little while.

"Solinari," the death knight whispered. "The white moon of Krynn."

The people of Sithicus interpreted the moon's appearance in myriad ways. Some thought it a harbinger of doom, others a sign that the time of troubles had ended. To Soth, though, the meaning of that pale white orb was clear. He was one step closer to home.

"What will you do about Malocchio?" Inza asked, interrupting Soth's musings.

The death knight regarded the girl coolly. "You think him responsible for the assassins?"

"Who else could it be?" Inza looked to the other members of the troupe. They remained silent, just as she had expected.

Soth didn't notice. He had started across the camp, to the spot where Sabak's corpse lay. A salt shadow protruded from its open mouth, struggling to free itself from the body. The death knight withdrew the dagger from the hound's skull. Quickly the shadow slithered up the nearest *vardo*'s wheel and into the open window.

"Whose wagon is this?" Soth asked.

"Mine," Inza replied. "As is the knife."

Soth studied the dagger for a moment. "Impressive," he said as he handed the weapon to her. He presented it handle first. As the girl took it, the blade's needle point scored the fingers of the dead man's gauntlet.

Soth did not ask for permission to enter the *vardo*; like all things in Sithicus, the wagon was his property.

He was startled to find the interior so similar to the cluttered wagon kept by Madame Girani. A high stack of manuscripts collected dust in one corner. A cloth-covered table held a heap of trinkets and small boxes crammed with charms. Cages housing all manner of strange birds hung from the rafters; they chittered and chirped nervously at the death knight's passing.

"Why would the shadow hide here?" Inza asked from the doorway.

Soth tossed aside the carpet covering an ornately carved chest hidden toward the back of the wagon. Salt was scattered on the floor all around the box. "Because this is where it, and all the others, had been hiding for days," Soth rumbled.

He threw open the box. The shadow hung on the underside of the lid like some monstrous spider. It dropped onto the salt heaped in the chest, trying to bury itself. Soth snatched the thing up and slowly crushed it.

Inza crowded close. The chill of Soth's presence didn't seem to bother her in the least. "How did Malocchio hide the shadows in there?" she said.

Soth slammed the chest shut. "It wasn't Malocchio who sent the assassins. It was Azrael."

SEVEN

Azrael should have realized something was wrong when the voices at the Lake of Sounds went suddenly silent.

When it happened, the dwarf was listening to the dark describe what his kingdom would be like. There were other things he should have been tending to—the hunt for the White Rose, eavesdropping on Soth or the Wanderers—but those were tedious, empty pursuits compared to the construction of the new Sithicus, even if only in his mind.

As always, the dark had been describing his realm with the stolen words of others:

"You've never seen such a look of *terror*."

"It *will be* easy to get her to leave."

"*All* of this needs to be cleaned up."

"It was *Azrael*."

Somewhere at the back of his mind, the dwarf dimly recognized that last voice. He had no time to identify the speaker, though. A hush had settled over the lake, a fear-thick pall that seemed to make the purple twilight tremble. Azrael's white brows knitted together in consternation. "What's going on?" he murmured.

The question had not died upon his lips when the answer came. A hand gauntleted in ancient, fire-blackened armor gripped Azrael's shoulder. "Traitor," said a hollow voice. The word reverberated across the still, black water. A heartbeat later that sound was joined by the dwarf's groan as he slammed against the cavern's salt-crusted wall.

"Mighty lord," Azrael gasped, scrambling to his knees before Soth, "what have I done to offend you?"

Soth did not answer, merely traced a symbol in the air. The glyph hung there, burning with the same orange fire that lit the death knight's eyes. It appeared an instant later on Azrael's forehead. The brand flared, then vanished.

The dwarf stiffened, and a strangled cry of agony rasped from his throat. Rivulets of blood trickled from his snout and ears.

The death knight clamped his hands to either side of Azrael's head and lifted the dwarf from the ground. Slowly, he began to tighten his grip, pressing his palms together like the jaws of a vice. Azrael howled in pain. With fingers ending now in a badger's thick black claws, he tore at Soth's arms. "Mercy," he cried.

"You showed Magda no mercy," Soth replied coolly. In his hands the dwarf's face shuddered, bones sliding into their hybrid configuration. In response, the death knight shifted his thumbs up from Azrael's cheeks to the dwarf's tearing eyes.

"I did it to protect you!" The werebeast thrashed like the captured animal he was. He clawed at Soth's helmet, kicking his armored chest "She'd joined the Thorns," he snarled. "Allied with the White Rose. She was plotting to destroy you!"

Soth's grip went slack, and Azrael dropped to the cavern floor. He writhed there for a time, retching from the pain. The ringing in his skull made him claw at his temples. Finally he slumped back against the cavern wall.

"Proof," Soth said. "Convince me of what you say, or you will die."

"After the meeting with Aderre, Magda went off alone into the Iron Hills to find the White Rose," Azrael replied. He wiped the vomit from his muzzle. "She must not have thought you capable of protecting her. Or maybe she had been in league with the Rose all along."

"Conjecture," Soth rumbled.

"No," Azrael said quickly. With one clawed hand he indicated the vast and silent lake. "This place allows me to eavesdrop on her and on almost anyone in the land. Magda wouldn't speak of her mission to her people, or tell them she doubted your ability to protect her, but she whined about those things incessantly to that flea-ridden hound of hers as they traveled to the hills."

"What did the White Rose say to her? What was their plot against me?"

Azrael shifted uneasily. "I, uh . . . cannot hear the White Rose's voice, or that of anyone within her presence."

"Feh," Soth snorted. "You stall for time." His sword scraped from its scabbard.

"Magda was carrying a white rose," Azrael offered desperately. "It was a symbol of her allegiance. The flower can be grown nowhere in Sithicus but the Iron Hills, in the territory controlled by the Thorns. That's proof she met with the rebels."

Soth sheathed his sword and paced along the stony shelf. "She handed me the flower as she died," he said at last.

Azrael nodded. "She wanted you to think the Rose might help you escape this place. That was her intent all along, to make you a party to your own destruction. It's the only way they could defeat you, mighty lord."

Emboldened by the death knight's hesitation, Azrael struggled to his feet. He slipped his chain of office from his neck and held it out to Soth. Head lowered, he said, "I thought I was doing my duty in sending the shadows against her."

Sardonic laughter escaped Soth's lips. Another seneschal had spoken similar words of contrition, in a time and place far removed from Sithicus. Back in the days when Soth's heart still beat, before his damnation to eternal unlife, he had confronted that minion with the disappearance of his first wife. The Knights of Solamnia had accused Soth of murdering Lady Gladria, to clear the path to his bed for the elf maid with whom he had betrayed his marriage vows.

"A hundred times I'd heard you voice a wish that the woman be gone," Caradoc had said. He, too, had presented Soth his chain of office. "I thought I was doing my duty in sending her away."

Soth had been unable to deny that he'd secretly longed for Gladria's demise, that Caradoc had only acted upon desires he himself had been incapable of acting upon. The man had merely done what he thought best for his lord, for the land.

So, too, with Azrael. The dwarf could see Magda's treachery where he had been blind. He should have seen the white rose as a sign of her alliance with the rebels. Instead, he had misinterpreted it as a sign of hope. And hope is something better left to fools and madmen in Sithicus, Soth reminded himself bitterly.

"I no longer have need of a seneschal," the death knight said. He took the heavy chain, letting it dangle from his mailed fist. "The office seems to corrupt whoever holds it. There is another mantle for you to wear, Azrael—one to which you are much more suited."

"Anything, mighty lord."

"Devote yourself, and whatever agents you can muster, to the eradication of the White Rose's allies. She is a general, a clever one, but a general is nothing without troops."

"And the Rose herself?"

"I will deal with her when the time comes," Soth replied.

Azrael turned to go, but the death knight held up a restraining hand. "Do not mistake this stay of execution for a pardon," Soth said coldly. He tightened his fist and crushed the heavy chain. "Know that my gaze will be upon you as you do my bidding. You are my minion, Azrael. Reach above that station again, and your death agonies will be legend, even in Sithicus."

Glumly, Azrael nodded.

"Good." Soth dropped the broken chain. The metallic *clank* rang out over the lake. "You will explain this place to me," he said, turning to the water. "I can see that it might be quite useful."

Azrael chronicled how he had discovered the lake and explained the water's properties. He failed to mention that the dark spoke to him in special ways, that those voices told him of the palace he would raise upon the ruins of Soth's crumbling keep. The death knight's anger and the narrowness of the dwarf's escape had engendered a new caution in him, even a little fear. But he did not fear anything enough to betray the dark.

When the dwarf had gone, Soth removed his helmet and his right gauntlet. Cautiously he dipped two fingers into the lake and touched the salty liquid to his scarred, scabrous lips. Voices filled his ears, a riot of sound more staggering than the banshees' keening. The babble overwhelmed him, and he sat stunned on the stony shore.

Finally, Soth's consciousness found an anchor: his name. Someone in the domain had spoken the death knight's name.

Slowly, warily, the master of Nedragaard Keep gained control of the clamor. He listened for hours as his subjects spoke of him, as he would many times in the coming days. From those confused, fractured exchanges he plucked bits of his story that he had forgotten. These divers tales could not completely mend the death knight's ravaged memory; there was too much of his life that the peasants did not know. Yet each new breach that was filled, every gap bridged, let him realize how much of himself he had lost and made him all the more certain he would recover every bit of his forgotten life.

* * * * *

Evening at Veidrava usually found the day-shift miners and their spouses at Ambrose's store. The place was more than a market; it was a meeting hall and tavern, even a hospital when circumstances demanded. On most nights, people crowded together in knots, trading tales of woe or laughing at execrable jokes. The men congregated at the makeshift bar Ambrose set up in the empty area used for gatherings and weddings and such. They talked of the pit. The women milled in the store proper, poking through the knicknacks and sundries, discussing life aboveground. Grubby children dashed between the two camps, and everywhere else, until Kern or Ogier or one of the other "regulars" chased them outside.

That was before Azrael commenced his hunt for agents of the White Rose.

The dwarf had always been an unwelcome presence at the mine. He was brutal and prompted the pit bosses to be the same. The seneschal had ears in every wall, it seemed. Sometimes he would recite the most intensely private conversations as if he had been right in the room when they'd been spoken.

Now, though, Azrael and his police—the Politskara, he called them—loomed large over every aspect of life at Veidrava. He recruited the most vicious of the pit bosses, the toughest miners, and most feared soldiers. It was their job to root out traitors. They suspected everyone of subversion, of secretly supporting the White Rose and her Thorns. When they found the least bit of evidence to support that suspicion, people simply disappeared.

The workers and their families feared the Politskara like nothing Ambrose had ever seen. Worse, they'd come to mistrust their friends and neighbors. Old grudges prompted brothers to inform on their brothers, wives to turn in their husbands. Almost no one came to Ambrose's now. It was better to stay at home and wait for the reign of terror to end.

This night only a half-dozen or so stalwart souls lingered at the store. Ambrose, Kern, and Ogier hunched over the bar, arguing their way through a game of Stones and Bones. The three were all but inseparable and had been ever since they'd first gone down the pit together. Only Ambrose's accident kept them apart during the day. The other two still went down the mine, as they had every sunrise for the past thirty years.

Ganelon slumped against the store's counter, fighting off boredom. Two women were picking over Ambrose's supply of cloth, and a rag-clad little girl, some maltreated miner's child, wandered in and out of the aisles. Ganelon suspected she was hiding from someone by the way she looked over her shoulder at every odd noise. She also kept the hood of her threadbare cloak pulled up around her fine-boned face. Probably on the run from some drunken lout of a father, Ganelon mused. Still, he watched her carefully, in case her skittishness proved the sign of an inexperienced thief.

A sudden cough of Ambrose's phlegmy laughter startled Ganelon out of his scrutiny.

"Here's a first," Ambrose wheezed. "Ogier comes out the victor in a battle of wits!"

The big man nodded proudly. "That's a bottle of Malaturno you owe me," Ogier said. The prize was a dear one, wine from an obscure Invidian vineyard.

Kern still stared down at the remnants of the game. "Bleat away," he said, tugging at his thin beard. His foul mood radiated from him like heat from a well-banked stove. "I still think you've pulled the wool over my eyes somewhere here, Sheep."

Ogier's thick head of curls, now gone white with age, had inspired that nickname. His gentleness made it stick. From Kern's lips, though, the name was a direct comment upon Ogier's low intelligence. The big man's smile drooped into a pout.

Kern regretted the insult the moment he saw its effect upon his friend. "Two bottles," he offered. "If you think you're a big enough boy to handle that much—and Ambrose can provide the goods."

A decade past, Kern might have trekked across the border himself for the prize. He always was the most adventurous of the trio. Like Ambrose and Ogier, though, concern for Helain kept him closer to home these days

The shopkeep clapped the smaller man on the shoulder. "I'll see what I can do," he said. "The Vistani haven't been much for trading with me since Magda died, and no one else is going to be caught dead bartering at the border. How about another game? See if you two can even things up and save me the trouble."

The store's main doors burst open. One of the wooden panels shattered; it fell to the floor like so much kindling.

Framed by the doorjamb were two of Azrael's Politskara. The miners knew one of them, a heartless tough named Markel who'd been conscripted from the pit. He brandished a small silver axe. Each *politska* carried one, though Markel seemed intent on using his every chance he got. Hence the shattered door.

The other was an elf. He regarded Ambrose, Ganelon, even Markel with a look of open disdain. Azrael hadn't exempted the citizens of Mal-Erek, Hroth, or Har-Thelen from service; the wild elves were their enemies, too, though it was hard to imagine them despising the savages any more thoroughly than they did the humans.

"We have a report of a stranger hereabouts," Markel announced. "Seen on your doorstep, in fact."

The pair offered no more of an explanation before splitting up to search the store. They pulled Ganelon from behind the counter and shoved him roughly to the floor. When he tried to protest, the elf kicked him in the ribs. "You've gotta teach the boy manners," Markel shouted to Ambrose.

The two *politskae* moved on, shoving aside any barrel or crate in their way, causing as much casual chaos as they could manage. When they came to the two women, they snatched the cloth bags that held their purchases.

"Sorry to have to do this, dears," Markel said as he upended the sacks. He poked through the scattered contents with the toe of his boot, searching for the white rose carried by the Thorns.

"I've never even seen a white rose," one of the women cried.

"No one around here has," her friend added, "not in ten years."

"The Politskara knows otherwise," Markel said smugly. He slapped both women hard enough to drive them to their knees.

Ganelon watched the brutality with growing anger and indignation. He pushed himself from the floor. Someone has to stop this, he decided. His hands curled into fists, and he took a step toward Markel.

"Don't even think about it, son," Ambrose warned in a quiet tone. He wrapped one flabby arm around the young man's shoulder. "You've got to remember your promise to Helain and stay out of trouble. That oath might be the only thing she has to hold on to. Let them break a few chairs, feel big about themselves. They'll be gone soon enough."

Helain's name struck Ganelon like a dash of ice water. For her sake, and his own honor, he would stay true to his oath.

"All right," the young man growled. He moved to the counter, limping heavily on his left leg. He still didn't know how he'd injured himself, but whatever strain or sprain he'd suffered wasn't getting any better. At the moment, it felt as if unseen hands were twisting the limb, wringing it like a wet cloth.

Markel didn't bother to interrogate Ogier or Kern. Instead, he headed up the wooden stairs to the second floor. Ganelon turned pleading eyes toward Ambrose, begging for permission to act.

"I said stay out of this, and I meant it." A dark expression clouded the shopkeep's face, one Ganelon had never seen there before. "Trust me. I'll handle this," he whispered.

Ambrose trundled to the foot of the stairs. "There's a sick girl up there, Markel. Azrael himself told me that she wouldn't be disturbed."

The *politska* regarded the door before him. "Which room's she in?" he asked. Before Ambrose could answer, Markel kicked in the door. "Not this one, I hope."

Shocked from sleep, Helain let out a terrified shriek. Ambrose was up the steps much faster than Ganelon would have suspected possible, though he was clutching his chest as he lumbered across the landing. If he's not careful, his heart will burst, the young man brooded. Another thought followed that, as disturbing as it was sudden: No, it can't. Ambrose is already dead.

A high-pitched scream from the store's shelving made Ganelon start. "The little girl," he hissed.

He found Markel's partner shaking her violently. "Why are you here?" the elf shouted. When she didn't respond, he slammed her against the heavy wooden shelves. The impact shook loose a box of iron nails; they rained down onto the floor like metallic hail. Keeping the girl pinned against the shelving with one hand, the elf reached down for a nail. The use he intended for the spike was clear in his hate-filled gray eyes.

"Leave her alone!" Ganelon shouted. "She's only a child!"

One eyebrow quirked in surprise, the elf regarded the young man. "Hey," he called out to his partner, "this bumpkin is interfering with my interrogation."

Over the sounds of Helain's frightened weeping, Ganelon could hear an argument building on the second floor. The interplay of murmurs had devolved into an exchange of barked insults.

"Markel?" the elf shouted. But the argument had become a scuffle. The *politska* tossed the child aside. He barely spared her a second look as she tumbled into a pile of Borcan cloth. "I'm coming," he called.

Too late. From the landing came a gasp of pain and a wet, lingering death rattle. A heavy *thud*,

thud, thud told of a body bumping down the wooden stairs. Ganelon's heart stopped. They'd killed Ambrose!

When the young man emerged from the shelving, the elf close behind, he found not Ambrose but Markel heaped at the foot of the stairs. The shopkeep was crouched over the corpse. The silver axe clutched in his hand was dark with the *politska*'s blood.

Ambrose gestured with the axe toward the two women. "Get them out of here." His voice was deep and resonant, unburdened by the constant wheeze caused by his accident. "Now!"

Kern and Ogier were as startled as anyone at the change in their usually mild-mannered friend, but they didn't hesitate to follow his orders. "An unfortunate accident," Kern said as he shepherded the women into the night. "The man tripped and fell upon his own weapon."

Ogier scowled. "But the wound's in the middle of his back."

"No more unusual around these parts than someone strangled by his own tongue," Kern replied with a sigh.

The elven *politska* shouted after the women, "You'll be called as witnesses. Don't think I've forgotten your faces."

"I'm sure they've already forgotten yours," Ambrose said. He raised the axe and started forward. There was something liquid to his movements, a grace he'd never demonstrated before. He swayed like a serpent, or a shadow cast by a flickering fire.

Ganelon found himself backing away along with the elf. "Ambrose," he said softly.

"Shut up," the innkeep hissed. "See to the girl."

"She's my prisoner," the elf said, though he never took his eyes off Ambrose. To lower his guard, to turn away for just an instant, would be death. He could see that in the shopkeep's grim face.

Head swimming, Ganelon hurried into the aisles to find the little girl. He found her lying in the midst of a jumbled pile of Borcan cloth. She was dazed and struggling to free herself.

"Here," Ganelon said. "Let me help you up."

He pulled her to her feet. As he did, the tattered hood fell away, revealing short blond hair and pointed ears. This was no little girl but a young elven boy. The tattoos curling from his temples down the sides of his neck—a scattering of triangles and swirls—marked him as belonging to one of the feral Iron Hills tribes. Ganelon looked again at the tattoos. Not triangles and swirls, he thought, thorns and stems.

The *politskae* had been correct. The stranger was a spy, a Thorn of the White Rose.

"Why are you here?" Ganelon gasped. "What do you want with us?"

"With *you*," the elf said. "I bring a message from the most holy and terrible White Rose."

Ambrose came around the corner, a silver axe in each hand, a trail of bloody footprints behind him. "What's this?" he boomed.

The Thorn's face went pale with fear. It wasn't the weapons or the blood that inspired that fright.

Something else he recognized in Ambrose prompted him to whisper a prayer against evil and flee the shop.

"Wait," Ganelon shouted. "The message."

"Your hope lies with her," the Thorn called as he dashed out the door.

The young man crossed the room as quickly as his aching leg would carry him. Ambrose caught him well before he reached the door. "Where do you think you're going?" the shopkeep growled.

"I want to know what this is all about." Ganelon tried to pull free of the older man's restraining grip but found that he couldn't. In fact, Ambrose's fingers were digging painfully into his arm. "You're hurting me, Ambrose."

"You're hurting yourself," was the cold reply. Ambrose released his hold on Ganelon and turned away. "You're hurting Helain, too."

Crouched at the top of the stairs, Helain choked back a cry of despair. She clutched at her long white nightgown, at the flesh beneath, until half-moons of blood welled up. Her eyes displayed an overwhelming sorrow that seemed to stain her soul more deeply with each word the two men uttered.

Ganelon covered his face with one hand. "You're right," he said. "Why shouldn't I be tempted to join the fight when all this is going on around me?"

"Because you promised her you wouldn't," replied Ambrose. "Because you love her, and she loves you."

With a howl of anguish, Helain raced across the landing and threw herself at a closed window. The glass shattered, its jagged edges claiming gory ribbons of flesh from her arms and back. Blood stained her white nightgown the same fiery red as her hair.

Helain dropped to the ground with a bestial grunt. Cringing in the light of the new white moon, she wondered if she had hoped for death. That was not to be, at least not tonight. Some terrible benefactor had spared her from serious harm. She could not hear his voice, as she thought she would, but she knew she must go to him. Tears streaming down her cheeks, she ran off into the night.

From the store's doorway, Ganelon caught sight of Helain just before she disappeared amongst the crooked towers and heaps of broken earth at the mine. She was heading over the hill. He didn't hesitate, didn't pause to ask for Ambrose's blessing or his help. Ganelon damned his aching leg and set off after his fiancée.

Ambrose watched him go, then closed the shop's shattered doors as best he could. Ogier and Kern would be back in a moment, to help him dispose of the bodies. There was no need for secrecy, but they wouldn't understand that. They did not know about Ambrose's pact with Azrael or his other, more terrible secrets. He would have to come up with some explanation for his actions tonight, a reason his infirmities seemed to vanish the moment the fight started and blood was spilled.

He glanced down at Markel's corpse and felt the fury well up inside him again. "This is your fault," Ambrose said through gritted teeth.

He snatched up one of the silver axes. With frenzied strokes he hacked at the body until it flew apart. When there was too little left of Markel to satisfy his rage, Ambrose started in on the elven *politska*. He did not stop until that corpse, too, had been reduced to gory lumps.

Fury spent, Ambrose paused to survey his work. He didn't even realize what he was doing as he slowly crushed the silver axe between his palms. The twisted blade cut into his fingers. He did not cry out, merely watched the blood spatter onto the floor.

As Ambrose turned away, the dark drops slithered across the warped boards to join his shadow.

EIGHT

The pursuit was hopeless. Ganelon realized that from the moment he began it. His aching leg left him little chance of keeping pace with Helain. The strangling character of the Sithican wilds left him even less chance of finding her should she abandon the road. Somehow, though, he managed to keep her in sight for several hours.

After her initial wild flight from Ambrose's place, Helain made her way more slowly through the foothills of the Misttop Mountains. She kept to the narrow but straight road that ran north to the Musarde River and eventually ended at the wide east-west trade route known as the Merchants' Slash. Bathed in the light of the strange new moon, torn nightgown fluttering behind her like broken wings, she seemed a phantom, a will o'wisp leading Ganelon in to peril. He half-expected her to vanish from before his eyes.

Shortly after they reached the Merchants' Slash, she did.

Helain only stayed on the hard-packed trade road long enough to cross it. Scorched earth edged the Slash on the north for its entire length, from the elven city of Har-Thelen to the border with Kartakass, one hundred and fifty miles to the east. Without a heartbeat's hesitation, Helain ventured into that wide band of blackened waste. From his position back on the Veidrava Road, Ganelon cursed. She was heading for the Fumewood.

Decades past, merchants slashed and burned the gap between the trade road and the stinking tangle of forest and mire that bordered it to the north. They'd hoped the buffer would make it more difficult for the Fumewood's denizens to ambush travelers and caravans. It didn't. The merchants maintained the buffer anyway, even after trade along the route diminished to a trickle. Effective or not, the band of scorched earth let them feel they were doing something to drive back the dark.

For just an instant, as he crossed the trade road, Ganelon took his eyes off Helain and peered anxiously at the Fumewood. And in that instant, she was gone.

When he saw that he had lost her, Ganelon stood for a moment and braced his hands against the pain lancing his sides. "Where are you?" he whispered between exhausted huffs. The cold night air transmuted each heaving breath into steam. Even the wisps seemed to taunt him; the white shapes lingered before his eyes for an instant—Helain in her flowing gown—before they, too, disappeared.

Fighting back despair, Ganelon tried to reason out the situation.

Helain couldn't have reached the tree line. She simply wasn't moving that quickly. There was nowhere for her to hide, nothing between the road and the forest large enough to conceal a house cat. She might have fallen into a ditch, but when Ganelon surveyed the landscape, he was stunned at how absolutely flat it appeared. The merchants had done a remarkable job driving back the wood and keeping the buffer clear. Ganelon couldn't imagine how anything could creep across that blasted waste and surprise someone on the road, though he knew such attacks were no rarity on the Slash.

Ganelon didn't call out. Helain wouldn't have answered him even if he did, and the noise would most certainly draw unwelcome attention from the Fumewood. Instead, he started across the buffer. As he stepped off the road, a prayer came to his lips. It was an old soldier's benison, one he'd never particularly liked. Somehow, though, it felt right now. "Fate favor me," he said. "Fear flee me."

Swirls of ash blew across the blasted ground, obscuring any trace of Helain's passing. Ganelon did his best to remember her position when she vanished. Once he'd decided on a spot, he found a particularly tall oak on the edge of the distant Fumewood and made it his target. Since there was no landmark in the buffer to guide him, walking straight toward the tree would keep him from wandering off course.

The buffer turned out to be just as flat and featureless as it had appeared from the road. The way was so level that Ganelon's gaze tended to fix upon the more obvious danger of the Fumewood. More than once he thought he saw shapes moving against the trees, fleet figures that carried some sort of pole weapon.

Kendralihd has vomited up her denizens for the night, Ganelon thought. The village lay at the heart of the Fumewood. The creatures that dwelled there were the results of some unholy experiment at Nedragaard Keep. "Kender," they were called, gaunt little monstrosities with a penchant for thievery and a taste for human blood.

Ganelon shook his head. He had no idea where he'd learned about the kender, about Kendralihd. There were rumors of such creatures, campfire stories that told of vampires in the Fumewood, but the information he had was more like a military report, concise and detached.

Between his concern for Helain, the distraction of the sudden insight, and the looming menace of the Fumewood itself, Ganelon missed the small circle of darkness on the blackened ground before him. He stepped right over the hole and would have missed it entirely had his heel not sent a shower of dirt into the opening. The earth and small stones clattered noisily into the void, which made the young man whirl, ready for an attack.

When nothing sprang out at him, Ganelon crouched to examine the hole. It was the entrance to a narrow but expertly excavated tunnel. Not an entrance, he realized as he looked from the forest to the trade road, an exit. This was how the Fumewood's inhabitants managed to bypass the buffer. They used the tunnel—or tunnels—to cross beneath the open ground.

The hole had been hidden by a wooden cover disguised to blend with the surrounding blasted earth; if it hadn't slipped into the tunnel, Ganelon would have walked right over it. He looked back toward the road. He'd probably trodden over a half-dozen others already. A shudder gripped him. Suddenly, the Fumewood wasn't as far off as he'd thought.

He pushed that disconcerting thought aside and concentrated on his discovery. Scuff marks around the hole's perimeter and on the tunnel's lid told of a recent passing. Helain must have fallen into the hole; that would account for her sudden disappearance. Rather than climb back out, she'd simply plunged forward into the narrow, gradually sloping passage.

Ganelon climbed down into the dark. The creatures that had dug the tunnel had been smaller than men, but the way was just wide enough for him to proceed on hands and knees. He hesitated at the opening for a moment, wondering whether it would be best to leave the exit clear in case he needed to retreat in a hurry or replace the lid, so no other creatures would follow him into the tunnel. In the end, he decided to push the cover back into place. Should anything confront him underground, he'd have no chance to escape.

The tunnel's cramped quarters and lightless murk didn't bother Ganelon; his time in the pit at Veidrava had acclimatized him to those conditions. The smell most certainly did. Whatever creatures traveled in the tunnels did not wait to go aboveground to relieve themselves. Worse still, they seemed to devour their victims on the move, leaving behind gnawed bones and rotting flesh on their retreat to the Fumewood. That no rats or other scavengers ventured into the tunnels to claim these prizes did not escape Ganelon's notice, but he tried hard not to think about the reasons for their absence.

Ganelon felt the tunnel open up occasionally to the left and right. These spurs confirmed his suspicion that the buffer was laced with a network of cramped tunnels. He could only hope that Helain hadn't strayed from this route, wherever it led. If she had, he might never find her. Still, whenever he came upon an intersection, Ganelon paused to listen for some hint of her position.

It was during one such pause that he first noticed the snuffling. Something farther back in the tunnels was testing the air. It made a sound like a hound following a scent. Ganelon recognized the noise, but it sounded weird enough for him to guess that it was no dog there in the dark.

He tried to fight the panic, tried to push forward. Every time he moved, though, he lost the sound of the tracker. When that happened, his imagination placed the thing at his heels. He could almost feel its unseen hands wrapping around his ankles, its jaws locking on his aching legs. The tunnel was too cramped for him to fight back. Even if he could get turned around to face the thing, he had no weapon. He'd left the shop without so much as a kitchen knife.

At an intersection he paused once more. The awful sound came from both directions, louder now and undercut with a throaty chuckling. They—whatever they might be—were closing in on him.

He scrambled forward. Each scrape or scuff of his passing sounded like a cannonade to him, or maybe it was just the thundering of his pulse in his ears. Something sharp pierced his hand. Ganelon yelped in pain and surprise, thinking that one of the things had gotten in front of him somehow. It was merely a jagged piece of bone. He tore it from his palm and hurried on.

By the time he spotted the circle of faint light up ahead, Ganelon could hear the sound of his pursuers even over his own clumsy flight. Their passing produced a steady hiss, as of something being dragged across the dirt. Worse still was the huff and snort of their breathing and the rumble of their obscene laughter. The growing din told of a dozen creatures, maybe more, sliding through the darkness behind him.

He expected them to fall upon him at any moment. His left leg was useless. It trailed behind him as if death had already claimed it, hampering his already maddeningly slow flight. Once something took hold of that limb, but Ganelon kicked it away with his right leg. The pursuing thing chuckled more loudly.

Ganelon could scarcely believe it when he scrabbled out of the tunnel and clambered up the steep ring of excavated earth that circled the entrance. He'd made it! He stood a chance in the open. There might be something close by he could use as a weapon. Perhaps the creatures wouldn't even follow him out of the hole.

That last hope was dashed almost as soon as it formed.

The light of the white moon was faint here, choked by the canopy of trees overhead, but it lit the entrance enough for Ganelon to get a clear look at his pursuers as they burst from the tunnel. Not for the last time that evening, the young man wondered if all the nightmares in Sithicus had come alive somehow.

When the first bony hand emerged from the gloom, Ganelon rightfully mistook it for part of a giant bat. The three digits were thin and clawed, perched halfway along a larger limb webbed by a leathery membrane very much like a bat's wing. That semblance ended with the creature's head. It was bulbous, with the faceted eyes of an insect. Its mouth, too, was that of some monstrous bug. Its mandibles clacked open and closed, sucking in breath and expelling it as the horrible chuckling that had so unnerved Ganelon.

A second bat's wing snapped forward, bending at joints it should not possess, in ways that defied common sense. Still chuckling, the thing pulled itself up out of the tunnel. Its torso ended in a mass of short, writhing tentacles. Like the rest of its grotesque form, the squirming limbs were the sickly blue-white of a drowned man's flesh.

Ganelon threw himself over the top of the embankment and rolled to the forest floor beyond. He couldn't stand; his leg wouldn't support the weight. He crawled into the scrub. Thorny branches tore at his face, but he didn't notice.

They were coming for him. Ganelon shut his eyes tight, but he could still hear them pulling themselves through the dead leaves carpeting the ground. Others took to the air, their leathery wings stirring the bushes and fanning him with cold night air. All the while, they huffed and cackled and clacked their mandibles together hungrily.

"Helain," Ganelon whispered, "I'm sorry."

The solid *clank* of something metallic right beside him made Ganelon wince. He braced for the blow, for the rending claws and tearing mouths, but they did not come. Instead, a horrible shriek filled the night. Ganelon looked up to find the creatures retreating. They darted into the trees or stumbled over each other to reach the safety of the tunnels. Slack-jawed and incredulous, the young man stared at the fleeing beasts.

"I believe this belongs to you," said a melodious, cultured voice.

Ganelon was too exhausted to be startled, so chilled by Death's proximity that he merely turned and gaped at the weird figure standing behind him. A flowing cloak obscured the man's form. His face was hidden behind a full mask that was itself partially lost in the shadow cast by a wide-brimmed hat. Every stitch of his clothing was the same pale color, almost like the light of the new white moon.

"You frightened them off," Ganelon said.

The stranger nodded. When he did, Ganelon could smell the fragrance of flowers from the mask's long, hooked nose. Roses, he realized numbly. Of course.

"Why were they afraid of you?" the young man pressed.

"Because they are surprisingly bright for such hideous beasts," the stranger offered. He shifted the odd-looking mass of metal in his right hand; he balanced it against the ground and leaned on it like a walking stick. The contraption clanked again, this time more softly. "As I said, this belongs to you."

Ganelon studied the clutter of twisted rods and padded screws. It was some sort of leg brace. He'd seen miners wear similar ones at Veidrava, but never as elaborate as this. "Sorry, but you're mistaken." He rubbed his eyes, wiped away the blood from the scratches on his face. The shock was wearing off a little. "Did you see a woman come this way?" he asked as he crawled out of the scrub.

"Helain is safe," the stranger replied. He presented the brace yet again. "I hate to sound the pushy merchant, but I really do think this item is yours. It's the only reason I came."

Ganelon shoved the brace aside. "What do you know about Helain? Where is she?"

"Safe," the stranger replied, "or very nearly. The things in the Fumewood give the mad a wide berth. In a few days she'll have reached her destination."

"Which is?"

"A place you'd really do best to avoid."

"I'm supposed to take your word for that, I suppose," Ganelon snapped. "I don't believe a word of this."

The stranger shrugged and removed his mask. Ganelon had expected a scarred and hideous visage, but the man was handsome, preternaturally so. "What you believe is irrelevant to the truth of the matter, Ganelon. If you want to get Helain back, you need to recognize that fact."

"How do you know my name?" the young man asked. "No, never mind. I don't have time. Just tell me how to find her."

"No," the stranger said simply. "Not yet."

Ganelon took a threatening step forward, but his left leg buckled beneath him. He pitched forward into the dirt.

As the young man lay there, the stranger let the brace drop to the ground right next to his head. "Put it on, then we'll talk."

The thing fit perfectly, as if it had been forged for him. But the scuffs and the spots of rust—no, of blood, Ganelon realized with a shudder—revealed the brace as older and hard used. More unsettling still, Ganelon's hands seemed to know how to adjust the elaborate system of screws and knobs that held the thing to his flesh. Yet if he concentrated on the task, tried to think about what he was doing, his fingers faltered.

"Don't worry," the stranger said as he watched Ganelon make the last of the alignments, then struggle to his feet. "You'll get used to it if you allow yourself to. The memory is there. It's just obscured by the nature of this place."

Ganelon shook his head as if that might disperse the fog of confusion clouding his thoughts. It didn't. "Who are you?"

"You already know that, too," the stranger replied. "I'll give you a hint anyway."

He held out his gloved hands. The mask was gone. In its place he held a leather case, the same pale hue as his clothes. Even before the stranger let the case drop open like a well-read book, revealing the silver tools aligned so precisely within, Ganelon knew that he stood face to face with the Bloody Cobbler.

The Cobbler was a legend in Sithicus, a phantom who stalked through camp tales and bad dreams. He meted out rough justice to those who betrayed their callings. If the stories were to be believed, men and women who steadfastly refused to walk their intended paths through the world could expect a midnight visit from him. With his silver tools, he would slice the soles from their feet and use them to shod someone else, someone who only needed to be prompted back onto a road they truly wished to follow.

Bodies turned up now and then with parts of their feet missing, but it was easy for the skeptical to dismiss the damage as a scavenger's handiwork.

When someone suddenly switched careers, answered a calling that had long beckoned him, no supernatural agency had to be involved. After all, never remembered the Cobbler's visit—though Ganelon realized now that the phantom could have visited them nonetheless.

"Your repair was a bit more complicated than I'd anticipated," the Cobbler offered. His eyes twinkled with a mischievousness Ganelon found disarming, despite the menace of the gore-flecked knives in the case. "I should have realized that some of the more serious debilities of the, er, *donor* would carry to you. The brace will allow you to walk your road with a surer gait."

"Why?" the young man stammered.

"Why choose you? Because a life of adventure was the destiny you desired," the Cobbler replied. "It was a life you deserved."

"No," Ganelon said. "Why do this at all? What are you?"

"That sort of curiosity could get you in trouble," the Cobbler said darkly. "It killed the man for whom that brace was first crafted."

"Tell me anyway. I have to understand at least *that* much to be able to go on."

A satisfied smile lit the Cobbler's face. "Just the attitude I'd expect from a traveler on your lonely road," he said. Brushing back his cloak, he settled against a tree. "The best way to explain my purpose is to tell you a little story. You've no doubt heard variations on this unpleasant epic before, but never the truth.

"Once," he began grandly, "a long time ago, there was a knight of great renown. The man was graced with an agile intelligence and a strength of limb that perfectly suited him for his role as a champion of virtue. He possessed wisdom enough to recognize his destiny." The Cobbler laughed, the mirth tainted with a surprisingly potent bitterness. "A blind man could have recognized this knight's destiny—to lead his land, perhaps even the entire world, into a new era ruled by the just. Of course, you know the identity of this fabled warrior. He is the father of this black place."

"Lord Soth," Ganelon offered tentatively.

"Just so," the Cobbler replied. "But this was in the days before he died for his sins, when a heart still beat within his chest. He was a good man then, who saw the road to glory stretched out endlessly before him and chose instead to tread the gutter alongside."

A burst of icy air swept from the moonshadow of a twisted oak. "That tale outstrips your talent as a storyteller," said the death knight as he stepped from the darkness. "It also takes far longer to tell than you have life to live."

Ganelon prostrated himself before Lord Soth. The Cobbler remained where he was, leaning idly against a tree. He crossed his arms over his chest and shook his head. "You never were a fair judge of talent," he said. "Just consider your success with seneschals."

"There is a difference between bravery and foolishness," Soth rumbled. "Let me teach it to you."

The death knight traced a glyph in the air, watched as it took fire and flew toward the Cobbler. But the magical symbol passed right through the man's pale form. It struck the tree, which began to shudder. Its branches curled, fingers clenching into a fist. A sound went up from the trunk like an agonized groan.

"I learned all the lessons you had to offer quite a long time ago," the Cobbler said. "If you let me bid my friend farewell, I will demonstrate how well I mastered them."

Soth moved between the Cobbler and Ganelon. "I will deal with this spy, too," he said, "and without the lenience I showed him when Azrael first brought him to me."

"You mistake him for someone else," the Cobbler said. "It's the brace that fooled you. Ho, Ganelon! Let your sovereign see your face."

The young man looked up at the death knight, and saw those burning orange orbs regard him from within the tasseled helmet. "I am your loyal subject," Ganelon said. "I'm a worker from Veidrava."

"What are you doing here?" Soth asked.

The Cobbler answered for him. "Hunting for his ladylove," he said. "Surely that is a pursuit that can draw some sympathy, even from you." He chortled. "Especially from you."

Soth stepped aside and waved Ganelon away. The Cobbler extended a gloved hand to the young man. "I can tell you where to start your search," he said as Ganelon got to his feet, "but you must swear never to reveal the information to anyone."

"Of course," Ganelon replied quickly.

The Cobbler frowned. "It'll have to be more formal than that, I'm afraid. What should you swear upon, though?" He regarded Soth coldly. "The Measure, perhaps?"

The reference to the code of conduct of his former order surprised Soth. The death knight regarded the cloaked figure more intently.

"I swear upon my love for Helain," Ganelon offered.

"Perfect," the Cobbler said. He leaned close, the scent of roses clinging to him still, and whispered, "Continue north, to the Iron Hills. The place where she is heading is the first thing in the hills touched by the morning sun."

Ganelon thought to ask for better instruction, for a weapon, perhaps, but one glance at Soth told him that he was lucky to escape this meeting with his life. He hurried off into the night. The Cobbler could hear the steady clank of his brace long after the Fumewood had swallowed his form.

"Alone at last," the Cobbler said. "This meeting has been a long time coming."

"You know my history," Soth said, "so you must serve Kitiara."

"The White Rose," the Cobbler corrected. "I have other names for her, too, ones you could never use."

Soth snorted his derision. "Are you her lover, then? She's had many, boy. All dead by her treachery."

"You're one to speak of treachery," the Cobbler said. "How many thousands of lives are on your conscience?"

"None," replied Soth. "To feel guilt I would have to believe what I have done is wrong. I do not."

The Bloody Cobbler scrutinized the master of Nedragaard, as if his pale blue eyes could see beyond the death knight's blackened armor. "You remember all that you have done and been?"

Soth did not reply. He had pieced together most of his past through the power of the Lake of Sounds. In fact, he had been at the lake, listening for those still-elusive fragments of his history, when the Cobbler spoke his name. "I remember that I am at war with the White Rose," Soth said after a moment. "I know what I will do in the days to come to defeat her."

"You forfeited your title to the future when you abandoned the path of the Rose Knights and allowed the gods of Krynn to wreak havoc on the world. The past is all you have," said the Cobbler. He gestured to the blackened rose on Soth's partially melted breastplate. "You wear its symbol. That cold that chills your bones is its breath, the dead sigh of a million misused lives. They all have claims upon you."

Soth grabbed the Cobbler by the arm. "If those lost souls concern you so much," he snarled, "I will add you to their ranks."

The Cobbler's laughter was more cutting than any blade that had ever touched Soth's flesh. "I already am part of their ranks," he said.

The Cobbler vanished, and Soth's fist closed on empty air. Twined scents lingered in his wake, roses and burned flesh. His laughter persisted, too, until it finally diminished to a noise that had lost all its mirth and derision.

In the instant before it silenced, the Cobbler's laughter became the agonized scream of a child.

NINE

A chill lingered with Ganelon long after his meeting with Soth and the Cobbler. It wasn't the harbinger of some sickness. Neither sunlight nor a fire's warmth could lessen the sensation. By his third day in the Fumewood, he came to think of it as an icy shroud that had enwrapped his soul, one he could not shake off.

Thoughts of Helain only seemed to make the pall cling to him more fiercely. The Cobbler had called her "mad," not "sick" or "distracted" or any of the other euphemisms Ambrose and the others used. Ganelon knew that the mysterious man had been correct.

That fact didn't disturb him as much as it once would have. The whole world seemed mad now, full of walking dead men and living nightmares. Since no creature in the wilderness had so much as sniffed around his camp since that first night, Ganelon had to wonder if he, too, might not be crazed. That was what the Cobbler had said, wasn't it? "The things in the Fumewood give the mad a wide berth."

No, Ganelon could cope with Helain's madness and had no trouble envisioning himself caring for her. He still loved her, after all. What saddened him was the growing certainty that he had played some part in bringing on the insanity. Perhaps she'd mistrusted his promise to curb his wanderlust. Fear that her one true love would leave her might have driven her mad.

As he looked around him now, at the expanse of stunted pine that marked the vague border between the Fumewood and the Iron Hills, Ganelon could not deny the quickening in his blood. The Cobbler had told him that an adventurous life was his destiny. He'd even killed someone else to set Ganelon back on that path.

A ragged sigh escaped Ganelon's lips. He was on the right road, but it was a lonely one. All the times he'd wandered off from the mine, Ambrose and Kern and Ogier had known where he was going. It was a sort of game they played. He dropped hints in between demands to be left to his own devices. They carefully noted his plans, all the while grumbling about being kept in the dark. Ganelon's friends thought of themselves as safety lines, like the ones the miners used down in the pit when someone explored a newly discovered cave. It was a role they treasured.

They couldn't pull him back to safety now, though. No one could.

Ganelon glanced up at the late afternoon sky, swiftly darkening to match his mood's grim hue.

Rain was on its way, and soon. For the hundredth time that afternoon, he cursed himself for his hasty departure from the shop. He'd managed to compensate for most of the things he'd left without. Soon after parting ways with the Cobbler, he had literally stumbled across a hunk of timber suitable for a club. The clanking of his brace prevented him from sneaking up on any small game and putting the makeshift weapon to use, but he knew enough woodlore to keep his stomach filled with roots and berries. Nothing in the forest, however, would suffice as a cloak.

Best find a place to spend the night, Ganelon thought, though his prospects didn't seem to include shelter from the storm. The Iron Hills were still too far away for him to hope for a fortuitously placed cave. He was well clear of any woodsman's paths, where he might find a lean-to or some other improvised haven.

The trees in this part of the Fumewood didn't offer anything in the way of potential building material either. Much of the growth here was old pine, blighted and misshapen. The trunks crawled with some sort of termite that devoured flesh as readily as it did wood. The fallen limbs and needles burned only grudgingly and produced a thick smoke that reeked worse than anything Ganelon had ever smelled. If he tried to harvest a living branch, it seemed to struggle against him. It was as if the woods knew what he was doing, just as in all the childhood stories Ganelon had ever heard.

That was reason enough for him to leave the trees alone. As the past few days had taught him, those old stories held more truth than he'd ever suspected.

So it was that the thrashing of branches and cracking of limbs behind him brought to Ganelon's mind an image of an angry uprooted tree instead of a more mundane traveler in the forest. At the sudden commotion, he dashed behind a fallen log and camouflaged himself as best he could beneath a blanket of pine needles. He had barely finished his work when the large figure blundered into view.

Ganelon couldn't see his face at first, but his hulking frame was clad in tatters of once-bright Vistani clothing. Scratches crisscrossed his bare arms. A gash in his side wept dark blood that told of a deep infection. The man reached up with both hands and pushed a branch away from his face; the dirty remains of bandages circled the wrists.

As the branch came away from the stranger's face, Ganelon gasped. It was Bratu. There were only mangled stumps where the man's ears should have been. Pus and dried blood smeared his face. The Vistana's bald pate was blistered from sunburn. His ponytail had come undone, and the tangled hair trailed down his neck like a horse's mane. Gone was the pompous bully of a fortnight ago. A ragged madman swayed in his place.

Ganelon decided to take a chance. Just after the Vistana passed the log, he pushed himself to his feet with his makeshift club. "Bratu," he called quietly, "what are you doing here?"

The Vistana didn't turn, didn't pause. With a silent curse, Ganelon hurried after him. It was obvious. With wounds like that to his ears, the man couldn't hear.

As Ganelon got close, he could hear the constant rumble of odd, feral noises coming from Bratu. He was delirious with pain and probably starving. That made him dangerous. Ganelon hesitated, his hand part way to Bratu's shoulder.

Whatever senses left to the Vistana had alerted him to the presence of something behind him. With a bestial grunt, Bratu turned to Ganelon. The frenzy in those eyes made the young man back away.

"It's Ganelon, from Veidrava." He let the club drop to his side and extended his other, empty hand. "I'm a friend."

Bratu rolled his head from side to side, eyes fixed on Ganelon's face. Whether he recognized the younger man or not, he seemed calmer. With a broad gesture at their surroundings, he opened his mouth to speak. All that came out was a pitiful moan of rounded vowels divided by blubbered Bs and Ws. His tongue was gone.

Ganelon turned away in disgust. Bratu's own people must have done that to him. It was probably part of some banishment ritual. This way, he couldn't speak of their secrets.

"I'm so sorry," he whispered. But when he turned back, Bratu had already started off again.

Ganelon stood there for a time, uncertain what to do. There was nothing he could do to help the

Vistana. Truth be told, he wasn't even doing a very good job of helping himself. If he was going to make it to the Iron Hills and find Helain, he was going to have to keep to his own path and let Bratu wander off on his own.

As the first drops of rain began to fall, Ganelon decided that the log and the pine needles were going to be the best shelter he could hope for tonight. He wedged himself against the wood and heaped needles over his legs and stomach. It would have been warmer to cover himself all the way to his neck, but that would only serve as an open invitation for the roaches and weevils to venture up to his face. They needed no extra help finding his ears and nose.

He fell asleep with a nightmare already half-formed in his brain: Blood-red beetles pressed into his mouth. Razored pinchers clacking in anticipation, they scurried to the root of his tongue and set to work.

* * * * *

The next morning, Ganelon awoke feeling more rested than he had any right to expect. The rain hadn't been as bad as the clouds had threatened, and the insects had only bothered him a little, despite his nightmare. He lay there for a time, eyes closed, willing away the last vestiges of the night's unquiet dreams. Finally, he stretched his arms and cracked open one eye at the morning light. The bright glare made him hiss and clamp his eyes closed again. What was going on? The sun couldn't possibly be that bright through the canopy of branches overhead.

"Don't think of reaching for that stick, sleepy head," admonished a decidedly female voice. "It's already gone. Besides, it wouldn't have done you any good anyway. Not against this."

Ganelon felt the slightest of stings on the tip of his nose. He opened his eyes again and saw the cause: a dagger, its thin blade shining with reflected sunlight. The dagger shifted slightly and the reflected light flared, blinding Ganelon again.

"Get up," the woman said. "Slowly."

Ganelon propped himself on his elbows and, from this half-reclining position, was able to assess the situation. It could have been better.

After meeting Bratu the previous evening, Ganelon was only moderately surprised to discover Inza Kulchevich on the other end of that alarmingly sharp dagger. The striking, dark-haired Vistana had swapped her flowing skirt for leather leggings, and had tied her hair back with a scarlet ribbon. She also sported a heavy cloak, Ganelon noted enviously.

"All right," the girl continued imperiously, "your nap is over, *giorgio*. I've got some questions for you."

As he looked up into the girl's green eyes, all Ganelon could think of was Bratu's wordless groans. Monsters, he thought, you and all your kind. He cast a disdainful eye over the half-dozen other Vistani arrayed behind Inza and said, "I don't have the answers you want."

Inza flicked the dagger toward Ganelon's left leg. The blade touched the brace so lightly that he didn't feel its impact. It scarred the metal nonetheless.

"Think of the damage such a weapon would do to your face," Inza said.

"Or tongue," Ganelon offered.

The defeat in the man's voice made Inza smile. It was not a pleasant thing to see. "Then you do have some answers for me." She motioned to one of the other gypsies. "Bring him something to eat, and some clean water. Oh, and a cloak, too." She nodded to Ganelon. "Don't think I didn't recognize the envy in your eyes, *giorgio*. There isn't a Vistana alive who doesn't know what it's like to be cold when all around her are warm."

Inza waited until Ganelon had splashed some water on his face, wrapped himself in the brightly dyed woolen cloak, and sat down to a plate of bread and cheese before she spoke again. "It was Malocchio Aderre's men who cut out Bratu's tongue," she said, "though we were ready to do so, too. He was passing secrets to the Invidians."

"Why would the Invidians want his tongue cut if he was working with them?" Ganelon asked between mouthfuls of bread.

"He'd been found out. They were afraid he would reveal the names of their other agents in Sithicus," Inza replied casually. "So, tell me, how long did you travel together?"

"We didn't," Ganelon said. "We crossed paths in this very clearing. He went on, I stayed here."

Inza scowled. "I heard the men at Veidrava describe you as kind and compassionate, but they must be liars. You let an injured man wander off into the night without so much as offering to share your fire."

Ganelon overturned the now-empty wooden plate. "You said you were going to cut out his tongue if the Invidians hadn't beaten you to it. What do you care about him?"

"There is punishment and there is torture," Inza said. She impaled a millipede on the end of her dagger and watched it squirm. "To be lost from the tribe is torture for poor Bratu. We would have kept him safe with us, even after justice was meted out."

Ganelon missed the grim looks exchanged by the other Vistani, who knew that Inza had proposed a far different fate for Bratu. Instead, the young man had his eyes fixed on the matted pine needles that had been his blanket. "It should be obvious that I had no fire to share with Bratu," he said. "I offered him help, but he couldn't hear me. Did the Invidians cut his ears off, too?"

"He harmed himself," Inza replied distractedly. "You haven't told me your cause for being here, *giorgio*. Maybe you're a spy, too." She gestured at the leg brace. "They only make those in Invidia. Your price for betraying your homeland, perhaps?"

"I'm looking for Helain," Ganelon said. "I should be going if I'm ever going to catch her."

Inza gave the man a knowing smirk. "Ah, the sick girl from the store. She finally heard him, eh? It was only a matter of time."

"Heard who?"

His look of puzzlement was too genuine for Inza to think him a liar. "The Whispering Beast," she said. "Just like Bratu, she answers the Beast's call."

Ganelon stood and brushed off the borrowed cloak. "Nonsense," he snapped. "The Beast only speaks to those who lie and cheat. Helain is nothing like that."

The coarse laughter of the Vistani men fanned Ganelon's anger. He turned on them. "What would any of you filthy wretches know of honesty?"

Inza wrapped a hand around Ganelon's wrist and eased him back to a seat beside her. "If we are all liars, *giorgio*, then you should pay all the more attention to what we say. Liars have to know the truth well enough to avoid it." She lifted the cloak back to his shoulders. "No one is saying that your Helain is like Bratu, you know. It might just be guilt that drove her to him. Sometimes that's enough."

"Guilt about what?"

She shrugged. "It only matters that you find her before she gets to the Beast. Once she's in his hands—" The Vistana mocked a shudder. "Horrible. And there will be no way to find her. His lair is hidden."

The words of the Bloody Cobbler came back to Ganelon then: "The place where she is heading is the first thing in the hills touched by the morning sun." That place, he realized with a terrible certainty, was the lair of the Whispering Beast.

Inza leaned close and lifted Ganelon's chin with one finger, positioning his face so that their gazes met. The young man could feel himself slipping into the green depths of her eyes. He realized distantly that those eyes were very much like the Fumewood. Both had a certain intolerant lushness to them. For all they seemed full of life, they were actually choked with death.

"Something brought you here," she said softly. "You couldn't have kept pace with her, not with the brace, not pausing to sleep at night. How do you know where to look?"

"I don't know. I'm following her trail."

Inza gave a subtle signal. "I told you before that liars must be acquainted with the truth," she said. As a pair of callused hands clamped down on Ganelon from behind, the girl added, "We're also quite aware when we're being lied to."

The Vistana lifted Ganelon and locked him in a bear hug. The young man dug back with his elbows. Both connected, but the Vistana didn't flinch. The kick from Ganelon's braced leg drew a howl of pain, but his captor didn't release his hold. If anything, the blow made him squeeze harder.

Dagger in hand, Inza stood before Ganelon. "Who told you how to find the Beast's victims?" she shouted into his face. When he refused to reply, she rested the blade on his earlobe. "Who told you?"

The slightest twist of her wrist, and his earlobe dropped to the ground. When he'd stopped screaming and struggling, she placed the blade against his other ear. "We move to the eyes from here."

"The Cobbler," Ganelon hissed.

The answer shocked Inza into silence, but only for a moment. "You're lying," she snapped. The dagger's point pierced the lobe and continued into the corner of his jaw.

"A few nights ago," Ganelon said through gritted teeth. "He gave me the brace then, too."

The girl paused again and regarded the brace more closely. After a moment, a look of recognition crossed her face. "Well, well," she said finally. "You have some important friends, *giorgio*. Tell me what I want to know, and you can count me one of them."

"I can't tell you what the Cobbler said."

"*Won't* tell me," Inza corrected. "You're capable of doing so, at least right now."

"I swore an oath. I can't break it."

Inza raised the blade again. "You'd be surprised at what you can do, given the proper motivation."

As she brought the knife down, Ganelon didn't struggle. He went slack. To compensate for the sudden weight in his arms, the Vistana holding him jerked backward. The moment he did, Ganelon pushed up with his legs.

Instead of slashing Ganelon's face, the blade struck the Vistana's arm. It was a glancing blow that should have left nothing more than a scratch. But the dagger Inza carried was enchanted by magics older than the Vistani themselves. Its steel bit down to the bone.

Ganelon crashed to the ground and was immediately set upon by the other Vistani. They kicked him and pummeled him, blackening his eyes and loosening more than a few teeth. The man who had been holding him tried desperately to stop the bleeding from his slashed arm. His attempts proved as futile as Ganelon's hopes of escape. Before long he had slumped against the log, his lifeblood flowing into the dirt.

Only Inza remained calm. Once Ganelon had been subdued again, she cleaned her dagger's blade and walked slowly to where he lay pinned to the ground.

"I swore on my love for Helain," he cried. "I will not betray that."

"Of course not," Inza said. She lifted the dagger, positioning the blade so that it would catch the sun. The flare of light struck Ganelon full in the face. At the same time, she focused her eyes on his.

When his eyes cleared, Ganelon found himself stretched out within a beautiful bower. Vines curled around him, caressing him and shading him from the sun. The leg brace was gone, as were his wounds and the terrible chill that had clung to him since the meeting with the Cobbler. He was safe here. Nothing could harm him, not the Vistani, not the beasts of the Fumewood, not even Lord Soth.

He marveled at that sensation of utter security. It was one he had experienced before only rarely and only in Helain's arms.

"As it should be," a cool voice said. "You are only truly safe with someone who loves you absolutely."

Ganelon shifted, looked up, and was startled to find Helain cradling his head in her lap. The taint of madness was gone from her face. She smiled down on him in perfect contentment. One hand rested upon his cheek. The other was entwined in her red hair. How vibrant that hair was, a bright flame against the forest's deep green. Her eyes sparkled like two still pools reflecting the first morning sunlight as she said, "You freed me."

She bent to kiss him. As she did, her tresses flowed around his face. Ganelon's senses reeled. He breathed in her perfume and hugged her fiercely. They lingered there as the morning became afternoon and the afternoon dwindled to twilight.

Finally, Ganelon broke the embrace.

"I can't believe you're here," he sighed as he pulled back a little to study her face.

Hugging him again, this time more playfully, she replied, "Believe it. You have yourself to thank. Only you could have saved me."

"You're really here."

Helain mocked annoyance and pushed him away. "If my method of proving that isn't sufficient for you, sir, I suggest you find another lap to rest your head upon."

"It is far beyond sufficient," he said, laughing. "It's just . . . I think I must have lain here too long. I'm having a hard time recalling exactly what happened."

"Oh, come now," Helain scoffed. "Surely you remember finding me in the lair of the Whispering

Beast." At his blank look, she said, "You're starting to worry me, love."

A wave of dizziness washed over Ganelon. Disoriented, he put his hand to his eyes. "I remember the Cobbler helping me. You're right—"

Helain took his hand from his eyes and pressed it between her palms. Her brow furrowed with concern. "Why don't we start at the beginning, from when the Cobbler told you how to find me. That will help you put things back together."

Ganelon tried to sit up, but Helain held him fast. "Rest," she said. "Please, love." A shadow of worry stretched across her face, making her blue eyes appear green.

As green as the bower.

As green as the creeping vines that were even now encircling his legs.

Somewhere in the back of his mind, Ganelon felt panic rise. "No!" he shouted

With trembling hands he grabbed Helain by the shoulders and began to shake her. She shouted for him to stop, but it was too late. Streaks had begun to appear in her hair, the crimson tresses quickly darkening to the black of ravens' wings. Her eyes gave up their facade of blue. They were the green of serpent's scales and just as emotionless.

"Enough," Inza said. She slumped forward, exhaustion withering her young face. As in the dream, the day had run its course and night once more perched upon the Fumewood. "Your heart may resist me," she said wearily, "but there are other ways to break you, other agents to impose my will upon you."

Inza nodded to one of her tribesmen, a grim-faced man of middle years named Alexi. Like most of the Wanderers, he'd been left without a family by the butchery Duke Gundar inflicted upon the Vistani in his domain. After joining with Magda, there were few creatures of the night he had not faced. In all the world, the only thing that truly frightened him was the girl who now led their caravan.

At Inza's signal, Alexi pulled Ganelon up from the ground and brought him to the small cook fire the gypsies had started. There was no smoke, and the logs seemed to burn readily enough. Ganelon wondered numbly if the Vistani had some sort of magic that made the wood more compliant. Perhaps they'd hauled wood with them somehow.

"You don't have to hang on to him," Inza said. "Find a decent tree and pin him to it."

"As you wish, *raunie*," Alexi said.

It took only a short time for the Vistana to bind Ganelon to the trunk of a large, moss-covered tree. As he did, another of the Vistani made a show of setting a trio of large metal pokers in the cookfire's coals. Inza supervised silently, her form bathed in the fire's glow. "I will have what I want from you," she said to Ganelon. "Make no mistake. I always win."

The young man snorted, displaying a bravado he most certainly did not feel. "Hot pokers? Isn't that a bit primitive for the Vistani?"

"Oh, those are only my reserve tools," Inza said cheerfully.

The *raunie* reached into a hidden pocket in her cloak. With a smile of satisfaction, she withdrew a small, ornate box, and presented it in her palm. "One last chance, Ganelon, before I loose this on you."

"I will not dishonor myself or my love for Helain," he answered simply.

Inza gave the young man a last thoughtful look before she placed the tiny box on the ground and opened it.

A soft black shape slid out of the box. It expanded as it slithered forward, its saline stench overpowering every other odor in the camp. Ganelon gaped at it for a moment before the shock wore off and the horror set in.

He closed his eyes and conjured an image of Helain. It would be the last time he could envision her with the same passion in his heart. The shadows knew nothing of love and did not tolerate such emotions in their slaves.

The gasps of the Vistani and Inza's loudly uttered curse made Ganelon open his eyes. The shadow pooled at his feet. Tentatively, it extended a tendril toward his boots, then recoiled as if burned. The thing was like a dog rooting after a bone that it knew was near but remained tantalizingly out of reach. Finally it grew frustrated and slithered back to its box.

With a cry of frustration, Inza grabbed one of the pokers from the fire. "The Cobbler's plied his trade on you, hasn't he?" She looked to the other Vistani. "He has a dead man's soles. The shadow can't see him."

With her free hand she snapped the box shut and tossed it to Alexi. The man cringed as he caught the captive soul but did not drop it or put it down. Secretly the *raunie* smiled. Her mother never inspired such unswerving, unquestioning loyalty. Magda's kind heart had always interfered.

That weakness had never plagued Inza. In fact, she intended to demonstrate to this maddening mine rat just how cold her heart really was.

"I'll never give in," Ganelon proclaimed as Inza came close. His fear was gone. The salt shadow's defeat had vanquished it. The young man knew that he was going to die, but he knew, too, that he would not break his oath.

Ganelon heard it first in the hissing of the poker as it approached his face. A voice whispered to him. The susurrus spread to the pine trees and the cookfire, gathering strength. Just before the iron touched flesh, the whisper exploded into an unearthly howl that drove the steaming poker from Inza's hands and scattered the Vistani like frightened birds.

Of all the people in the little camp, only Ganelon saw his rescuer clearly. It reached from the shadow trailing behind the tree to which he was bound and pulled the young man in. At the sight he screamed until there was no breath left in his lungs.

Inza saw only the thing's gangly arm, covered with matted hair, pluck away her victim. Ropes, still knotted and looped, sagged on the tree trunk where they had held Ganelon fast a moment before.

There was no time to lash out with blade or blaze, but the *raunie*'s hatred offered up this parting blow: *No love, no light, but that which causes pain. Everything you hold dear will perish by your own hand.*

That curse, swift as a vengeful thought, followed Ganelon into the darkness, just as it would hound his every step for the rest of his life.

TEN

"It's time," Azrael said cheerfully. "I want you and your little friends down in the pit right now. They're almost done loading the crates. Make certain they don't leave anything behind on the landing, then get started on that other business we discussed. Understand?"

Ambrose did not respond. As the dwarf tromped out of the store, the shopkeep got stiffly to his feet. "You heard him," he said to Kern and Ogier.

The two miners exchanged puzzled looks. "What about the wine?" Kern asked. He held up a half-full bottle of Chateau Malaturno. Its twin stood empty in front of Ogier. "We've enough left for one decent toast. After all the trouble *I* went through to get this stuff, it'd be a shame to waste it."

Ambrose missed Kern's unsubtle jab. The shopkeep had never looked into finding the bottles for Kern, despite his initial offer to do so. As a result, Kern paid twice the wine's worth in order to fulfill his debt to Ogier.

" 'Sides," that white-haired stalwart now chimed, "you said we was going to do another job for Azrael. That meant we wouldn't have to lug crates with everyone else."

"That special duty is still yours," Ambrose said rather sadly.

"A mysterious errand for the homicidal dwarf, *and* we get to cart boxes besides," noted Kern. He held his empty glass up in salute. "Only a true friend would set us up with that kind of deal."

Ogier elbowed the smaller man. "Leave him be. He's doing the best he can."

Still glowering, Kern filled his glass to the brim, then did the same for Ogier. He went to top off Ambrose's mug with the remaining wine but found that the shopkeep hadn't touched a drop that had been poured for him. With a shrug, Kern handed the bottle to Ogier. The big man put it to his lips and drained it in two gulps.

Kern raised his glass again, this time in earnest. Solemnly he said, "To absent friends, who leave us shadows until their return. May it be soon."

Nodding his approval, Ogier tipped back his glass. After a moment's hesitation, Ambrose raised his mug. "Friends and shadows," the shopkeep said flatly.

The statement was no more cryptic than anything Ambrose said these days. Ever since the night Helain and Ganelon disappeared, he'd been acting strange. Kern dismissed it as the man's way of mourning. In his own childlike fashion, Ogier noticed a deeper change in Ambrose. His voice was stronger now, missing the wheeze that had softened every word he'd uttered since the accident. He was more forceful, too, even cruel. Ogier knew that this was not the stuff of mourning. The murders of those *politskae* had changed him. Something grim and loveless had taken hold of Ambrose's heart.

Faces flushed from the wine, the three made their way from the store up to the mine. A hundred torches lit the grounds around the pit. Workers from both shifts carried boxes from the lift and loaded them onto heavy wagons, then trudged back for another load. The entire process was supervised by Azrael's Politskara. They were everywhere, silver axes at the ready. Whatever Azrael had the men unloading from the mine, it was more valuable than salt.

The dwarf clearly thought so anyway. He'd shut down the mine so everyone could focus on the task of moving the heavy crates. It was an unprecedented event, one that disturbed the workers more than the sudden appearance of the white moon. That was beyond their understanding. They knew what the work stoppage meant: lost wages, maybe even lost jobs. Worse, there were rumors that the mine was going to close down for good. To men with no other skills, that meant starvation and hardship as deadly as any creature lurking in the woods.

As Ambrose and the others got close to the lift, they could see apprehension, even fear, etched on every miner's face. It was not merely concern for their lives and their livelihoods that weighed so heavily on the men. They were frightened for their souls.

The dwarf had insisted the work proceed day and night, breaking every rule the miners had established to protect themselves from the salt shadows. Since the damned creatures could not survive in daylight without a host, nothing ever left the mine unless the sun was shining. Even if a shadow had attached itself to someone, a single shift was too short a time for it to completely possess him. Exposing it to sunlight quickly would reveal its presence. The unfortunate host might not be saved, but he could be destroyed before the salt shadow drove him to a life of corruption.

Azrael dismissed it all as superstitious nonsense and ordered the men to keep working after the sun went down. A few of the younger miners agreed, having never seen evidence of the shadows themselves. To them, the creatures were no more real than the Bloody Cobbler or the Whispering Beast. The older workers, though, kept a careful eye on the boxes, in case a shadow should be hiding on it. A few had even burned their palms and the soles of their feet, since dead flesh supposedly repulsed the creatures.

Ogier said a little prayer as the last of the boxes was unloaded and he, Kern, and Ambrose stepped into the lift. The big man did not fear the salt shadows, but he *was* scared of the trip down the pit. One of the lifts had broken free of its cable recently, killing everyone inside. Ogier asked the fates to keep this one safe.

Kern chuckled at the serious expression on his friend's face. He leaned close so the two dour *politskae* in the lift wouldn't hear and whispered, "You should be praying to the dwarf to keep us safe. The lift never falters when it's carrying anything important to him."

"Enough foolishness," Ambrose said more loudly than was necessary. Kern shot him an angry look, but the shopkeep met his gaze defiantly.

Ever the unknowing diplomat, it was Ogier who broke the tension. "Even if you're right, Kern, Ambrose is important to Azrael, and we're important to Ambrose. We'll be safe."

Silence fell upon the three men as the lift started its descent. They listened to the creaking of the pulleys and the groaning of the ropes. After a time, they could make out quiet voices from a cross shaft far below. The mine usually rang with the shouts of workers and the impact of hammer and pick on stone. The muted sounds took on an eerie quality for the men so accustomed to that din.

With a jerk, the lift came to a stop. The landing was crowded with men and crates. Kern and Ogier didn't recognize the miners. Grunts from the night shift, they assumed.

"Last load," said the group's foreman. Ambrose walked past him as if he hadn't heard. He went straight for a knot of six *politskae* gathered where the landing narrowed into a tunnel. They were a sullen bunch, half-concealed in the shadows. As Ambrose quietly discussed something with them, the rest of the workers set to loading the lift.

Ogier was quick to lend a hand, hefting even the larger boxes with ease. The crates were a mismatched lot, everything from salt barrels to children's coffins. The only things they had in common were their weight and the clanking sound they made when dropped or jostled. Even someone of Ogier's meager intellect could guess what was inside.

"An attack's coming," one of the workers muttered to Kern. "That's why we're moving this. Azrael don't want the Invidians to get it."

Kern, who was poking around the boxes in search of the lightest burden, yapped a dismissive laugh. "We're about as far from the border as you can get. Besides, if a raiding party attacks Veidrava, this stuff would be safer down here."

"If the Invidian army shows up," someone noted wearily, "we'd all be safer down here."

"Not in this tunnel," hissed an old man named Divelg, who'd been down the pit longer than anyone else at Veidrava. "Better to be sitting in Malocchio Aderre's lap than here. You know what that leads to?" He gestured toward the tunnel.

Ambrose was suddenly beside Divelg. He grabbed the old man by the throat and slammed him against the wall. "What's back there is something best forgotten," he rumbled.

"You're hurting him," Ogier said quietly. "Ambrose, stop."

The shopkeep whirled to face the big man. "Shut your bleating, Sheep, and get back to the boxes."

Trembling with fright, Divelg looked up into Ambrose's face and whispered, "I know what you are."

With a curse Ambrose hurled the old man toward Ogier. Divelg tumbled over a chest, spilling the contents. To no one's surprise, a small fortune in gold and silver coins poured onto the cold stone landing.

"Think of all the bottles of Malaturno this could buy," Kern murmured, eyes as wide as the largest gold doubloon. He knelt down to examine the hoard. The coins came from every land surrounding Sithicus and a few places more distant. There were also currencies that Kern couldn't identify; they'd been struck with odd images and odder names, like *Cormyr* and *Iuz*.

The *politskae* surrounded Kern. "I wasn't going to take anything," the miner said, smiling up at them. The silver axes that appeared in the men's hands made it clear they didn't believe him or didn't really care.

"We're wasting time," Ambrose boomed. Even the stoic *politskae* jumped at the uncharacteristic fury in the man's voice. They parted for Ambrose, who pulled Kern up from the floor. "I should let them kill you," he rumbled, "but you won't get off that easily."

Kern and Ogier were herded to the back of the landing while the rest of the boxes were loaded. Ambrose ordered Divelg to gather up the money he'd spilled. The shopkeep and a tight ring of *politskae* encircled him, ensuring that every coin was returned to the cache. When the work was done and the lid was about to be hammered back into place, Ambrose plucked two coins from the hoard. He handed them to Divelg.

Kern craned his neck to see what was happening. "Did he just give Divelg some money?" he asked.

"Uh huh," Ogier replied, "but the old guy don't look so happy about it."

In fact, Divelg looked heartbroken. He stared at the small black coins in his hand, turning them over and over again. Finally he mouthed a short, silent prayer and faced Ambrose. "It's back there, isn't it? It really exists."

Ambrose wrapped an arm around Divelg's shoulder and led him away from the throng. It might have been the light from the guttering torches, but the shopkeep's expression appeared to flow manically between glee and sorrow. "Yes, it exists. In fact, that's where Ambrose had his little 'accident' all those years ago." With one pudgy hand, he closed the old man's fingers around the coins. "Keep a tight grip on these. You'll need them sooner than you might think."

When the last box was loaded onto the lift, Ambrose ordered the landing cleared. The miners, even the *politskae*, crowded onto the lift. Only Ambrose and his two friends were left behind as the elevator shuddered, then began its ascent.

Divelg had been one of the last onto the lift. He stood at the very edge of the press, *politskae* to either side of him. Just before the elevator passed above the shaft's ceiling, he crouched down. "You must've had the heart of a titan to keep control of it for so long," he said to Ambrose. A slight, sad smile on his face, he tossed the coins onto the landing. "Those two will need them more than me. I know I'm not coming back."

The last words echoed after the lift had carried the old man out of sight. Kern stomped on one of the coins, which was rolling crazily across the stone. Lifting his heel, he found a black Sithican penny. It had landed rose side up, a bad omen.

Ogier picked up the other penny. "I don't think I get it," the big man said.

A slither of dread shot up Kern's spine. He understood the pennies' significance perfectly. When a corpse was set upon its funeral pyre, a penny was placed upon each eye. Fired red-hot by the blaze, they would sear through the dead man's eyes. His ghost would be blind, unable to find his home should his spirit rise up from the grave.

The meaning of Ambrose's gesture, handing the two pennies to Divelg, was clear: The old man would soon be a corpse. That Divelg should think their need for the pennies was more urgent—Kern found that message even easier to read.

Fortunately, the coins' ominous meaning seemed lost on Ogier. "Don't worry about it," Kern said, patting him on the back. "Divelg probably meant us to have them for good luck."

"He sounded like something was wrong," Ogier said plaintively.

Such a large man and so little in the engine house, thought Kern. Out loud, he said, "What could be wrong? We have our friend Ambrose here, and he'd never let anything happen to us."

The shopkeep was standing far back on the landing, in the mouth of the abandoned tunnel. "I've already saved you from a nasty death on the battlefield."

At Ogier's puzzled look, Ambrose continued: "The rumors about the mine closing down are correct. Azrael is pressing everyone into the army. Well, almost everyone. A few choice individuals are being put into special service, away from the fighting."

Kern regarded his old friend coldly. "Which brings us to that 'special duty' you've lined up for us."

"Exactly," Ambrose said. "If you'll come this way, we'll start your training."

Ogier happily clomped over to Ambrose. The big man peered into the darkened tunnel, then turned back to Kern. "Let's go," he chimed. "The sooner we get this over with, the sooner we can relax."

"I couldn't have put it better myself," Ambrose noted. He held out an empty hand toward Kern, who shot him a look of utter disgust and went back to his search for a way off the landing.

Kern was not particularly surprised to find there wasn't one. All the emergency ladders had been removed, if any had ever reached the cross shaft. There wasn't even a way to call the lift back, not that he could see anyway. Ambrose had obviously planned this little ambush carefully.

"Come to think of it," Kern said, forcing a smile, "I've always wanted to see a big battle firsthand. You should too, Ogier. Broaden your perspective."

"It's far too late to change plans now," Ambrose said darkly. He moved behind Ogier and placed one hand conspicuously on the big man's shoulder. With the other he gripped a chunk of rock jutting from the wall. "We want to stay together, Kern," he noted. "This tunnel's a bit treacherous."

One squeeze, and the rock crumbled to dust.

Ogier spun around and whistled. "Hey, you're right. The walls are kind of quaky."

Scowling, Kern walked to the tunnel. "I think Ambrose had the better word for it," he said. "'Treacherous.'"

Kern and Ogier went first, though Ambrose never let them get out of earshot. When the tunnel broadened into a smooth-floored hallway, he positioned himself between them, a falsely friendly hand on each man's back. Ogier trudged cheerfully along, oblivious to the danger that Kern had recognized long ago. If there was nothing to be done to save themselves, Kern hoped to keep his friend blissfully ignorant until the very end.

"This place is pretty," Ogier exclaimed, eyes wide with wonder at the statues lining both sides of the hall. He pointed up at the ceiling, carved to give the illusion of clouds and birds and open sky. "Why don't we ever come down here?"

Kern stopped just short of the arched doorway

at the end of the hall. Torches had flickered to life in the room beyond, providing just enough light for him to glimpse the altar, the melted benches, the dark shapes flowing in a hideous, gleeful dance across the walls and floor. He'd never really believed the old miners' stories about the Black Chapel or the salt shadows that had been spawned in that unholy place. Kern realized now that he'd been wrong.

He realized, too, what Ambrose had planned for them.

The shopkeep stepped in front of Kern, blocking his view. "Down deep, I'm sure part of me is sorry for this," he said. An insane giggle bubbled from his lips. "But I'll be damned if I can find that part."

The shadows swarmed out of the chapel, flowing around and over Ambrose in a hissing torrent. Kern's scream finally drew Ogier's attention away from the hawks and butterflies on the ceiling. The big man wailed in horror. As that cry echoed through the hope-forsaken tunnels of Veidrava, it sounded for all the world like the bleat of a lost lamb.

* * * * *

It was known forever after as the Night of Skulls.

As the armies mustered at Veidrava and a half-dozen other places throughout Sithicus, Lord Soth and his thirteen skeletal warriors rode out from Nedragaard Keep. The hoofbeats of their undead mounts reverberated through the night, curdling dreams into nightmares. Their passing kicked up clouds of choking dust so thick they blotted out the face of Solinari.

The raiding party was already in full retreat when Soth's patrol caught up to them. The mercenaries were scrambling north through a steep-sided canyon in the Arden Valley, back toward the Invidian border. They'd obviously heard the thunder of the patrol's approach and fled without a second thought of meeting the charge. So, at least, they wished it to appear.

In his days as a Rose Knight, highest order of the fabled Knights of Solamnia, Lord Soth had ridden down a hundred such knavish bands. Their tactics inevitably hinged upon the same simple notion: Given a fleeing enemy, a soldier will always pursue. Soth had seen talented warriors do just that, their bloodlust stirred by their enemy's apparent weakness. He'd even laid ambushes himself that depended upon that sort of short-sightedness in his adversary. But he had never, in his years of life or unlife, been taken in by such a ruse.

As Soth and his warriors entered the canyon, he raised his sword and waved it twice. He and three of his skeletal soldiers charged ahead, hard upon the heels of the fleeing ogres and human mercenaries. The remainder of the patrol split into two bands of five. Without breaking pace, without the slightest hesitation, they stormed up the steep canyon walls.

The Invidian archers hidden atop the canyon, perched behind boulders and scrub trees, raised their bows. Most never fired a shot. The sight of the dead riders ascending the sheer rock cliffs was too much for them. They dropped their weapons and fled, turning the staged rout into an actual one.

The swords of the skeletal warriors ran red with Invidian blood. The dead men offered no mercy, untouched by the screams of the dying. They went about this grisly work as they did everything—dispassionately, with a murderous mechanical efficiency. The victory, the battle, it all meant nothing. Yet every one of those former stalwarts knew that it should stir his heroic heart. Such was their curse.

Soth, too, left a trail of corpses in his wake. Like his companions, he felt no exhilaration from the conflict. These sell-swords were feeble adversaries, unworthy of his blade. If these were the best troops Malocchio could muster, the war would be a short one.

The master of Nedragaard and his thirteen loyal retainers pursued the remainder of the Invidians until they were within sight of the border. Too many remained, and they were too widely scattered, for Soth and the others to kill them all before they crossed back to their homeland. The death knight reined in his horse. Sheathing his gore-spattered sword, he began to sing in a voice as deep as a bottomless chasm. His mournful dirge of oaths betrayed, destinies abandoned, filled the Sithican night.

The skeletal warriors ceased their pursuit, threw back their heads, and joined in the chant. Their voices rattled like ancient paper as they added the catalogue of their sins to their master's. Lust, greed, pride—they confessed to these and more. The worst of their crimes, the one that bound them forever to the Knight of the Black Rose, was idolatry. In life, they had honored Lord Soth above all else. In death, they shared his awful fate, forever damned alongside the one they had mistaken for a god among men.

Throughout Sithicus, others added to the song. They were, like Soth himself, unconscious of the things they confessed, unable to hear the secret vices their neighbors admitted. The dirge gathered at the border. There, the accumulated sins blossomed into a wall of spectral roses that touched the heavens.

Then the flowers withered and vanished.

The few surviving soldiers from the raiding party raced across the border to safety. Soth, sitting dazed upon his decaying steed, watched them go. He'd felt the song's undoing. More disturbing still, he'd also heard the dirge clearly in the instant before it was silenced. The awful weight of those confessions, the indisputable truth of those countless dark deeds, pressed down upon him still.

Slowly, the death knight approached the border.

From a distance the boundary resembled a low stone wall. As the death knight drew closer, he recognized it as a barrier of bloody human skulls.

They were lined along the border in both directions as far as the eye could see. Small and large, ancient and recent, the skulls faced Sithicus. Their empty eye sockets regarded the land and its lord with the utter detachment of the truly dead.

Soth dismounted and warily approached the barrier. He saw now that the skulls were not simply smeared with gore but covered with words penned in blood. The script was cramped, but delicate. He lifted one of the skulls and began to read.

The gods granted Soth enough self-knowledge to see how low he'd fallen. . . .

The death knight dashed the skull to pieces on the ground. He picked up another. It, too, held a fragment of his history.

For failing in his quest, for letting his own child burn to death before his eyes, Soth's elf maid bride called a curse down upon the once-noble knight. . . .

So it was with every one of the skulls. Someone had gathered Soth's history and turned it against him, even as the death knight himself grew confident that his past was once more under his control. This wasn't the work of Malocchio Aderre; the skulls were on Sithican soil, beyond his reach. That meant someone within the domain. The White Rose, then.

Soth paused. Such sorcery was far beyond Kitiara's abilities. But if not her, who? What other powers had set themselves against him?

A shadow of uncertainty darkened Soth's already desolate thoughts. With it came a sensation the death knight had all but forgotten. For the first time in centuries, Lord Soth felt the icy touch of fear.

ELEVEN

Ganelon awoke bathed in late afternoon sunlight, nestled in a bower strewn with white rose petals. Their heady perfume lay heavy upon his senses. He thought to sit up, but a lethargy inspired by the roses' bouquet overwhelmed him. With a sigh, he let himself sink deeper into the verdure.

He tried to recall how he'd come to this place. Bird song and distant laughter chased away the vague thoughts before they could coalesce into memories. It didn't matter. He was safe here.

"As it should be," said a cool, lovely voice. "You are only truly safe with someone who loathes you absolutely."

At the sound of Helain's voice the drowsiness lifted from Ganelon. Heart racing, the young man struggled from the sylvan bed. His leg brace foiled his attempt to stand quickly, and for just an instant, sunlight dazzled his eyes. When his vision cleared, he saw her.

She sat upon the green, her face aglow with madness. The smile upon her face was so wide that her dry lips cracked and bled. For all its prominence, though, that smile was empty. So, too, were her beautiful blue eyes, which stared blankly down at the thing cradled in her lap.

One of Helain's hands rested upon his scabrous cheek. The other stroked her own tangled red hair. "You freed me," she said as she bent to kiss the creature's chancred lips.

A cry of horror finally welled up from Ganelon's soul. "Helain!" he wailed.

Helain gasped and shrank bank. Chuckling, the creature raised its misshapen head from her lap. "Ah, roused at last," the thing said, glancing down at its own swollen crotch in case the double entendre had eluded Ganelon. It hadn't.

As he looked upon the creature's corrupt visage, the memories flooded back—poor lost Bratu, capture by the Vistani, Inza's magic and the torture she'd promised when that sorcery failed to make him break the oath he'd sworn to the Bloody Cobbler. This creature had rescued him, pulled him through the shadows even as the Vistana raised the red-hot poker to his face. The Whispering Beast. He and Helain were in the hands of the Whispering Beast.

"G-Get away from her," the young man stammered.

The Beast pushed himself to a crouch. Helain immediately threw her arms around his sunken chest. "What makes you think she wants to be left alone?" he asked. "I doubt she was ever this affectionate with you, little boy. If she was, it was wasted effort."

With one filthy hand, the Whispering Beast broke Helain's clinging embrace. He stood, revealing himself in all his hideousness.

He was starvation thin, taller than any man Ganelon had ever seen. Stringy hair covered his entire frame, gray-white where dirt and excrement hadn't matted it. Arms that seemed to bend the wrong way hung down past his knees. The hands at the ends of those misshapen limbs were graced with slender fingers that constantly twitched and traced vulgar patterns in the air. Those agile digits hinted at the most horrible thing about the Beast. Underlying the corruption were the faint remnants of a beauty so profound it could not be hidden by any amount of grime.

A leer split the Beast's twisted visage—yet his face, too, held vestiges of magnificence. His simian skull, all but fleshless at the crown, had the high cheekbones of a noble-born elf. Weeping sores all but obscured that feature, just as an orange rheum dulled his bright, piercing eyes. The pus welled at the corners and filmed the orbs. From time to time, it drooled down his cheeks, tears of festering corruption.

The sight of this malignant creature so transfixed Ganelon that he did not notice the crowd gathering around him. The hillside was filled with lunatics. They crawled toward the Beast like supplicants, hands outstretched, eyes averted. The creature smirked at their reverence and spat upon those who got too close.

Finally, when the mob was ready to close in, the Beast lifted the grim necklace from the tangle of his hairy chest. Upon that chain of fire-blackened steel dangled thirteen human ears. He raised one of these gruesome ornaments to his lips and whispered into it. As one the madmen screamed. Whimpering and barking like whipped mongrels, they disappeared over the top of the hill.

Helain, too, fled. Ganelon turned to pursue, but found befouled fingers wrapped around his arm.

"The best part of the joke is the poor ninny didn't even hear what I said."

The slaughterhouse stench from the Beast made the gorge rise in Ganelon's throat. The young man pulled away, gagging. "She's not yours," he managed to gasp as he fell to the ground.

"Technically correct," the Beast replied. "No one properly condemned her for breaking her oath. In a more practical sense, however, she's been mine from the moment she vowed to love you forever."

"Helain still loves me!" Ganelon shouted angrily.

The Beast rolled his eyes. "You still haven't figured it out? Helain loves the man you *were*, the daring dolt who swept her off her feet. After you got all safe and promised never to do anything dangerous again, she found you, well, boring."

"I did that for her."

"Don't you feel foolish, then," the Beast sneered.

Ganelon wept. The Beast watched him for a moment, disdain clear on his horrible face. "Wipe away those tears, little boy. The wronged lover act won't play with me." He leaned close. "I know that you've dreamed of breaking the promise to stay by her side. You've practically frothed at the mouth at the thought of roaming the countryside again."

The Beast held up one of the severed ears and placed it over Ganelon's. The young man could feel the maggots dripping off the dead flesh as the Beast whispered, "If you weren't so stone stupid, you'd realize how faithless you've been to poor Helain. Why, a cynic might even think you were glad she went mad and ran off. It gave you an excuse to be a hero again."

Ganelon shoved the Beast away. "I'm taking her away from here," he said.

"I told you: She likes it here. She thinks so little of herself, she's only at home with someone who detests her." The Beast thumped his hollow chest. "No one loathes the false more than I do."

His thoughts awhirl, Ganelon turned away. He looked out over the hillside, still strangely green when all the rest of Sithicus had long ago browned with autumn's first frosts. "If not to rescue Helain, why was I brought here?" There was silence for a moment, then the sound of the Beast's laughter. Ganelon turned back, an accusatory finger leveled at the creature. "I won't be mocked," he shouted. "I won't—"

The rest of Ganelon's angry rejoinder died on his lips. The Whispering Beast was no longer alone. It crouched subserviently at the feet of a figure in a pure white robe. Her face, her hands, and every inch of her frame were concealed by the habit.

"You were brought here at my insistence," the figure said. "I am the White Rose."

Her voice was gentle, loving, yet thick with a penetrating sadness that overwhelmed even Ganelon's broken heart. She moved toward him with an unhurried step. Even so simple an action as walking betrayed her grace and her station. She was clearly accustomed to setting the pace, not following another's lead. Ganelon wasn't even aware that he had bowed to the Rose until her hand, clad in a white silken glove, appeared before his downturned eyes.

"M'lady," he said and kissed the proffered hand.

In the shadow of her hood, a slight smile flared and faded. "How gallant," the Rose said lightly. "I have obviously chosen well. Come, let us talk of adventure." She began to walk slowly to the crest of the hill.

"And of justice," the Beast noted. He'd taken up a deferential station, loping along two steps behind the Rose.

"Justice, as always," the Rose confirmed. She reached down and stroked the creature's fleshless pate. The Beast leaned into the touch like an affection-starved hound. The sight made Ganelon's skin crawl.

"You kept your word to the Cobbler, Ganelon," the Rose noted without preamble. "You did not tell that monstrous gypsy where she might find the Beast's lair. She would not have forced it from you, even with the tortures she had planned."

Ganelon did not ask how the Rose knew. The Beast seemed able to look into his heart, to know things that Ganelon hid even from himself, so there seemed no reason why she could not share that power. Instead, the youth merely noted, "I swore upon my love for Helain. There is nothing I value more highly."

The Beast chortled, but the Rose silenced him with a gesture. "It is not in the Beast's nature to understand the dark urges that plague all mankind," she explained, "only to punish those who give in to them. I, however, appreciate those dark desires all too well. You appeal to me because you have fought them and won."

"For now," the Beast added.

The White Rose nodded but once. "For now. Yet that is sufficient for me to make you my servant."

"I don't mean to be rude," Ganelon said, "but why should I serve you?"

"Because I can free Helain from this place," the Rose answered simply.

The trio topped the hill. Upon the slope of the facing rise lay a vast and complicated hedge maze. Their vantage allowed them a clear view of the figures within that leafy labyrinth. Even in the deepening shadows of late afternoon, their distant movements were easy enough to distinguish.

Some wandered aimlessly, sobbing dry tears of penitence. Others paced back and forth along the same small span. Still others crouched in corners, heads clamped between their hands, as they moaned or sang or shrieked their sorrow. This was the racket that Ganelon, in the bower's languor, had mistaken for laughter and bird song.

"They can find their way in and out of the maze," the White Rose noted, "where a sane man who entered there would never return. It is the power of madness, perhaps—or the whims of the gods."

The Beast sidled up to Ganelon. His overlong arms dragged in the dirt as he moved. "Take that as a warning," he hissed, "in case you thought to storm our midden and steal our maiden."

Ganelon's mind reeled. It was all too much. He struggled to put this strange new knowledge into some perspective, but the feel of something wet and warm on his neck distracted him. He reached up with trembling fingers, which came away red with blood. The wound from Inza's dagger. He felt the ear, found the lobe missing. There were new, thick stitches there, but they must have come undone.

He stumbled, but the Rose's strong hands steadied him before he fell. "The Vistani were cruel to you," she noted, "and you've only had a few days to rest."

"Days," Ganelon repeated dazedly.

The Rose took him by the arm and gently guided him down the hill toward the maze. "In a day or two more," she said, "you will be ready to undertake a journey on my behalf."

At a touch from the Rose, Ganelon's wound stopped bleeding. She spoke of trifles as they walked, refusing to let the conversation drift back to the journey she had mentioned. Her only reply to Ganelon's direct questions about the matter was, "It will be easier for you to comprehend once you see."

With an ape's ungraceful gait, the Beast careened ahead to the edge of the maze. The few lunatics on the hillside itself scattered at his approach; they ran howling for the safety of the labyrinth, though none moved quickly enough to get there before their tormentor. When Ganelon and the White Rose finally arrived, the Beast was squatting upon one unfortunate. He'd propped his muddy feet on another, a bald and blubbering Vistana whom Ganelon recognized instantly.

"Bratu," he said as he moved to help the man.

The Beast bared long yellow fangs pitted with decay. "Don't interfere," he snarled, "unless you're willing to take his spot."

"He'd be better off with the Vistani," said Ganelon, a look of disgust on his face.

The Beast leaned forward. "What makes you think so, hero?"

"They would care for him," Ganelon replied. "Inza said—"

"You're taking the word of that twisted piece of work?" the Beast exclaimed. He kicked Bratu away. The brawny man scrambled up to the thick hedge, which parted just wide enough to admit him. After he'd passed through, the rift closed again.

"Inza only wanted the goon back to finish him off," the Beast continued, "to silence him for good before he got beyond her reach."

Ganelon remembered the glee on Inza's face as she came toward him with the hot iron. "She's the one who pulled out his tongue."

"Inza would have killed poor Bratu if her mother hadn't yet been alive," the Rose noted. "As leader of their caravan, Magda could have exiled her, cast her into darkness. There is no Vistana alive who does not fear that."

"There is no creature alive that does not fear its mother's wrath," the Beast added without a trace of humor.

"And now Magda's dead," Ganelon said, recalling the rumors they'd heard at the mine. "That makes Inza the Wanderers' *raunie*. She can do what she wants."

"Bright boy!" The Beast got to his feet, and the madman he'd been perched upon crawled away along the hedge maze's border. The thicket eventually opened and swallowed him as it had Bratu.

"Actually," said the Beast as he came to Ganelon's side, "you and the gypsy make a fine pair. You're both worse Oathbreakers than anyone here. You just haven't been caught—yet."

The White Rose dismissed the loathsome creature with the wave of her gloved hand. "See to the cauldrons," she said. "It's getting dark."

The Beast loped off along the maze's perimeter. Every few steps, he lifted his gory necklace to his lips and spoke into one of the ears. Ganelon could scarcely imagine what it was that the Beast said. He was certain, though, that he never wanted to hear for himself.

Twilight had settled upon the hills, and the cries of the madmen wandering the maze had taken on a singsong quality. For all its discord, the sound had an underlying motif. It was a chant, Ganelon realized. The lunatics were passing the song between them. Each uttered a few words before letting it pass to the next.

The White Rose turned toward the hedge, and the wall of green opened wide to admit her. She took Ganelon by the arm. "Come," she said and led him toward the break.

He hesitated, the Rose's earlier comments about the maze still fresh in his mind. "No fear," she said. "You are safe from the labyrinth's magic so long as you stay with me." After a slight pause, she added, "Or perhaps you are already mad, and the maze will welcome you."

Ganelon sputtered a reply, but the Rose's gentle laughter drowned it out. "My apologies," she said lightly. "Too much time in the Beast's company has tainted my sense of humor. You may trust me when I say that you are safe in my company."

The hedgerow closed behind them the moment they passed through. Ganelon felt a powerful wave of vertigo wash over him as the thick bushes knit together. He looked back at the seamless wall of greenery. There was no trace of the gap where they had entered. He wasn't even certain he was facing the right direction to retrace his steps.

The hedges were thick with roses, both black and white. The flowers' fragrance was overwhelming, even stronger than in the bower. Ganelon's disorientation grew more profound. He could only keep moving if he focused on the White Rose, her firm hand on his arm and the soothing lilt to her voice.

"We are agents of a justice older than Sithicus, older even than Soth," she began. "We are here to remind the Knight of the Black Rose that such justice reaches even into those places hidden from the gods."

"I don't see what I can do to help you," Ganelon said. "I don't really understand any of this."

"That is no surprise. You've been drawn into this struggle in ways not even we could have predicted." The Rose plucked a white bloom from the hedgerow. When she spoke again, that immeasurable sadness had returned to her voice. "Epic events, like blind giants, will trample upon even the innocent unlucky enough to stumble beneath their tread."

A pale glow suffused the path ahead. It reached above the tall hedges to drive back the lowering night. As Ganelon and the Rose walked on, the air grew close. Swells of heat washed over them. A thin sheen of sweat formed on Ganelon's brow, and his lungs ached from gasping in the superheated air.

At last they turned a final corner and saw the source of the strange light and the awful heat.

There, at the labyrinth's heart, stood a pair of mammoth cauldrons. They were five times a man's height, as wide around as a mine shaft. Scaffolding surrounded them both, the ramps and platforms concealed behind an ornate latticework of gorgeous metal flowers. Even as Ganelon watched, wild elves bustled up the scaffolding of the nearest cauldron, sacks of white roses upon their backs. They emptied the bags into the pot and hurried back down. All the while, the chatter of the madmen in the maze wove together as a chant that underscored the weird rite.

The second cauldron was the root of the blasting heat. A roaring fire raged within the huge iron pot. On the ground surrounding it lay a few sacks of roses—not white or black, but red. Such flowers were impossible to grow in Sithicus. Even blooms smuggled in from Invidia or Barovia blackened within a day or two.

The White Rose gestured toward the rare blossoms. "That is how you can aid us, Ganelon," she said. "The second cauldron has been purified and stands ready. We only need flowers enough to fill it."

At the puzzled look on Ganelon's face, the White Rose merely held up the pale bloom she had plucked from the hedge. The flower merged with the white moon overhead. "We've already brought Solinari to the heavens. When Lunitari shines its crimson light upon Sithicus, Soth will stand ready to receive our sentence. But we must hurry. As we speak, soldiers from Invidia are on the march, moving into place to besiege Nedragaard Keep."

"Even if I knew where to find enough red roses to fill the pot, I couldn't carry them back here by myself." Ganelon slapped his leg brace. "I can't ride, and I'm not even certain I could walk very far."

"Oh, boo hoo," whispered a voice in his ear. The smell of the Beast's breath struck him an instant later. "Always sniveling about yourself. Well, don't think twice about it, little boy. You stay home and play with your brace. I'll take care of Helain."

Ganelon lashed out with a spinning backhand. The Beast didn't move or flinch. Casually he caught the young man's fist in one grimy paw, then pulled him close. The two were face to face as the Beast said, "It's about time." He held Ganelon there for an instant longer, orange-filmed eyes glittering with perverse delight. "Maybe you can help us after all."

The Beast shoved Ganelon away. "The deal is this," he said, stroking the food-crusted hair on his chin. "You bring us red roses, and I lift the madness from Helain's mind. You'll find a field of crimson beauties just over the Invidian border. They're a bit livelier than most flora, but you'll manage."

"Cure her first," Ganelon said. "I'll do whatever you want if you cure her first."

"You must prove yourself before we can reward you," the White Rose answered coldly.

"We traffic in justice here," the Beast chimed in, "not mercy."

"I'm not leaving here without her."

"We did not intend for you to do so," said the Rose, though the Beast seemed surprised at the news. "You will take Helain, and as many of the Beast's wards as you wish, when you make your journey. They can carry the bundles back."

"What about the elves? At least they can follow orders."

"The wild elves who tend the cauldrons are the only ones left. The rest have already taken up the quest," the White Rose said. "You have heard our offer, Ganelon. What is your answer?"

Ganelon slumped onto the ground. "What choice do I have?"

"There is always a choice," the White Rose said. For the first time, anger had crept into her voice. It was a terrible thing to hear. "You walk the path of honor or you do not."

The Beast cowered, hands covering his hideous face. A chill swept over Ganelon, not a sensation born of fear, but a palpable cold that radiated from the White Rose. It damped even the heat of the cauldron's blaze.

The anger in the Rose's voice, the fear it inspired in the Beast, did not sway Ganelon to the quest. It was love of Helain that prompted him to accept. "I'll storm Nedragaard Keep if that's what it takes to save her," he said at last.

"Do not make such offers lightly," the White Rose noted. Once more she held out a silk-gloved hand for Ganelon to kiss. As she did, her sleeve rode up just enough to reveal a glimpse of her charred and skeletal arm. "You may be called to account for such oaths in ways you never expect."

With a shudder, Ganelon touched his lips to her stiff, cold fingers.

TWELVE

The day was unlike any other for the Wanderers. For the first time since Magda formed the troupe all those years ago in Gundarak, the dawn found the Vistani in the same camp they'd used the night before.

Superstition had prompted the troupe to seek a new site each day. Magda's ancestor, the fabled Vistani hero Kulchek, had suffered under a curse that required him never to sleep in the same place twice. As she carried Kulchek's cudgel and traveled with a hound descended from his own faithful Sabak, so Magda took his customs upon herself. Her tribe had no choice but to follow her wishes.

Inza felt no such compunction, even though she, too, carried more of Kulchek's legacy than some vague blood tie. The dagger she wielded was none other than the hero's own storied blade, Novgor. That needle-pointed, ever-sharp blade had freed Kulchek from the chains the nine boyars used to enslave him. With it he'd picked the lock to the tower in which the giant hid his beautiful daughter. Novgor was the only weapon sharp enough to cut the tree the Wanderer found at the top of the world, the tree from which he fashioned his cudgel, Gard.

It was the only weapon sharp enough to score that same unbreakable cudgel, to render it useless in Magda's hands on the night of the salt shadow attack.

That dark deed had caused Inza no discomfort. How, then, could abandoning Kulchek's habit bring her harm? The curse, after all, had been leveled against him, and he was long dead.

So Inza had stopped the caravan from breaking camp the afternoon before. "We've found no better site on the edge of the Fumewood," was the only reason she gave.

Some of the Wanderers grumbled. A few even took their bedrolls and went off to sleep in the woods. Most of the gypsies, exhausted from a week of scouring the Fumewood for some trace of Bratu, merely slouched off to their *vardos* to get a few extra hours' sleep.

Now, in the still moments before dawn, when the whole world seemed to hold its breath in anticipation of the day to come, Inza walked quietly through the sleeping camp. Alexi nodded a somber greeting to her from his station at the low-banked fire. She stifled the urge to laugh. Whether keeping watch over the *vardos* or celebrating a well-run scam on some *giorgio*, the man maintained the same comically grim expression. It was as if he'd just eaten something so sour he couldn't open his mouth again to spit it out.

Inza knew the man feared her, so perhaps the expression was one he reserved only for her. It didn't matter. Alexi did what she ordered, without question, without hesitation. If he was lucky, he might still be around to help her put her final plans into motion, but she wasn't counting on it. Better, she knew, to rely only upon herself.

Still musing on the value of self-reliance, Inza made her way down a winding path to a spring-fed pool she had discovered two days ago. It was one of the things that made the site so attractive for a camp. When she came to the cool, clear water, Inza neither drank nor washed her face. Instead, she sat on the mossy bank and waited.

Just after the sun topped the Fumewood's twisted trees, a shout of alarm startled the *raunie* to her feet. She drew Novgor from the special sheath in her boot and took a step toward the *vardos*. She paused as the single shout was echoed by a second and a third cry of alarm. Finally, when the screams of horses and the clash of steel sounded from the camp, she set off at a run.

Inza surveyed the cramped battlefield from the edge of the clearing. A group of ogres stormed through the camp. Instead of the usual flea-ridden furs and tattered rags, these brutes were clad in plate armor or chain mail. Decorated helms hid their warty faces and greasy locks, and they carried weapons of a fine enough forge to satisfy any soldier.

Though they wore no insignia and carried no standard, the colors of their cloaks—purple and black—declared their allegiance to Malocchio Aderre.

A quick count totaled the number of ogres at twenty. The Vistani were outnumbered, even if all of them were included as worthwhile fighters. Many of the older men and women simply were not. Still, the Wanderers seemed to be holding their own. Ten bodies lay bleeding into the dirt; the casualties were split evenly between the Vistani and the ogres.

Alexi in particular seemed to be acquitting himself well. At the moment he was driving not one, but two of the brutes into retreat. Whoever had shown the Vistana how to wield a sword, they'd taught him well.

"Regroup with me," Alexi shouted. Inza and the remaining Vistani retreated to his position, placing the arc of *vardos* at their backs. The ogres formed a semicircle of their own. Slowly they began to close in on the cornered gypsies.

"They were separating us," Alexi explained breathlessly. "We can hold off their charge, but only if we stay together." He gave Inza that familiar sour-faced look. "If there's some fey magic at your disposal, *raunie*, now would be the time to use it."

Inza didn't get a chance to answer. One of the wagons that the Wanderers had been counting on to keep the ogres from encircling them suddenly flipped over. Two Vistani were caught beneath the *vardo*, killed instantly. A second wagon toppled, then a third. The ogres surrounded them. With a cry of "Invidia!" they charged.

Greta, a blonde beauty who had promised to wed Piotr come spring, was trapped between two of the brutes. She fought valiantly. One blow from her staff and the shorter of her attackers dropped to the ground, broken nose gushing blood. The other snatched her from the ground even as she raised her staff to strike again. With a swiftness startling for his size, the ogre brought one knee up to waist height and cracked the girl over it like a bundle of dry firewood.

From across the camp, Piotr howled his anguish. He brought his sword down with such force that it bit into an ogre's armored shoulder and stuck there. The brute spun away, clutching at the weapon. In doing so, he dropped the pike he'd been carrying. Piotr grabbed it and charged the ogre that had killed his beloved Greta.

The pike's spiked tip lodged in the ogre's gut. The force of the blow knocked him from his feet. But the brute would not die. Even as Piotr twisted the polearm and jammed it deeper into his stomach, the ogre struggled to free himself. He was either too stupid or too tough to realize the severity of his wounds.

When it was clear that the pike was not going to finish the job, Piotr seized a large piece of firewood. As the brute wrestled with the blood-slicked weapon protruding from his stomach, the Vistana tore off his helmet and caved in his skull.

The screams, blood, and chaos set Inza's heart aflutter. She hung back from the brawl, Novgor clutched before her. The ogres left her alone. Time and again they ran right past her, as if she were invisible.

The rest of the Wanderers were not so lucky. Before long, Inza could see only four men standing. Alexi and Piotr were holding their own, but Katan, the troupe's youngest, was staggering from a nasty leg wound. Nikolas flanked him, offering some meager protection as the two tried to find some suitable place to make their final stand.

Inza smiled. It was time.

"On my mother's soul, upon your sacred oath, I call to you, Lord Soth! Defend me!"

The sound of the battle and the cries of the dying all but drowned out Inza's words. She knew, though, that Soth would hear them, wherever he was. If her mother had been telling the truth in all those dreadfully boring tales she used to tell over the campfire, Soth would uphold the oath he'd sworn to her. He would come to poor little Inza's rescue, if only to show how hollow and meaningless such noble actions were. After all, if a thing of darkness such as Soth could take on a guise of honor, who was to say that all men who appeared honorable might not secretly share his heart of darkness?

Just as some women who feign helplessness might share his warrior's spirit, Inza noted silently.

As if to prove that statement's truth, she lunged at a passing ogre. Needle-pointed Novgor bit through the plate mail covering his chest, through the flesh and bone beneath. The blade finally came to rest in the brute's massive heart. He was dead before the startled gasp left his snaggletoothed mouth and the iron-spiked club slipped from his thick fingers.

As the club struck the ground, Lord Soth emerged from the shadow of a shattered *vardo*. The cold of the grave rolled out of the darkness with him, washing over the camp like some icy tide. Orange eyes ablaze, he surveyed the carnage. There was no need for Inza to say anything. The situation was plain enough.

An unsuspecting ogre, startled by the sudden blast of cold, literally stumbled into the death knight's grasp. Soth clamped one gauntleted hand around the soldier's throat. No blow, no gasp for mercy could make him slacken that grip. He squeezed until the ogre's eyes bulged and his mottled tongue lolled from his mouth. Satisfied the brute was dead, Soth dropped him like a child bored with his toy and waded into the fray.

The battle turned immediately. Inza could see the astonishment register on the ogres' faces. "Betrayed!" some of them cried as they fled into the Fumewood. Others tried to reach Inza, their faces florid with anger. Novgor decapitated the first who rushed her. The rest turned back.

Like Death itself, Lord Soth strode across the camp toward Inza. Every Invidian in his path fell before him. At first he did not draw his sword. His fists were weapons enough. When two ogres charged him, he smashed their heads together with such force that the skulls split open like old melons. The two sank down in a heap, purple brains and gore staining the ground.

It was only when he came upon Alexi, locked in mortal combat with one of the brutes, that Soth drew his ancient blade. The death knight did not slacken his pace, merely called to the Invidian as he came.

"Face me," he rumbled, "or flee. There is no third way."

The ogre turned, hesitated. Soth slashed open the brute's throat and continued on.

As his opponent crumpled, Alexi stood staring at the Knight of the Black Rose. He felt certain that Soth had not even seen him. The death knight was simply clearing a path to Inza.

As abruptly as it had started, the battle was over.

Only four of Inza's troupe remained alive. Piotr and Nikolas tried to offer their thanks to Lord Soth. They hesitantly approached the death knight, but he did not acknowledge them. Instead, he stood stone still among the dead, eyes focused on something in the carnage.

Inza wiped the blood from Novgor and came to Soth's side. "They were Aderre's lackeys," she offered, "sent here to slaughter us."

When Soth remained silent, Inza followed his gaze to the ground. A burst of silver and gold coins spread across the dirt, spilled from a leather pouch one of the ogres had been carrying. The Vistana knelt. Some of the coins were Invidian, others Sithican or Barovian. She held up one silver piece whose mint she could not recognize.

"Where is Palanthas?" she asked.

"Far from here," Soth said, his mind awash in a memory of that city's never-conquered walls falling before his magic.

The death knight pushed the remembrance aside and walked to the next fallen ogre. With the tip of his blade he opened the corpse's purse. A similar fortune in gold and silver slid onto the ground. He turned and seized Inza by the arm.

Her arm went numb immediately from the unearthly cold of his touch. "What is it?" she asked, panic making her voice shrill. "What does all that money mean?"

"That someone within my domain has bought the allegiance of this rabble," the death knight replied flatly. "They are garbed as Invidian soldiers and surely crossed into Sithicus as such. Yet even Malocchio Aderre is not fool enough to pay his army before a battle is fought or let them take their wages on campaign."

Soth indicated the battlefield with a swipe of his sword. "If I am correct, then this has been a simple diversion."

"Diversion?" Inza sputtered. She pulled free of Soth's grip. "There are but four of us left standing. Our *vardos* are smashed, our horses frightened off. This is the stuff of a diversion? The Wanderers are extinct!"

"In the larger war that will be fought, you and your tribe are meaningless," Soth said coldly. "You have been a pawn in this, put in peril to draw me away from the main army's true objective. Come, we must return to Nedragaard Keep."

Alexi stepped forward as though he meant to challenge Soth, to demand he release their *raunie*. But Inza flashed him a warning look, and he stopped in his tracks.

"What about the rest of my people, mighty lord?" she asked.

"They are not my concern."

"But they are *my* concern," Inza snapped. "They were my mother's concern, too. In her name, if not in mine, help them." She swallowed hard, as if the next word were barbed in her throat. "Please."

Soth regarded the men coolly. "Very well. Make your way on foot to my castle. You will be permitted to stay there."

"Alone and on foot they will be dead before noon," Inza said. "Only you saved us from this 'diversion.' What if they encounter another?"

"You demand much of me, *raunie*," Soth warned.

"Only what is fair. My mother's benediction is surely worth this small beneficence for her people."

Turning to Alexi, Soth said, "I will summon guards to protect you, but their number will be yours to determine."

"How so?" the grim Vistana asked.

"Shall your fallen kin be part of this guard or no?"

Alexi's face blanched. "No," he gasped. "Our ancestors would—"

"Enough," Soth rumbled. "You have chosen."

The death knight strode to the center of the camp and raised his arms. A sudden wind howled around him, billowing his purple cloak. Soth clenched his hands into fists, and midnight-black clouds blossomed in the sky, obscuring the sun. The wind's howl grew more strident. There was another sound, too, faint at first but growing more insistent with each passing moment. It was the awful moan of souls in torment.

The slaughtered ogres rose from the battlefield. There was an awkward, disjointed quality to their movements that made them terrible to watch. They shambled toward Soth, eyes fixed sightlessly ahead. Their arms hung limp at their sides. The zombies carried no weapons, save those still buried in their flesh.

"You will follow this man's orders," the death knight said, indicating Alexi. "You will escort him and his companions to Nedragaard Keep, killing anyone who tries to detain or harm them."

With that, Soth turned his back on them and approached Inza. "Now," he intoned gravely, "we are leaving."

"Of course, mighty lord," the Vistana said demurely. She glanced at Alexi and called out, "Bring the chest from my *vardo*. It has supplies you'll need on the journey."

Soth put his arm across Inza's shoulders and ushered her into the shadow of a gaunt oak. The Wanderers watched their *raunie* disappear into the dark. When she was gone, Alexi turned to the others.

"We have our orders," he said brusquely. "We are to travel to the keep as quickly as possible. We take the *raunie*'s strongbox, but anything else that might slow us down must be left behind." He cast a meaningful look at Katan.

The boy's wounds were grave. He might survive the day, but without the medicines only Inza knew how to concoct, his wounds were all but certain to fester. Moving him would be tantamount to torture. But to delay, even for a few hours, might mean losing their *raunie* forever. Without her, the Wanderers would have to disband. The men would be outcasts, stray dogs in a society that valued the pack above all.

"Thank you for all you've given and done, Brother," Nikolas whispered to Katan. He kissed the boy on each cheek and then thrust his short sword between the youth's ribs. Katan died instantly. The zombies watched it all with patient, passionless gazes, as if they expected the boy to rise up and join their ranks.

"Shall I build a pyre?" Piotr asked, "or should we have the monsters do it?"

"Neither," Alexi said. "We break camp now. There is no time to build a fire hot enough to burn the bodies."

Piotr shook his head emphatically. "I will not leave my Greta to the crows," he said. "This is not our way."

Alexi clapped a hand on the younger man's shoulder. "Much we have done today is not our way, Brother." He stared sadly at Katan's corpse, at Nikolas, who lingered over the friend he had murdered.

"What good are all these sacrifices if we lose ourselves?" Piotr asked. "What are we fighting so hard to save?" He walked to the corpse of his beautiful Greta. With a short sword he found on the ground, he began to scrape the beginnings of a grave.

Alexi sighed raggedly. "Dig a grave," he told the zombies. "Make it deep enough and wide enough to hold all the Vistani you killed." He called to Piotr. "Let them do it. Come help me sift through the splinters of the *raunie*'s *vardo*. We need to find her strongbox."

By the time the zombies finished with their work and the corpses had been laid to rest, the sky had clouded over. A light rain fell upon the three men as they looked upon the shallow grave. Alexi said a few brief words in Patterna, commending the fallen Vistani to their ancestors and wishing them fair travels beyond the Mists.

"Now you are no longer bound to any lands. Now you are free," he finished quietly. The silence that followed was marred only by the hollow spatter of rain on the zombies' armor.

Only a short while after the Vistani left the clearing, bound for Nedragaard Keep with their shuffling guardians, a figure separated from the trees. His colorless clothes seemed to match the bleak, rain-sodden day, yet his spirits were bright as he approached the grave.

"A thousand pardons for the indignity I am about to inflict upon you," the Bloody Cobbler said in all sincerity to the figures piled beneath the mounded earth. "It would have been much simpler for everyone had they left you where you fell. Still, this is all in a good cause."

He raised his arms in much the same fashion as Lord Soth had earlier. "Up and out of there," the Cobbler ordered. "I summon you up, and you must obey."

Whistling an ancient traveling song once popular among the Knights of Solamnia, he turned his back on the shuddering, churning grave mound and walked to a fallen log. There he rested a booklike leather case the same pale color as his clothes.

The Cobbler glanced back once, just in time to see the first fingers claw at the dismal daylight. He smiled and let the case fall open. Carefully, he began to unpack the tools of his trade.

THIRTEEN

Ganelon looked down at the severed ear in his hand. Slowly, he brought the piece of rotting flesh to his lips and whispered into it. The effect was instantaneous. Bratu and the other lunatics, even his beloved Helain, hurried from where they had strayed across the hillside. They huddled together at his feet and looked up at him expectantly.

Beyond the cowering madmen, at the foot of the hill, lay their destination. The Invidians who lived in this part of the Border's Edge Mountains referred to the huge field as Malocchio's Dream Garden. How appropriate, mused Ganelon, that it should be so dismal and twisted.

A low wall of rough-hewn stone surrounded a riot of misshapen greenery. Emerald tendrils, almost like veins, crept from the garden through gaps in the wall. They did not seem intent on escaping the place, but shoring up the stones to keep trespassers out. From the looks of things, the garden had few enough of those.

The greenery was horribly overgrown, the paths choked with weeds. There seemed to be no clear pattern to the beds. They ranged in size from smaller than a child to larger than one of the massive carts used to haul salt at the mine. Some were bunched together, others isolated. The only thing they had in common was the sort of plant crouched upon each: a large, thorn-snarled rose bush with flowers the crimson of freshly spilled blood. Together the blooms formed a blanket of red that resembled a gaping wound slashed into the Invidian countryside.

The semblance was chillingly appropriate. The garden was located upon the site of a massacre, the spot where Malocchio Aderre himself had slaughtered an entire caravan of Vistani. As it was Malocchio's ambition that all Vistani be similarly butchered, so the field had been tagged his "Dream Garden." It was no less a monument to madness than the Whispering Beast's hedge maze. Ganelon hoped that the congruence would work in his favor as he readied his ragged band of lunatics to begin their perilous work within.

"Go to the garden wall and wait," Ganelon said to the two dozen or so soldiers in his mad army.

A few evinced some small comprehension. Most just stared at him blankly. He sighed and repeated the order into the ear the Beast had given him. They immediately turned to the task.

Ganelon wondered what they heard when he spoke to them, if the voice was his own or if the Beast's gruesome present gave it a sinister sound. From what the Beast had said about Helain, she couldn't hear the commands at all. She only aped the others, her guilty conscience goading her to take on their punishments and fears as her own.

It pained Ganelon to see his beloved so distanced from the person he knew her to be. Still, hints of her former self shone through now and then. When the lunatics were at their most manic, she would go suddenly calm. They whirled and capered about; she remained still. The breeze of their passing would stir her red locks and billow her torn, soiled nightdress. Through it all she stood unmoving, letting them swirl harmlessly around her like wasps swarming a gravestone.

He watched her now as she walked atop the low stone wall. She turned, as if she could feel his longing eyes upon her. No spark of recognition lit her face as she returned his gaze. Ganelon finally looked away. She was lost to him.

With a heavy heart, the young man focused again on the task at hand and took a quick accounting of his wards. Most had reached the wall. Once there, they took up their usual crazed behavior.

One woman, whose name Ganelon had forgotten, walked with direction and determination for short spans, only to stop suddenly. All sign of intelligence fled her thin face until, just as suddenly, she would pluck at her hair until she came away with precisely eight long strands. Tossing them over her shoulder, she would turn sharply and repeat the routine. A few more repetitions, and she ended up close to where she'd started.

Some lunatics wept openly, others sat on the ground and rocked back and forth. Only Bratu ventured into the garden. He wandered aimlessly among the maze of plants, slapping at his ruined ears and pointing at the beds. It was a gesture many of the others, still perched atop the low wall, soon copied. They were obviously frightened by something in the garden, something hidden from Ganelon's view by the weeds and the wall.

Ganelon hobbled down to the garden. As he wrestled his braced leg over the wall, he noticed that the roses' fragrance was twined with some other, more ominous odor. It was pungent and earthy, the smell of old rot. At first he suspected the black blight spider-webbed across many of the plants. A closer inspection of the nearest rose bush revealed the actual source of the smell.

The bases of the rose bushes were thick and woody, completely denuded of leaves. They resembled nothing so much as human bones, a trait that allowed them to blend seamlessly with the old skeletons from which they grew.

That was the thing that had so alarmed Bratu and the others. Each of the rose bushes was rooted in a corpse. Malocchio had left the butchered Vistani where they fell, then planted his victory garden amongst the dead. Some of the bodies were partially buried. Some lay atop the dark loam. The branches so resembled bleached bones that the remains were invisible from a distance.

As he walked the weed-choked paths Ganelon realized that some of the corpses were newer than others. They still retained some scraps of desiccated flesh or some tatter of clothing. Around a few of the beds lay coins and small trinkets, even a rusting knife or two. The remains of failed thieves, no doubt, he guessed.

The thought made Ganelon stop dead in his tracks. He peered more closely at one of the bushes. Through the mold-flecked leaves, he could make out wicked greenish-yellow thorns running along the stems and branches. Ribbons of mummified flesh dangled from some of the spikes. Others were dark with old blood.

An insight blazed across his mind: Those aren't thorns. They're teeth. These are corpse roses.

The intuition's clarity stunned Ganelon. He wondered briefly at its origin, but left that problem for another time. The information it had imparted was indisputable. They were all in terrible danger.

"Don't touch the roses," he said into the severed ear. "Stay on that side of the wall!" He directed Bratu to join the others. The Vistana was reluctant to leave the garden, as if he could sense that these poor souls were his people. Eventually, Ganelon took him by the hand and forced him over the wall.

His charges out of harm's way for the moment, Ganelon returned to his examination of the corpse roses. There was no way around it; without the roses, the Beast would not cure Helain. Cautiously he plucked one of the flowers. The stem shuddered and oozed blood as red as the bloom but did not lash out at him. So long as Bratu and the others could harvest the roses carefully, they'd be all right.

He walked back to the wall, giving the bushes as wide a berth as possible. Through the Beast's charm, he gathered the madmen who had strayed from the wall. That none of them had ventured into the garden, as he had ordered earlier, gave Ganelon some small hope as he outlined his orders to them. If he was precise enough in his instructions, they might survive this ordeal.

"All right," he said, "remember why we're here. We are collecting roses for the Beast." At the mention of their tormentor's name, the madmen whimpered piteously. "He does not want leaves or stems or thorns—especially thorns. Whatever you do, do not touch any part of the rose bushes except the flowers."

Ganelon slung the small pack he had been carrying from his shoulder. "The sack tied to your waist is for holding the flowers." He dropped the bloom in his hand into his pack. "Like this. Just the flower, nothing else."

One of the older men, scarcely any hair left on his head, grabbed the canvas sack from his neighbor. He hugged it to his chest as if it were a long-lost friend. Ganelon returned it to its owner quickly, before a brawl broke out; then he led the old man into the garden.

"See, Grandfather," he said kindly, "we want all the pretty flowers, but only the flowers." Ganelon beheaded a few blossoms to demonstrate. With palsied hands, the old man slowly pulled the roses free. Ganelon bit his lip as he watched the man's shaking fingers pluck at the blooms, but the man seemed to catch on quickly. With a quick word of praise, Ganelon was off to get the others started.

At first he kept a careful eye on the demented souls as they went about their task. As the afternoon wore on, though, Ganelon found himself less and less attentive. It was tedious watching them work, or attempt to work. And after three days with the madmen, leading them from the Beast's lair to this field just across the Invidian border, he had little stomach left for the manifestations of their sad, awful, infuriating sickness.

Thoughts of Helain were quick to provide distraction. The fragrance of the roses reminded him of the plans they'd made for the wedding, how they would transform Ambrose's store into a blossom-filled chapel. He was caught up in imagining what that happy event might have been like when a soft voice startled him from his reverie.

"They smell like churches should smell," Helain said quietly. In her hand she cupped a single red rose. "Though they're the wrong color. White roses are my favorite."

Ganelon's heart sang. Even when she turned away in mid-sentence, making it clear that she wasn't speaking to him so much as to herself, the happiness lingered. The old Helain had surfaced for just an instant, long enough for him to realize she still existed. It was enough.

Helain knelt to collect the blossoms from a particularly thorny bush, and Ganelon moved to her side. Even if she weren't aware of his presence, he might bask in hers and hope for another glimpse of her old self.

She hummed a work song from the mine as she plucked the flowers. It had been one of Ambrose's favorites. The stout old fellow sang it endlessly around the shop. Helain went through three verses as she stripped the bush, pausing only when she dropped a large blossom. It fell onto the skeleton beneath the bush, into its open rib cage, where it sat like a suddenly resurrected heart.

Ganelon warily reached into the bones and retrieved the rose. He marveled at the bloom's color, a crimson so deep it was nearly black. He held it out to Helain. She looked first at the blossom, then up into Ganelon's face. Without a word, she slowly shook her head from side to side.

Before Ganelon could ask her why, a shriek of fear rent the garden's calm.

Bratu stood before a particularly large bed, face contorted with terror. One of the partially buried skeletons was moving. The bare bones trembled, seeming to push up out of the ground. Ganelon was at his side in an instant. He immediately spotted the rat, disturbed by the Vistana's proximity, as it burrowed deeper into its home within the bones. Bratu, however, was too blind with fear to recognize his terror's mundane cause.

Mouthing silent prayers to his ancestors, Bratu backed away from the rose bushes. He could not hear Ganelon's murmured words of reassurance or the frightened squeals of the other madmen. He shoved Ganelon's hands away when the young man tried to grab hold of him. An instant later, the Vistana toppled backward onto a plucked rose bush.

The struggle was brief, too brief for Ganelon to react in time to aid the Vistana. The thorns bit into Bratu's back. He howled in agony and tried to stand, but the branches entangled his legs. He reached down, frantic to pull himself free. The limbs of the bush bent to meet his fingers, and the thorns buried themselves in his hand. As they drank in the Vistana's blood, they pulsed and swelled in the wounds until they were all but impossible to shake loose.

More branches wrapped themselves around him, eager for his blood. Finally, the brawny Vistana got his feet beneath him. Using all his considerable strength, he pushed himself up. Some of the branches tore loose. Their thorns etched gory streaks in his flesh as they fell away. Most of the bush kept its awful grip upon him, so that when he stood, the skeleton from which the corpse rose had sprouted jerked to its feet, too.

The skeleton appeared to wrap its arms around Bratu, though it wasn't clear if it was acting on its own or merely animated by the vines and branches of the corpse rose.

The sight of the skeletal remains clinging to Bratu shocked Ganelon into action. He reached for the Vistana's hand, but the corpse encircled Bratu's arms and pinned them to his sides. A steady, wet slurping sound came from the thorns as they drank in the man's blood. Even as Ganelon watched, new roses budded upon the stems and blossomed. Their petals were dewed with Bratu's blood.

The feeding frenzy of one plant sent the rest into motion. Branches lashed out, snaring arms or legs or faces with their inch-long thorns. Panic swept through the garden. Most of Ganelon's mad army not entangled by the bushes fled. Because the sacks had been tied to their belts, they carried the precious blooms with them as they scurried over the wall. A few froze, paralyzed by fear, Helain among them.

Ganelon tore one of the madmen free of a bush; the thorns claimed ribbons of flesh from the unfortunate's face as he came away. Shoving him toward safety, the young man stormed through the garden. Bones and branches crunched beneath the heavy tread of his braced leg. He found Helain huddled at the garden's center. Corpse roses snaked all around her, but luck or some unseen hand kept them from her fair flesh.

"I've spilled my flowers," she said, gesturing to the red roses scattered across the path. "There can be no wedding now."

Ganelon tried to pull her up from the ground, but she resisted. A branch snagged his leg. He wrenched himself free, heedless of the deep cuts the thorns left in his calf. However, the blood spilled from those wounds drew the unwelcome attention of another rose bush, and it lurched forward hungrily. The corpse at its base stirred, too. Like a half-dozen others around the garden, the ravenous plant uprooted itself. Supported by its skeletal host, the corpse rose shuffled forward in search of blood.

Ganelon stuffed his own small, rose-filled pack into Helain's hands. "The Beast wants these. Hurry."

He protected her flight from the garden as best he could. The mobile corpses moved slowly enough for Ganelon and Helain to evade them. The lunatics already immobilized by the stationary plants were not as lucky. Crazed with hunger, the ambulatory roses descended upon the doomed men and women. The sounds of their feasting followed Ganelon up the hill, away from Malocchio's Dream Garden. The young man knew that the moist tearing and the agonized screams would forever echo in his nightmares.

When he was far enough from the garden to slow his pace, Ganelon removed the Beast's token from his pocket. "Back to him," he whispered into the ear. "Take the roses back to the Beast."

Ganelon hoped the madmen heard him. He had little chance of catching them now.

As he topped the hill, though, Ganelon was stunned to find the survivors of his mad army kneeling on the ground, groveling before a youth clad entirely in black. The sinister figure paced back and forth through the whimpering crowd, hands clasped behind his back. The steady *clank* of Ganelon's leg brace drew his attention away from the madmen, and he waited patiently for the newcomer to approach.

"Do you know the penalty for disturbing my garden?" Malocchio Aderre asked impatiently. "I'm going to kill you whether you do or not, of course. I'm just curious as to whether you are ignorant or foolhardy."

The tone was playful, but Ganelon recognized an undercurrent of deadly earnest there as well. He would have to deal with this carefully. Still, he felt an odd sense of comfort in the Invidian lord's presence. He'd spoken with this man before, many times. He just couldn't remember when.

These were more phantom memories caused by the Cobbler's graft, he realized. While Ganelon couldn't recollect the incidents that spawned them, he did remember the Cobbler's advice to him in the Fumewood: for these half-forgotten impulses to be useful, he needed to relax and simply let instinct take over.

"Neither fool nor imbecile, great lord," he said, bowing as deeply as his leg brace would allow. "I am merely an obedient servant on a mission."

"The only servants I tolerate in this land are my own," Malocchio replied. "And you and this . . . *rabble* are most certainly not servants of mine."

"Perhaps we are," Ganelon corrected mildly, "after a fashion."

Malocchio kicked one of the madmen. "Only if the fashion this season is for mewling lunatics," he snapped.

"The fashion is whatever you say it is."

A slight smile quirked Malocchio's lips. "Indeed." He studied Ganelon for a moment, then said, "Come closer."

As the young man hobbled forward, a light of recognition flashed in Lord Aderre's dark, penetrating eyes. "Where did you get that brace?"

"A benefactor," Ganelon replied. "He thought it would help me travel the hard road I have chosen for myself."

The Invidian lord reached down and tapped the metal. "This is mine, forged in my keep, by my smiths. It was crafted for a friend."

"I'll return it, then," Ganelon said. He began to undo the straps, adding, "Though a friend wears it still."

"How so?"

"The one I serve is set against Lord Soth," Ganelon said. "That gives us common ground for friendship."

Malocchio snatched up one of the bags of roses, overturning it. "This petty theft gives me reason to know you as an enemy," he snarled. With the toe of one black boot he kicked the petals. "Foes of Soth, you say? What use will these be in battling him? Do you hope to litter his path with them so that he trips and falls down the Great Chasm, perhaps?"

Ganelon finished removing the brace. His leg, free of the weight, felt odd. "I don't understand fully," he said. "I know only that the White Rose has a plan and that it will bring Soth to a reckoning for his crimes."

"The White Rose." Malocchio clasped his hands behind his back again and paced through the prostrate lunatics. "She really does exist?"

"I've seen her myself. She sent me after these roses. They play a part in some ancient sorcery she will wield against Soth. I believe she intends to time the spell so that it coincides with the siege of Nedragaard Keep."

"What siege?"

A puzzled look crossed Ganelon's face. "Why, your own. The Rose told me that your troops were even now moving against the keep."

Malocchio swore bitterly. "Is the Rose part of the siege?"

"I don't think so," Ganelon replied. "She spoke as if it were something she had no part in."

The black-clad man rushed to Ganelon's side, lifting him from the ground. "Is this the truth?" he shouted.

Ganelon averted his eyes from Aderre's face. It was frightening in its fury, marked with traces of the youth's demonic heritage. "It is the truth until you tell me it is not," said Ganelon meekly.

The phrase was one familiar to Malocchio's underlings. The lord of Invidia slowly lowered Ganelon back to the ground. "Put the brace back on," he said, "and tell me more about how you obtained it."

Ganelon did as Malocchio demanded, relating the tale told to him by the Bloody Cobbler. It seemed clear to him as he spoke that Aderre had known and perhaps even valued the Cobbler's victim. That fact could only work in his favor, Ganelon realized. Perhaps it might even afford him influence enough to see Helain and the others back safely across the border.

"Yes, of course they can go," Malocchio said distractedly when Ganelon inquired after the fate of his mad soldiers. "In return for my generosity, though, you will remain here with me for a time. We have plans to lay and treachery to punish."

The Invidian lord dismissed the lunatics with a wave. A few got to their feet, but Ganelon had to take out the Beast's token and tell them to flee back to the White Rose before most would leave.

As Helain adjusted the small pack filled with roses for the long journey ahead, Ganelon took her by the arm and studied her face. Wrinkles creased the corners of those gorgeous blue eyes, the leavings of worry and despair. So, too, the frown that tugged at her mouth. These would vanish after the Beast doused the fire of guilt consuming her from within. She would be whole again, the Helain he cherished in his heart.

If she reaches the Beast, Ganelon thought sadly. The words of Inza's curse were always fresh in his mind; he could not help but wonder if, by sending Helain off, he was not fulfilling it somehow. His direction, his hand, would be her doom.

"Tell her to go back to the Beast," Ganelon said suddenly to Malocchio. "Lord Aderre, please be the one to tell this woman to go."

Malocchio smirked. "Can't bear to do it yourself? Very well. Run along, girl. Deliver your flowers."

She turned, but Ganelon held her hand in his for an instant longer. "I only wish one thing, dear heart, and that is for you to remember me."

Helain's blank expression was too much for Ganelon to bear. He released her hand and bowed his head. Mournfully he watched her hurry off—then stop and turn back to him.

Slowly, eyes fixed on her lover's face, Helain returned. Without saying a word, she took Ganelon's hand and placed in it a perfect red rose. She smiled down on the bloom, then at Ganelon. He fixed that smile in his memory, letting it linger in his thoughts even as she hastened over the hills and disappeared into the forest beyond.

"Now that the wench is disposed of," Malocchio noted glibly, "we can discuss what it is I require of you."

"Yes, lord," Ganelon replied in a subdued tone.

"What do you know of Veidrava?"

"The mines? I know them like the veins on the backs of my hands."

"Fine, fine. You will go there and be the agent of my wrath against that treacherous beast Azrael. I want you to kill him, if possible."

Ganelon laughed bitterly. "Is that all, lord?"

Malocchio did not bridle at the grim joviality, for he knew the last laugh, as always, would be his. "Azrael must be made to pay for his betrayal. Those troops you say are now marching toward Nedragaard were never meant as more than a diversion. They were supposed to stay close to the border, to buy the little monster time in which to perform a rite to oust the death knight from the throne. He would take over Sithicus, hand over Magda and her Vistani as thanks for my help, and the world would be a better place.

"He's obviously got something else in mind. He must have bribed my men, purchased an army he could not hope to raise in Sithicus." The Invidian frowned at Ganelon. "What's your concern? You may speak."

"How am I supposed to challenge Azrael?" The youth held up his empty hands. "I don't even have a sword."

"A blade will do you no good against a thing like Azrael," Malocchio noted. He reached into his black cloak and brought out a small bag. "This, however, will make his twisted little brain boil in his skull."

Ganelon undid the drawstring on the silken bag. The pouch contained nothing more than poppy seeds.

"Slip enough of the seeds into his food, his drink, and he will be the Sorrow of Sithicus no more," Malocchio said brightly.

Aderre reached into his cloak again and produced a clear crystal orb. He rolled it in the palm of his hand, letting the sunlight flare upon its flawless surface. "This will be of use to you against his minions at the mine."

"What does it do, lord?"

"Azrael surrounds himself with creatures of the living dark, salt shadows and the like. This is a conduit for their opposite." He held it up to the sun. The orb flared brightly, almost as brightly as the sun itself, before resuming its appearance of mundane glass. "You need only speak a single word to activate it."

"What is the word?"

"Whatever you choose," replied Malocchio, "though you'll want it to be a word you won't forget."

"Helain," Ganelon replied softly.

The smirk returned. "The wench again." Malocchio murmured something as he passed his fingers over the orb. It darkened for an instant before he dropped it into Ganelon's outstretched hands. "I think you'll be able to remember the trigger."

"There's one thing I don't understand," Ganelon said as he tucked the orb and the seeds into a pouch. "Why are you trusting me with this task?"

"Your dearest Helain," the black-clad youth said. "The rite Azrael hopes to perform will destroy her—and everyone else you love in Sithicus. He'll gain control of their shadows, and they'll be his slaves. I'm certain you can imagine what Sithicus would be like if that were to happen."

Ganelon could imagine. That horrible thought drove him on through sleepless nights and exhausting days as he trekked back across the border, through the Fumewood, and on to Veidrava. At the same time, Inza's curse taunted him. If, as she had promised, everything he held dear would perish by his own hand, was he returning to the mine to save Sithicus, or to destroy it?

FOURTEEN

Nabon's daydreams had once been simple. In them the giant wandered faraway hills, to places familiar and places fresh. Beyond that, their content was inconsequential. Freedom was all.

Freedom was, of course, something Nabon no longer possessed.

That theft darkened the giant's fantasies. He dreamed now of roaming the land, but not in idle explorations. Nabon ranged the Sithican wilds in search of the one who had first ensnared him: Inza, a Vistani girl with hair as black as her soul and a viciousness in her heart the likes of which the giant had never seen in all his wide travels.

Deep in the Fumewood, Nabon had responded to her cry for help but found himself set upon by the girl instead. With a cudgel of unbreakable wood she shattered first one kneecap, then the other. As he lay on the ground, howling in pain, she beat him unconscious.

The greatest indignity of all was the purpose the assault served. Inza had captured him and broken his legs so she could barter him to Azrael for a mere dagger. The dwarf had been given the blade by Malocchio Aderre as a symbol of their recently forged alliance. Inza wanted it, and Nabon was the substantial price she was willing to offer.

Azrael was wont to torment Nabon with this tale on nights the giant slacked in his ceaseless toil. Nabon loathed the dwarf and wished him harm more times than he could remember, but his chief hatred was reserved for Inza. Had she not preyed upon his kind nature, he would never have fallen into Azrael's hands. Worse, the Vistana had hunted Nabon only after hearing stories that lauded the giant's gentleness of spirit. That, Inza explained as she hauled him to the salt mine that first night, made him the perfect slave.

With the mine shut down, the men all shuffling off to war, Nabon passed the time in a fitful drowse. He envisioned himself inflicting his revenge upon the girl in myriad ways, but only after he had pursued her through the Sithican wilds. The chase made the kill all the more satisfying. In those dreams, his footfalls shook mountains and sloshed rivers from their banks. His legs were whole. He was free.

One morning, in the quiet moments before dawn, he awoke to find the dream had become reality. At least parts of it, anyway.

The pain was gone. The shrieking ache of mangled flesh and broken bones had left his legs.

He squinted into the darkness, reached down with trembling hands. It was true. His legs were sound again. The shackles that had pinned him to the filthy floor were broken.

The joy in Nabon's heart was overwhelmed an instant later by a terrible dread. This had to be a trick. Surely Azrael lurked in the darkness. Worse still, maybe Inza was there. When he moved, when he got the first fleeting taste of freedom after his long imprisonment, they would descend upon him. This time they'd cut off his legs and rob him of any hope at all.

The giant cowered against the wall of his lightless, stinking prison.

"No need for that," came a soft voice from the darkness.

A lantern glowed to life. Its light revealed a figure dressed in pale clothing, a fine cloak, and a wide-brimmed hat. He removed the mask that concealed his features. The friendly smile on that handsome face made the giant gasp. It had been so long since he'd seen such a sign of goodwill that he scarcely knew how to respond.

"You really are free," the Cobbler said, "and well shod for the road that awaits you." He held the lantern toward the giant's feet. "Tell me, how do they feel?"

Nabon let his eyes trail down his legs. The wounds had all but vanished. The only traces of his abuse were some faint scars. Around his ankles, though, he could detect some heavier puckering. He ran his fingers over the marks. They were like the stitching that joined a sleeve to a coat or held together the pieces of a shoe.

"They're much bigger than the ones I normally make," the Cobbler noted casually.

He leaned close to admire his handiwork. It had taken the Cobbler much of the night to dress the giant's feet. The work had required much more from the Vistani corpses than the soles of their feet, but the magic had taken hold. That much was obvious from the way Nabon's bones had knit. The boots didn't look half bad, either.

"She betrayed them too," Nabon said softly as he ran his fingers over the leather. "Her own people."

The Cobbler smiled more broadly. This was clearly the best match he had ever made.

"Inza orchestrated the attack that took their lives," the pale-clad figure confirmed. "She paid the murderers in advance, with money stolen from the gypsies' own *vardos*."

"But why?"

"The slaughter gave her a reason to call upon Lord Soth for aid," the Cobbler replied. "She needs to be inside Nedragaard Keep for what she has planned."

Nabon stood. He wobbled a bit at first and bashed his head upon the Engine House's beams. He soon got his balance again, though. When he did, he offered a quick but sincere thanks to the Cobbler, then bulled his way through the huge building's back wall.

The Bloody Cobbler was chuckling to himself as he emerged from the rubble into the morning sunlight. The smile didn't abate, even when he found Azrael standing before him. "You're fortunate he didn't wait around to hammer you into the ground like a tent peg," the Cobbler said.

The dwarf's face was so colored by fury that even his bone-white mustache and sideburns seemed tinged with crimson. He let the jugs and candles he'd been cradling in his arms crash to the ground. "I still needed him," he rumbled. "Now I'll have to climb down to the chapel."

"You could use the exercise," the Cobbler replied calmly.

Azrael's stubby fingers sprouted thick black claws. The bones of his face shifted, grinding into a profile that reflected both dwarf and badger. "Who do you think you are to challenge me here?" Snarling, he locked one hand around the Cobbler's arm.

"You're wasting your time," the pale-clad man said lightly. "I can leave any time I want."

"Not from here you can't," Azrael said. He pushed the Cobbler against a pile of shattered timber.

It was then that the Cobbler noticed the items the dwarf had dropped into the dirt. A thick black sludge oozed from the shattered bottles. It stank of salt and of sorcery. Concern stole across his handsome features. He reached for a shadow in the rubble, expecting to enter it. His fingers met solid wood. The way was blocked.

As swiftly as he could picture it, a pale leather case appeared in the Cobbler's hand. Before he could extract one of his knives, though, Azrael batted the entire thing from his grasp. The silver tools scattered.

"I sealed the place off," Azrael said. The Cobbler's lost smile was on the werebadger's lips now, all pointed teeth and malicious glee. "You're not going anywhere."

The beast reached down for one of the silver scalpels.

"You can't kill me," the Cobbler said defiantly, "even with that."

"Oh, good," Azrael replied. "That will make this a lot more interesting."

* * * * *

In her two days at Nedragaard Keep, Inza had grown insensitive to the smell of death. The whole place reeked of it, from the web-choked dungeons to the top of the shattered tower. That was hardly a surprise. Skeletal soldiers patroled the battlements. Banshees howled through the corridors. Death had never frightened Inza, though, and the walking dead held no special place in her nightmares. Despite the lingering fetor of decay—perhaps even because of it—she found the castle much to her liking.

Soth had abandoned her soon after they arrived. They stepped into the shadows at the battlefield and emerged an instant later within Nedragaard's circular throne room. Soth informed Inza that she was free to roam the keep—at her own peril, of course—but that he had more important business elsewhere. He left her standing in the darkness.

Since then Inza had marched through every hall and explored every room of Nedragaard Keep. The inspection was long and largely tedious. The castle revealed little about its master that the Vistana didn't already know.

Now, at last, Inza had returned to the hall from which she had started her explorations. She lingered at the triple-tiered chandelier that lay in a heap at the room's center. The damage to the floor, flagstones shattered by the chandelier's fall, was both ancient and recent. Soot and melted wax from a fresh blaze masked far older scarring.

Inza found the juxtapositions unsettling. It was like standing in two times at once, suspended precariously between the past and the present. "Better to keep your gaze fixed on the future," the Vistana muttered. Unconsciously she tugged at the fine silver chain hanging around her neck and fingered the small black charm dangling from it.

She then made her way to the dais, with its warped and moldering throne. Her lips curled in a moue of distaste at the sight of the worm-eaten wood. It could be salvaged, she supposed. The rotting lumber might be reinforced with strips of metal. The joints could be joined more tightly with pegs or nails.

Or badger's teeth, thought Inza, smiling darkly to herself. They would do quite nicely.

Something winked on the floor behind the throne, distracting the Vistana from that pleasant thought. She knelt upon the cold stone flags to get a better look.

Shards of glass lay scattered across the back of the dais, pieces of the large oval mirrors that had once hung behind the throne. Inza gasped. These were fragments from the memory mirrors Soth had once used to prompt his reveries. Her mother had told her about them. The mirrors tapped into a person's memories and fantasies to create a waking dream that could be experienced as if it were reality. There were few men strong enough to resist a memory mirror's seductive powers. Most who used them quickly abandoned the real world for the mirror's tantalizing illusions.

Inza picked up one of the larger shards. As she looked into the mirror fragment, she saw not her own reflection, but a knight clad in gorgeous silver armor patterned with roses and kingfishers. This was Soth as he had been before his curse—at least, how he remembered himself.

The Vistana moved to slip the fragment into the pocket of her leather breeches. Before she could, something white and fleeting snatched the glass from her fingers, slicing them in the process. Inza cursed. She reached for Novgor, but an unseen force grabbed her long black hair and toppled her backward. Thrashing like a landed fish, she finally got the blade in her hand. She brandished it at the three apparitions floating above her prone form.

The trio of ghostly women scowled, a particularly unattractive expression on their angular elven faces.

"Not for your eyes," one banshee moaned.

"Unless you wish to share the dead man's dream," the second added.

"Unless you wish to share the dead man's fate," cried the third.

Inza pushed herself up onto her elbows. "I make my own fate."

Howls of ear-splitting laughter ripped through the hall. It echoed up the stairs and shook the dust from the rafters. The banshees circled the Vistana. Evil mirth twisted their faces.

"Away from me, wretches," Inza finally shouted.

She lashed out with Novgor at the nearest of the trio. The needle-sharp blade bit into the tattered, ghostly shroud that cloaked the spirit's frame. Another howl went up, this one of pain and fright.

"I am cut!" the banshee shrieked. "I am wounded!"

The hall's main doors creaked open, and Lord Soth stalked into the room. At first Inza thought the banshee's cries had drawn the death knight, but he ignored the unquiet spirits' calls for vengeance. "Your men approach, Inza Magdova," Soth stated without preamble.

The Vistana let a sigh of relief escape her lips and closed her eyes briefly. When she opened them again, Lord Soth was gone.

The smirk on Inza's face was almost as sharp as Novgor as she turned to the banshees, still lingering near the throne. She held the dagger up for them to see. "Another sharp word to me, and I'll cut out your tongue," she murmured. "I've done it to my own kind. I'll gladly do it to you lot of howling bed sheets."

The banshees were silent for a moment. They regarded Inza with pale, dead eyes, then said, "We serve the mistress of Nedragaard faithfully, as loyally and honestly as we have served all those who have gone before."

Though the pledge had been voiced without any hint of sarcasm or anger, Inza knew it was a threat. The words had the weight of a curse, a promise of something unpleasant to come.

The sound of Alexi's voice drew her attention away from the banshees. The last of the Wanderers were shuffling through the main doors. They looked terrible, little better than the undead ogres who staggered in behind them. The forced march had pressed them to the brink of exhaustion. Their faces were pale, their clothes ragged and dirty. A grimy, makeshift bandage encircled Nikolas's chest. Piotr had one hand, or all that remained of it, wrapped up tight. The ogres, too, had been hacked and battered. Some were missing arms. Another had been slashed across the face with a blade of some sort. Its swollen black tongue lolled from the hole in its cheek.

"The whole Invidian army is right on our heels. They've been pursuing us all night," Alexi said. He slumped onto the floor. "Soth's soldiers cut the bridge away the moment we crossed."

Neither the news of the Invidians nor the suffering of her people mattered to Inza. She was interested only in the whereabouts of the chest.

"Where is it?" she growled, grabbing Alexi by the collar.

"Outside, *raunie*," he replied. "Safe."

"Safe?" Piotr groaned. "Nothing here is safe. We're surrounded by dead men, and there's an army on the doorstep."

"I'll keep you safe from the dead men," Inza purred. "As for the Invidians, I'm certain Lord Soth will know how to deal with them. He is a warrior, after all, one used to seeing armies camped before his walls."

The same thought occurred to the Knight of the Black Rose as he climbed the spiral stairs up to the top of Nedragaard's central tower. This, at last, was a problem he could face head on. It had been centuries since he had looked upon the banners of a besieging force, but his warrior's instincts and knight's training left him in no doubt of the course he must take.

He and his thirteen loyal retainers had held off an army of Knights: Sir Ratelif and the best soldiers the Solamnic orders could muster. They'd been flesh and blood then. Hunger and cold and despair had been their foes as much as the besieging Knights. Not so now. With his thirteen deathless warriors, Soth was confident the keep could withstand the charge of the entire Invidian army, with Malocchio himself at the vanguard.

Lost in thought, he continued his march to the keep's upper floors. The interior stair wound in a circle, tighter and narrower as it ascended. Soth barely noticed as the number of steps passed one hundred, then two hundred.

It was not until he reached a small landing high in the keep that he paused. In life, it had been his practice to run his fingers over an inscription etched crudely into the stone: *Est Sularus oth Mithas*. My honor is my life. The sacred Oath of the Knights of Solamnia.

He'd carved the words there over many days as a boy of five, starting on the afternoon he rescued Caradoc's sister from the chasm spider. His father had rewarded his heroics with a real blade. The small dagger was unfit for combat, but it seemed a formidable weapon indeed when compared with the blunted wooden play swords he'd been given up until then. With that knife he declared his intent to become a Knight of Solamnia, if only to the watchmen and to the rodents that frequented that isolated part of the keep.

Here now was that declaration again. The words were faint, just as they had been in Dargaard Keep. The original inscription had been worn down by Soth's fingertips, which he traced over them year after year as he marched to the highest platform to watch the sun set on the Dargaard Mountains. Nedragaard had always lacked this detail. Yet it was in the right place, in a child's awkward scrawl. *His* awkward scrawl.

Soth had been so caught up in his concerns with Invidia and the White Rose, he'd failed to notice how closely the keep was beginning to resemble its original on Krynn. He'd called the place Nedragaard because of the small but noticeable flaws that differentiated it from Dargaard. Ruined doors hung where there should have been ones intact. Hallways extended a few paces too far or stopped a few paces too soon. The oath Soth had carved on that landing had always been missing. Until now. Those flaws, along with the more substantial imperfections brought on by the death knight's inattention, were apparently being corrected.

As he pushed aside some rubble that marked the stair's end, a cold wind tugged at Soth's cloak. Ignoring the chill that surely signaled the coming of winter, the death knight stepped onto the keep's highest vantage. From the ruins of the tower's upper floors, he surveyed the fortress's defenses.

The shadows that filled the Great Chasm were roiling, as they did on some bright mornings, almost as if the sunshine made them angry. This day they swirled with particular ferocity against the high cliffs that surrounded the keep on three sides. The darkness lapped, too, at the shores of the isthmus that connected it to the chasm's eastern cliff.

Or rather, had once connected it to the shore. Just outside Nedragaard Keep's front gate, a group of undead ogres were even now completing the task of drawing in the wooden bridge. A thirty-foot gap between the crumbled outer wall and the isthmus gaped blackly.

The reason for this defensive precaution milled on the chasm's eastern shore. A massive force, at least a thousand Invidian troops, had claimed the overgrown garden-graveyard there. More were straggling south along the Chasm Road. Soth could hear the ragged cheer that went up from the army as each wayward company arrived.

A banshee rose up before Soth. The sunlight made it appear even more insubstantial than normal, less a spectre than the memory of one. It was joined by a second, then a third. Leedara, Marantha, and Gisela, his three primary tormentors, the leaders of the shrieking host, stood before him.

"The wolves are at your door," Marantha began.

"They have claimed the graveyard, claimed your buried dead," Gisela added.

Leedara, whose phantasmal form still gaped from the wound Inza had inflicted upon her, hovered directly before the master of Nedragaard. "Your dead are all you have, withered rose. Lose them, and lose yourself."

"There is no chance I'll be defeated," the Knight of the Black Rose said smugly. He gestured to the east and the south. "In Sithicus, the living and the dead heed my battle cry. Even now my fleshy army comes to drive the curs from our stoop."

They totaled twice the Invidian thousand, elves from the east and a ragtag army of miners and farmers from the south. At Soth's bidding, Azrael had mustered the troops. They were intended as an invasion force, a sword point the death knight meant for Malocchio Aderre's throat. If they had to fight first on Sithican soil, all the better. The slaughter of the invaders would harden them and give them a taste for Invidian blood.

Soth watched in anticipation as the elves fanned out, forming their favored order of battle. The miners, too, arrayed themselves for the clash to come. Their lines were irregular, befitting the assortment of picks and flails and axes with which they armed themselves. The difference in formations mattered little. Soth was certain either army could easily break the siege.

A cry went up from the garden-graveyard, the fitting place where the three armies met. It was not the clamor of war Soth heard, nor the outraged roar of the dying. It was a cheer of fellowship. The three armies were now one.

The siege of Nedragaard Keep had begun.

FIFTEEN

The tripartite army's cry of unity reverberated from the walls of Nedragaard Keep, echoed across the Great Chasm, and finally faded. The leaders of the three allied forces stood for a moment, bathed in the glow of fellowship, before turning to consider the seemingly inviolable fortress looming before them. The good cheer fled, and the relief at having finally ended their long marches soured into exhaustion.

It was Gerhard, commander of the miners and farmers from the south, who gave voice to the question vexing them all. "Well," he asked gruffly, "now what do we do?"

"The isthmus is too narrow for any large-scale frontal assault," noted the elven general Ulrisch, an effete nobleman from Har-Thelen. "Perhaps we could mount a sneak attack from the chasm and have a few dozen men attempt to gain access to the keep from below. They could reset the bridge, allowing the rest of—"

"Who'd be idiot enough to climb down into those shadows?" interrupted Gerhard.

"Why, your miners, of course," the elf sniffed. "They're used to the dark. Besides, all those stories about the chasm are silly. It's just another hole in the ground."

"Well, then, your elves can go," Gerhard snapped. "It's your idea, after all."

The commander of the former Invidian forces, a particularly gruesome ogre named Onkar, snorted his amusement. He immediately scratched furiously at the gaping hole where his nose once had been. Snorting always made the tattered flesh there quiver.

"What for do you think we carry all this wood?" Onkar asked, gesturing to the heaps of timber piled at the center of the garden-graveyard. As each company of ogres and mercenaries arrived from the north, jingling with the gold and silver Azrael had used to buy their loyalty, they dutifully deposited more logs and beams onto the stack. There was enough there now to construct the frame for a fairly large house.

"Siege engines," the elf noted, "Of course. That would have been my next suggestion. Only we have nothing to hurl at the keep."

"Elves," Gerhard grumbled. "We have plenty of elves."

Onkar removed his foot from the large granite headstone upon which he had planted it. The stone was ornately carved, inscribed with the name *Gelbmartin* and the badge belonging to the lord steward of the keep. The ogre reached down and yanked it from the ground. "These make good crash," he said. "When we run out, we dig up the dead guys and fling them, too."

Gerhard and Ulrisch stared at the brute. "Crude, but creative," the elf said at last. "You supervise the stockpiling of the . . . missiles, Onkar, and we two will begin construction of the catapults." He encircled Gerhard's shoulder with an arm and steered him away from the brute. "Let us discuss the division of labor."

When they were safely out of earshot, the elf murmured, "Is there anything about this situation you find odd?"

Gerhard shrugged. "Odd? Like you pointy-eared wine sippers showing some spine for once—that kind of odd?"

With an exasperated grimace on his face, Ulrisch rolled up his shirt sleeve. His arm was a mass of scars from elbow to wrist. "I was captured by my Iron Hills kin. They flayed my arm, and a few other parts of my body you wouldn't care to see, before I managed to escape." He let the sleeve slip back into place.

Gerhard patted the *politska*'s silver axe hanging at his belt. "I've peeled a few people in my day, too. None of 'em escaped, of course. Still, you're all right by me if you stood up to that sort of torture."

"I'm so glad," the elf said blandly, "but you still haven't answered my original question." At the blank look on Gerhard's face, Ulrisch prompted,

"Our situation. Do you find anything odd about it? Where, for example, is Azrael?"

"Back at the mine," Gerhard said quickly.

"And what, exactly, are we supposed to accomplish here without him?"

The *politska* remained silent.

Ulrisch nodded curtly. "You're catching on. Even if we do manage to get inside the keep, who here will stand against Soth?"

"We've been tricked," Gerhard rumbled.

"Used," the elf corrected. "We are a diversion, nothing more."

Gerhard kicked the dirt and muttered a string of obscenities as vile as any creature lurking in the Great Chasm. "So what do we do about it?" he asked after he'd calmed a little.

"Play the role assigned us," the elf replied.

"Why not leave?"

"Azrael stationed some of your axe-wielding comrades in Har-Thelen just before we left," Ulrisch noted mournfully. "I thought it an uncharacteristically thoughtful gesture on his part to guard the city while we fought. I suspect now that none of us would find our families alive upon our return should we betray him or not do a creditable job in this siege."

Gerhard closed his eyes tightly, picturing the camp where the families of his troops awaited their return. It, too, was guarded by the Politskara. "We're all dead men," he murmured.

"Not necessarily," the elf said. "I suggest we keep the Invidians—pardon me, *former* Invidians—to the front ranks. From the clank their purses make, they've been paid too well to notice their peril." He paused to survey the fire-blackened walls of Nedragaard Keep. "And hope."

"For what?" Gerhard asked.

"For Soth to discover Azrael's plan, whatever that may be, or for the dwarf to succeed in his scheme." The elf sighed raggedly. "It doesn't matter which, so long as it happens before the lord of Nedragaard decides to sweep us from his stoop."

* * * * *

"To me, my knights!"

From the gallery overlooking the main hall, Lord Soth watched the thirteen undead warriors arrive from their various stations around the keep. The first to enter was Wersten Kern, most loyal of his men in life. He was the most loyal, too, in death—if loyalty was a trait these shuffling skeletons could possess. The shadow of that quality lingered in them at the very least. For Soth, that was enough.

Farold, Valcic, and Vingus, the inseparable Knights of the Sword, arrived together. Meyer Seril took up his usual station beside the main doors. As if pulled away from some other, more important task, Derik Grimscribe straggled in last. Once, the Sword Knight had been a master of words. His explanations for his tardiness would have amused the gathered knights no end. Now his jaws moved soundlessly, his tale trapped on the remnants of his rotted tongue.

The thirteen gathered warriors turned their eyeless skulls to their liege. Before Soth could speak, though, another voice sounded in the hall.

"How goes the siege, mighty lord?"

The skeletal knights looked to the shadow-shrouded dais. They hesitated, then dropped to one knee. Soth leaned over the gallery's rail. He had to look straight down the wall to see the Vistani girl perched upon a heavy wooden box set next to his throne. Long ago, another chair had been positioned there, the one belonging to the mistress of the keep, Soth's wife.

"My knights mistake you for someone else," Soth said coldly. "You mistake yourself for someone other than a guest." The death knight's harsh tone made it clear that he did not readily dismiss such improprieties.

"No insult was intended," Inza replied. "I thought it best to speak to you of my concerns before you sent your troops anywhere."

"You have nothing to fear. I will keep my word to your mother. You are safe in my—"

The crash of stone against stone resounded through Nedragaard as the bombardment, which had stopped for nearly half an hour, finally resumed. The missile had not struck the keep itself, though; it had crashed into the rocky ledge to the north. The aim of the engineers directing the catapults had not improved in the five hours they'd been directing sporadic fire against the keep. Far from offering Soth relief, their ineptitude only infuriated him.

The death knight gestured in the general direction of the besieging army. "You would have nothing to fear from them were you alone in this place. This is no assault. It is an annoyance—one I intend to silence before another moment passes."

Inza stood and walked toward the center of the hall. As she stepped from the shadows, the skeletal warriors rose from their deferential stances. " 'Annoyance,' " she mused aloud. "Perhaps. This assault most definitely offers no threat to you. Unless . . ."

"Out with it, woman," Soth rumbled. "You do not play coy well."

"This hopeless siege provides a distraction from the deeds of some great power," she replied bluntly, "an enemy more worthy of your attention."

Soth began to descend the curved stair from the gallery to the hall. "I do not lack in enemies," he said as he came. "I see all of their hands in this—Aderre, the White Rose, that treacherous cur Azrael."

"Azrael. He must be the one who set your own people against you," Inza said. The clatter of a missile finally striking the castle underscored the comment.

"He is the one who foolishly heaped gold on Aderre's raiders, paying them to join in this inept siege," Soth added. "He is no 'great power,' just a traitor with an inflated estimation of his own cunning."

The death knight had reached the hall now, and Inza bowed to him respectfully as he approached. "There is the White Rose to consider, mighty lord," the Vistana said. "When I read your fortune in the tarroka cards, her presence loomed large. Come, let me show you."

She led Lord Soth to the dais. There, upon the seat of the throne itself, lay nine cards arranged in a cross. They were large and crammed to the borders with intricate drawings. Soth could see the red tinge to the ink, even in the gloom shrouding the platform. This deck had been crafted with pigments mixed with blood.

The card at the center of the cross was a knight outfitted in plate armor, roses and kingfishers graven upon the breastplate. There could be no mistaking the figure for anyone but Soth, though the rendering depicted him before his damnation. "It was my mother's deck," Inza explained. "Who else would she portray upon the master card of swords? It is the suit of warriors."

The Vistana pointed to the two cards arrayed below the Warrior. The first depicted a ghost rising from a crypt. "This is your near past," Inza said. "A force arises to collect an old debt, to remind you of old obligations you have forgotten. The card below it is your distant past: the Innocent."

"There are no innocents in my past," Soth said.

"The card can signify someone who was powerless to defend herself at a particular moment in time, someone you might have taken advantage of," Inza noted. "She might have been quite formidable otherwise. Both these cards depict the Rose, I think. From what my mother told me, you think she is some warrior from your past, someone with a score to settle."

"Kitiara," Soth said.

While no innocent, Kitiara had been helpless, dying, when the death knight took her body from the Tower of High Sorcery. She feared him then, feared that he would raise her from the grave as his eternal consort. That had been his intent, of course. Had he not been dragged from Krynn into this nether-realm, it was an intent he would have fulfilled.

"Perhaps," Soth murmured. "Perhaps."

"Your adversaries are easier to identify," Inza said. She gestured to the first card on the Warrior's right. "The Traitor. It can be only Azrael. Behind him is the Charlatan. This woman is your real foe. See the picture—she hides behind a mask, a false identity like this White Rose of yours."

Soth indicated the rest of the cards with a sweep of his hand. "Do these tell me what they plan or how I may stop them?" he asked.

Inza suppressed a smile. She had arranged the cards with just that purpose in mind, to direct Lord Soth as she required. But when she looked down at the remaining four—the cards revealing Soth's allies and his future—a wave of fear washed over her. They were not the ones she had so carefully chosen.

"Well?" Soth said impatiently.

"These cards to the Warrior's left are the forces that fight on your side," she said, desperately trying to forge a suitable meaning for them in her thoughts. "Though you may not recognize their actions, they are important to you."

She lifted the first card, the two of coins. "The Philanthropist. Someone who gives unselfishly, seeking no return but the act itself." Another card, stuck to the first, dropped onto the ground. It was the eight of glyphs, the Bishop. "This person is bound by some rigid code. Or perhaps there are two allies who are connected somehow, one who gives, the other who enforces a code."

The next card, the one that revealed Soth's most important ally, was supposed to have been the four of stars, the Abjurer. The connection of the card's image—a raven-haired woman with a crystal ball—to Inza herself would have been obvious, even to Soth. But the card laid out was the Myrmidon. The unarmed, unarmored figure faced three men shrouded in mist, uncertain of their identity as friend or foe.

"Your other ally seems to be me," she lied. "The figure is helpless, surrounded by threatening figures: my situation in the forest before you came to my aid."

The remaining two cards foretold events to come. The near future was dominated by the Beast, symbolizing anger and fury. The Donjon, with its lone figure trapped within a moonlit tower resembling Nedragaard Keep, indicated the distant future. Were Inza trying to interpret the fortune correctly, she would have suggested that anger might continue Soth's imprisonment. Instead, she told him just the opposite. "If you give in to your fury and slay the Beast," she announced solemnly, "you will break free from your prison."

"Then your cards confirm the course upon which I have already decided." Soth turned and strode from the dais. "I want them slaughtered to the last man," the death knight told his skeletal minions. "The banshees will ride alongside us. Let them ready their chariots of bone."

The skeletal warriors shuffled out to the undead horses already milling in the courtyard. Inza called out to Soth as he was about to follow them. "Surely a coward such as Azrael would not place himself in harm's way."

"Of course not. He is hiding somewhere, probably at the Lake of Sounds, eavesdropping on the fight he should be leading."

"The Lake of Sounds!" Inza exclaimed. "If he and the Rose know about that place then the battle is already lost!"

"What are you saying?"

"The salt shadows that killed my mother are spawned from that place," Inza explained frantically, "but they are the least of its dangers. There are rituals using the lake's water that could grant someone control over all the shadows in Sithicus."

Soth did not reply. Instead he drew his sword and stepped into the darkness near the throne. An instant later he returned. His orange eyes blazed in fury. The cold radiating from him made Inza gasp at its intensity. "The way is blocked. He has sealed the area around the mine to me."

"They have begun!" Inza moaned. "You only have a few hours. They'll try to complete the rite late in the afternoon, when the day's shadows are longest."

"They cannot bar me from the mine for long," Soth rumbled, already heading back to the shadows.

"There is some small magic I can perform," Inza shouted after him. "It will help shield the keep from whatever dark sorcery Azrael and the Rose conjure."

"Protect yourself however you see fit," Soth replied, even as he vanished once more into the darkness.

The death knight did not see Inza throw open her wooden trunk, did not glimpse the large black bottle, swaddled like an infant, that rested within. However, he felt a shiver of apprehension as he emerged from the shadow of a massive outcropping on the road just outside Veidrava.

The death knight strode boldly into the open. As he marched toward the mine, his own shadow ranged beside him. He could not help but glance now and then at the wavering image. There was power in such things as shadows, he knew, as there was in the true names of plants and animals. Though a thing of fell sorcery himself, Soth disliked such magic. It seemed cowardly somehow, the stuff of assassins, not warriors.

He mused upon that subject even as he passed through the abandoned mining camp, which already looked as if it had been that way for a decade. Rats scurried incautiously between the hovels. Insects clustered on the window sills. Carrion crows searched for scraps on two corpses hanging at the camp's crossroads. They eyed Soth warily as he passed, trying to decide if he was a rival for the few bits of gristle left on the well-picked bodies.

The anger that had hurried the death knight from Nedragaard had diminished somewhat by the time he passed Ambrose's store. Rage had resolved into a cold determination. The mine's towers lay ahead, their shadows reaching down the hill to beckon him. If Inza was correct, his enemies would attempt the rite soon, before the shadows began to merge. Soth did not hurry his stride. He was lord of this domain. They could not escape him.

Even when he encountered the invisible wall, the same barrier that had barred him from entering the mine directly from Nedragaard, he maintained his grim calm. With his ancient sword he battered the unseen shield. Blow after blow fell upon the wall. Each slash produced a shower of sparks and left a blue-white scar in the air. The rifts healed swiftly, but Soth followed each strike with another and another. Soon the hillside trembled with a chest-rattling thrum, the sound of the mystic wards buckling before Soth's onslaught.

Another, more terrible sound rang out before the wall collapsed—the triple-toned shriek of Nedragaard's banshees. Their keening split the air over Veidrava as they materialized beside Lord Soth. Their once-beautiful elven faces were contorted with an awful mixture of anguish and glee.

"Betrayed!" the trio of the unquiet spirits howled.

"Deceived," Leedara screamed.

Marantha interposed herself between Soth and the unseen wall. "Plundered." she added.

A wide grin full of obscene mirth curled Gisela's phantasmal lips. "Lord Loren Soth," she said at last. "Lord Cuckold of Nedragaard Keep."

The words were familiar, almost identical to those the elf maids had used all those years ago to alert Soth to the infidelity of his wife, Isolde. The death knight paused in his assault on the barrier only long enough to say, "Begone. This is no time to replay scenes long grown stale. I have no mistress to cuckold me."

"This outrage is new," said Leedara, "but it is as old as your damnation."

"You have let a viper into your home," Marantha whispered. "She has warded the place against your servants."

"What?" Soth rumbled.

"While your knights and our sisters sallied against the besiegers, the gypsy witch erected wards that bar us from our home," Gisela said. She wove a pattern around the death knight, taunting him. "She barred you from your home, too, no doubt, but she will not be lonely."

"The halls of the keep will be filled with life," noted Leedara.

"She has thrown open the doors to the enemy," Marantha explained, "even as she bars us from entering. The keep is in their hands."

The fire that blazed to life within Soth's breast was as old as it was familiar. The fury consumed all, conquered all. Reason and logic collapsed before it. Whatever fragile shreds of mercy remained in his unbeating heart scorched and withered. "By my honor I kept her alive," the death knight said. "By my honor I will see Inza Magdova dead a thousand times for each affront she has heaped upon me."

Lord Soth turned away from the mine. He did not doubt that Azrael lurked there or that the dwarf intended some malefic rite. He did not even doubt that the ritual could grant the traitor power over all the shadows in Sithicus. Soth himself had seen the Lake of Sounds and felt the potency of its waters. None of that mattered. Vengeance was all.

As the death knight vanished into the shadows, the banshees trailing in his wake, Ganelon crept from his hiding place behind a crowd of discarded barrels. He had spotted Lord Soth from Ambrose's store, where he had gone to look for some sign of his old friends. For a time, as he watched the death knight hammer at the unseen barrier, his heart had soared. Here, perhaps, was an ally, someone more worthy to stand against Azrael. But it was not to be. This task was to be his alone.

The soft clatter of his leg brace seemed as loud as the banshees' keening as Ganelon made his way up the now-silent hill. He reached the spot in the road where Soth had stood. The air still smelled of heated steel and something else, a salt tang far stronger than the usual fetor that hung over the mine. Ganelon reached forward with one hand. He expected to encounter whatever invisible wall had barred Soth's way. Instead he found a minor resistance, as if the air had been transmuted to cold, still water. He closed his eyes and stepped through.

As he crossed the barrier, a line appeared on the ground below him. It was the uneven, dark splash made by water spilled onto dry earth, and it encircled the entire hilltop. When Ganelon reached down to touch the dark line, it retreated from his fingers. The thin black band squirmed like a serpent, the ripples flowing along its length in both directions until they disappeared. Finally, when it could retreat no farther, the line broke. It flared blue-white for an instant before dissipating.

"A fine trick," someone called from up the hill. "You must teach it to me."

Ganelon recognized that melodious voice and hurried to find the speaker. In the shadow of the Engine House, in a small circle cleared amongst the debris of the shattered wall, he found him.

The Bloody Cobbler struggled in vain to push himself up from the dirt. Gore spattered his ripped and tattered clothes. Most of it now was from his own wounds. His fingers had been broken, the flesh stripped from his chest. Clumps of his fair hair lay upon the ground alongside the blood-soaked tools of his trade. The silver snips and needles and knives had all been bent or broken.

As the Cobbler looked up at Ganelon, it appeared for an instant as if he had no face, only a mass of pulped flesh.

"I'm here to stop him," Ganelon said simply.

"I know the path you walk," the Cobbler replied through swollen lips.

"Of course you do," Ganelon said. He reached out to help the Cobbler to his feet and felt that same sensation of cold, still water. There were wards here, too, tight around the Cobbler to keep him from escaping. When the line appeared in the dirt, he reached down and broke it.

" 'No one who has died may cross it,' " the Cobbler repeated in a singsong voice. " 'No one who is merely alive may break it.' Azrael used to taunt me with that during our little . . . chats. He set up the wards so not even he could break them." He wiped the gore from his face with his cloak. The damage was not as great as it had seemed. "I'm certain he never imagined there was someone who could."

Ganelon looked down at his feet. The dead man's soles made him more than "merely" alive but not truly dead.

The Cobbler sat up. "I'd stitch myself up if I had time," he said absently. He lifted one of his needles from the ground, frowned at its sorry state. "There's little of that left for any of us, though."

"Then, it's over," Ganelon said.

The Cobbler gestured toward the late afternoon sky, just beginning to dim with the first hints of twilight. "No," he said. "We are finally ready to begin."

Ganelon followed the Cobbler's crooked finger with his eyes. There, marring the boundless blue overhead, hung a small crimson smudge. A red moon, Ganelon realized after a moment.

"They made it back to the Rose," the Cobbler offered. "Helain and the others."

"Is she—?"

"The Beast kept his word." The Cobbler laughed brightly. "As if he could even imagine breaking it! No, Helain's madness has been lifted."

As the Cobbler stood, it was clear to Ganelon that his wounds were already healing. Even his clothes seemed to be mending themselves. The pale-clad man extended a hand to Ganelon. In it he held a silver knife, the least damaged of his tools. "Take it," he said. "I would stay to help you, but—"

"Your path leads elsewhere," Ganelon concluded. He gratefully took the blade and tucked it into the small duffel he carried slung over one shoulder. "After all," the young man added cryptically, "he needs you."

The comment baffled the Cobbler for an instant. Then he nodded gravely; the Invidian spy had asked him his identity just before he died. Ganelon share that knowledge.

With a smile and a flourish of his broad-brimmed hat, the Bloody Cobbler disappeared into the Engine House's lengthening shadow.

As he made his way to the mine entrance, Ganelon thought about the reunion that awaited the Cobbler, about the reunion he imagined for himself and Helain. It seemed unlikely, but then, so many impossibilities had come true in the past few weeks he could not let the hope die. Even now, a second new moon struggled to be seen in the sky overhead, one as red as the rose Helain had given him when last they parted.

Ganelon carefully dug the bloom from his duffel. He'd armored it in a tin cup to keep it safe, but he saw now that the effort was wasted. The crimson petals had, like all others of their kind kept too long on Sithican soil, turned black.

He let the wilted rose slip from his grasp. After a moment, he followed it into the pit.

SIXTEEN

Ganelon knew by the screams that he was headed in the right direction.

The shrieks and moans welled up from deep in the pit, much farther down that he'd ever gone. There were scores of abandoned tunnels in the depths of Veidrava, some that had been flooded, others that had stopped yielding enough salt to be worthwhile. One of those deserted shafts supposedly housed a chapel. Ganelon knew almost from the moment he'd begun the long, tedious process of lowering himself from level to level with emergency ropes that the chapel was his destination.

He came at last to the tunnel from which the unearthly sounds originated. Human voices were not making the clamor, of that Ganelon was certain. He'd heard the cries of the dead and damned enough in the past few days to recognize them now. He was not surprised to find the uncanny sounds so close to the place he'd called home. Rather, he marveled that he'd been so blind to it before.

Cautiously, he started down the tunnel. Before long, a faint blue glow suffused the rubble-strewn passage, and Ganelon extinguished the lantern he'd taken from the surface. He left it, still smoking, in an empty niche hewn into the wall.

Ganelon did not notice the flowers carved around the niche, barely recognized the elaborate statuary of hounds and harts and other creatures that stood to either side of him as the tunnel opened into a broad hallway. The ceiling, which reflected the light of the torches in the hall as a sky-blue glow, scarcely drew his eye. Once the workmanship of these objects would have filled him with wonder. Now he only saw them as places to conceal himself from his enemies or places from which those enemies might strike at him.

The weird cries echoed all around Ganelon as he crept from statue to statue, ever closer to the fire-lit room at the hallway's end. Through the open arch, he glimpsed shadows wheeling across the walls. He expected to find a hundred men in there, all dancing in anticipation of the grim rite Azrael intended to perform. When he got close enough to get a better look at the room itself, though, at the melted benches and the scarred altar, Ganelon realized that these shadows had no mortal anchors. They were darkness incarnate, salt shadows, and they were celebrating the strife to come.

It was only their sheer number, the combined clamor of hiss upon hiss that made the shadows' voices heard. That same quality made it impossible for any of them to speak above the din or to raise a discernible alarm when Ganelon stepped into the Black Chapel.

The floor was dark with massing salt shadows, but Ganelon's footfalls sent them splashing back like so much fetid water. As in the Vistani camp, the lost souls recoiled from the dead flesh on his feet. They whirled about the vaulted room, curling over the repulsive statues lurking in the corners. In some places the most agitated shadows forced their bodies off the floor. They scurried toward Ganelon like misshapen spiders. Yet they could not bring themselves to envelop his death-tainted flesh.

The altar stood ready for Azrael's ceremony. A black cloth covered the stained and profaned block, while a chalice carved of ebony stood at its center. Around the cup were arranged bits of plants and animals. Ganelon opened the small bag of poppy seeds Malocchio Aderre had given him. Carefully he emptied a few into the cup, then secreted others among the bits of greenery and grue. He had returned the bag to his duffel and was considering what to do with the large vat that stood before the altar when a familiar voice made him stop short.

"What are you doing here?" asked Ambrose.

Ganelon turned to find the pudgy shopkeep standing in the mouth of a rough-hewn tunnel, which led from the chapel deeper into the earth. His face was pale, his eyes devoid of any of the good humor that had once shone in them. "What are you doing here?" Ambrose repeated.

As Ganelon started forward, arms outstretched to embrace his old friend, he noticed the shadows teeming at the shopkeep's feet. The darkness slithered up Ambrose's legs and reached out with tendrils to caress him. "You've been touched by Death," Ambrose said in a voice only vaguely like the one Ganelon remembered so fondly. "I can smell it on you."

"What happened?" the young man asked. A fist of grief closed around his heart at the sight of his friend so changed, so defiled. "How—?"

"I claimed this body a long time ago," the thing within Ambrose said. "It just took me some time to drown the last bits of that fat slob's personality. He lusted after Helain, you know."

"No. I don't believe it."

A vapid smile quirked Ambrose's mouth. "It doesn't matter what you believe. He lusted after her all the same. I tried to goad him on—Helain would have been quite a conquest—but he was too cowardly to let me guide him."

"You can't even tell love from lust," Ganelon said coldly. "No wonder Ambrose kept you at bay for so long."

The youth reached into his duffel for the crystal orb. Before he could close his fingers around it, Ambrose was at his side. The shopkeep's quickness startled the young man, as did the savagery of his attack. The bag slipped from Ganelon's grasp as the blows began to fall. Soon he was on the chapel floor beside it, curled tight against the relentless hail of punches and kicks.

"What's going on here?" Azrael snarled as he emerged from the tunnel. In his wake came Kern and Ogier. The two men carried a massive bucket filled to the brim with water from the Lake of Sounds.

"A spy," Ambrose said. "I don't know who sent him."

Azrael took one look at the leg brace and snarled, "He's Malocchio Aderre's man, but he's supposed to be dead." With his iron-shod boot, the dwarf rolled Ganelon over. "Wait," he said when he saw Ganelon's face. "This fellow used to work at the store, didn't he? He's no spy."

"Yes, he's from the mine, but the shadows won't touch him," Ambrose noted. "There's something strange going on."

"It doesn't matter what he is or why he's here," Azrael said. "It's too late for him to stop the ceremony, and that's all that matters." He motioned to Kern and Ogier, who had just finished emptying the huge bucket into the vat before the altar. "Keep him out of the way."

To Ganelon, supported by Kern and Ogier, much of the ceremony was a blur of dark shapes and flashes of light seen through a haze of pain. Azrael chanted for what seemed like hours. The words burned in the air as he spoke them, then floated down to the vat of black water. They extinguished one by one with a hiss that was echoed by the salt shadows.

As the last of the words drowned, the water began to churn. The salt shadows eagerly circled the vat. The stinking liquid followed their lead, spinning until a whirlpool formed in its center. At last, Azrael raised the ebon chalice. Ganelon gritted his teeth in anticipation; he said a silent prayer that he'd put enough poppy seeds there to kill the werebeast outright.

Azrael overturned the cup. The poppy seeds scattered onto the chapel floor, unnoticed by the dwarf or his minions. The sight struck Ganelon like a blow to the gut. He bowed his head. His ragged sigh carried with it the last of his flagging hope.

"I demand the power to remake this kingdom in my own image," Azrael intoned. "I demand dominion over the people and the beasts and the land itself. They will be as my shadow, so they have no need of their own. Come to me, then. Fill my cup so that I may drink down all the darkness in the world."

The black water in the vat rose in a spout toward the overturned chalice. As it whirled, the salt shadows that had been circling so close darted in and out of the column. Ganelon, too, felt the pull of the vortex. It did not snatch at his hair or his clothes, though, but at his shadow. He could feel it being drawn away from him toward the altar.

Azrael took the bits of flesh and flower from the stone block. As he tossed each scrap into the vat, he called upon the powers of darkness to grant him supremacy over the thing it represented: bird, tree, beast, and man. With the naming of each new sort of minion to the catalogue, the spout turned faster and faster, until it was little more than a black blur before the altar.

Ganelon felt his shadow ripped from him. It tumbled across the cavern floor like a sheet of parchment in a hurricane, only to be drawn into the vortex. A sense of loss filled Ganelon's heart, and a strange weakness washed over him. He slumped forward. Kern and Ogier, fighting the weakness wrought by the loss of their own shadows, let him drop to the cavern floor.

From the Fumewood to the gray-walled elven city of Mal-Erek, from the Iron Hills to the farthest reaches of the Merchants' Slash, all the shadows in Sithicus felt the summons. They struggled against it, but none were strong enough to ignore the call. One by one they fled their source. Like ebon-hued arrows they darted over the land. Some poured into the pit at Veidrava. Most were swallowed up by the Great Chasm, where, by a circuitous path of caves and tunnels, they eventually descended upon the Lake of Sounds.

Just to the north of Nedragaard Keep, along the cliffs of the chasm, Nabon the giant felt his great mainsail of a shadow billow, then slip away into the abyss. It was swiftly joined by those of the hundreds upon hundreds of corpses scattered in Nedragaard's garden-graveyard. The poor fools had been caught by the skeletal warriors and the banshees before Inza opened the keep to the besieging army. Most of the casualties were turncoat Invidians, along with Onkar and his slow-witted ogre cohorts. Their shadows seemed almost grateful to abandon them.

The keep provided no shelter from the dark rite. Ulrisch and his elves, Gerhard and his ragtag army of miners and farmers, all watched helplessly as their shadows fled. Alexi, Piotr, and Nikolas retreated to the keep's lightless gatehouse, but the Vistani weren't quick enough. Their shadows joined the rest as they slithered from the castle into the Great Chasm's murk.

On the isthmus connecting the keep to the cliffs, Lord Soth and his minions had just begun to batter at the wards barring them from their home. The skeletal warriors turned sightless sockets to the ground and gaped as their shadows deserted them. One even fell to its knees in a vain attempt to catch the dark shape before it escaped.

The shadow of Lord Soth, blacker than all the rest and burning with the cold of the grave, held out the longest. It clung to him like a frightened, frantic child. But the death knight would not be distracted. Vengeance was all that concerned him now. Even as his shadow slipped away and a profound lethargy settled into his limbs, he struggled to raise his age-tarnished sword to strike the wards again.

The shadow of only one creature in all of Sithicus defied the awful summons, that cast by Inza Magdova Kulchevich as she stood upon the dais in Nedragaard's main hall. The dark shape clung to the charm around her neck. Anchored by that bit of enchanted silver, which Inza had created with just this moment in mind, her shadow flapped around her like a cape in a maelstrom.

Deep within the pit at Veidrava, Azrael did not notice that one missing shard of darkness. Neither did he sense the powerful magic resisting his incantation. He was too caught up in the spectacle before him. The stolen shadows swirled around the Black Chapel and merged with the vortex. Each new captive bit of dusk darkened the inky waters until, at last, they were a deep, profound black. Finally, the vortex rose into Azrael's overturned chalice, distilling itself into a single cupful.

Azrael righted the chalice. A silence fell upon the Black Chapel as thunderous as the cacophony it had succeeded. From where he lay on the floor, Ganelon looked up just in time to see the dwarf raise the cup to his lips and drink.

In the stillness of the Black Chapel, as the bitter ebon ooze worked its way down Azrael's throat, a voice spoke to the dwarf. "Terror will be all," it promised.

Azrael recognized the words instantly as those the dark had used time and again to describe Sithicus under his reign. The voice, too, was familiar. Free from any sorcerous masking, it was easy to identify Inza's mocking tone. A frisson of dread crept up Azrael's spine.

"Yes, terror will be all," she continued, "but you will be dead."

The awareness that he had been betrayed raged through Azrael's mind. Inza had used the dark against him. She was the comforting voice at the Lake of Sounds. She'd told him of this rite and goaded him into revolt against Soth. Now she would claim his reward and snatch control of the realm from the death knight's weakened grasp.

A stabbing pain in his gut drew Azrael's thoughts from Inza. He dropped the empty ebon chalice, which cracked and rolled away. All the captured shadows writhed inside him. Another lance of pain pierced the dwarf's side, drawing black tears of misery from his eyes. The darkness trickled down his cheeks and slithered back into his mouth, eager to rejoin the corrupt mass roiling inside him.

Ambrose and the others moved forward on unstable legs to aid their master. Like them, Ganelon hadn't heard Inza's threat, but he saw that there was a problem with the rite. He took advantage of the confusion to crawl to his discarded duffel, still heaped next to the vat.

As he was rifling through the bag in search of the Cobbler's blade, he felt a strong hand on his leg. He looked over his shoulder to find Ogier looming over him.

"Don't make me hurt you," Ganelon pleaded. His fingers closed around the orb Malocchio had given him.

Ogier's lips curled in a snarl more fitting for a wolf than the gentle animal to which he'd been compared so often. "I think you got it backward," he said, tightening his grip around Ganelon's leg until the bones creaked. "You should be begging me not to hurt you."

"Helain," Ganelon whispered.

* * * * *

The wards Inza had raised around Nedragaard Keep were a dozen times more powerful than those Azrael had set at Veidrava. They were structured to withstand the might of the banshees, the skeletal warriors, and Soth. Once their shadows had been taken and their strength sapped, the death knight and his minions should have been powerless against them—but Inza had not reckoned on the might of Soth's fury.

When his sword proved ineffective, the death knight drove his armored fingers into the magical barrier. The enchantment fought against him, heating Soth's gauntlets until the metal glowed white. As he widened the rift, sparks showered down upon him and lances of lightning flashed around his head. None burned as brightly as Soth's eyes. "Vengeance!" he cried, and threw his entire being into the assault.

Blue-white light played upon the invisible barrier, revealing its form as a gigantic dome. Soth drove the rift even wider, and a tear stole up from the ground to the dome's peak. With a sound like every tree in the Fumewood splitting from root to crown at the same moment, the barrier tore open. A faint radiance lingered for a moment, a ghost of the sorcerous wall. Then that, too, faded.

Soth pushed himself forward, moving as much by instinct as any conscious thought. He strode through the breach in the keep's outer shell, stalked through the bailey to the double doors leading to the main hall. Elves and men cowered at his passing, but he paid them no heed. His only interest was the woman who had betrayed him, the faithless Vistana.

Not so with his minions. The skeletal warriors and the banshees set about slaughtering every trespasser that crossed their paths. The massacre continued until the bailey was choked with the dead and dying, and the besiegers who thought Nedragaard Keep impossible to invade learned that it was even more difficult to escape.

The Knight of the Black Rose found Inza in the main hall. She was crouched before the throne like a cornered animal. Her green eyes narrowed to slits when she saw the death knight and heard the clamor of battle in the courtyard. She drew Novgor, the ever-sharp dagger of Kulchek the Wanderer, and brandished it. "This will shear your thorns as readily as any rose's, *giorgio*," she warned.

Soth paused. With an edge of mocking laughter in his voice, he said, "An ill considered admission, witch. If the blade is enchanted, the Measure allows me to use my own magic to even the fight."

With one finger, Soth traced a symbol in the air. The glyph hung there, glittering with a fire the same hue as the death knight's burning gaze. Before it could speed toward Inza and deliver Soth's gift of agony, though, a single white rose slashed down from the gallery and dispersed it.

"I don't think Vinas Solamnus had creatures such as you in mind when he wrote the Measure, Loren," the White Rose said. She stood in the musicians' gallery overlooking the main hall, the Bloody Cobbler on her left, the Whispering Beast to her right. "Your mocking references cannot stain that most treasured code of knightly virtue. In making them, you only demean yourself further—if that's possible."

Soth did not reply. He stood and waited as the Rose descended the curving stairs. As she did, the Beast slipped over the gallery's rail and dropped down onto the rotting throne behind Inza. The Vistana turned, ready to lash out with Novgor. The sudden pressure of a silver shoemaker's knife at her own throat made her freeze.

"Nice blade," the Cobbler said cheerfully. His wounds and bruises had healed, it seemed, at least those that were visible. His face was hidden behind his pale mask, but Inza could hear his voice clearly enough when he added, "Put it away before I lop your head off."

At the center of the hall, by the wreckage of the triple-ringed chandelier, Lord Soth bowed stiffly to the White Rose. She returned the courtesy with an equally artificial curtsy.

"I never thought to see you again, Isolde," said the death knight.

The White Rose nodded slightly, only a hint of a sad smile visible in the darkness of her hood. "Nor I you, my husband."

* * * * *

The orb in Ganelon's hand flared to life, radiating light that cut through the Black Chapel like a thousand shining scythes. The bodiless salt shadows curled under the blaze of sunlight. Their perpetual hiss became a gasp of pain, a statement of agony rivaled only by Azrael's intermittent howls.

A look of surprise flashed onto Ogier's face. It was much the same as the expression of good-natured bewilderment his friends had seen there all his life—so close, in fact, that it made Ganelon's heart ache to see it. That baffled look was the first thing the light melted. The big man's white curls were next, just before the rest of his shadow-tainted flesh burned away.

Kern, too, burned under the orb's intense light. Ganelon caught a glimpse of him as he scrambled from behind the altar. He might have been using Ogier to shield his escape from the chapel, but Ganelon knew somehow that the soft-hearted cynic was trying at the last to push the big man from harm's way. The ashes of the two friends mingled on the dirty chapel floor.

Only Ambrose withstood the light long enough to speak. The bitter, hate-filled face of the thing possessing him softened. For just an instant, the kindly man Ganelon had loved so dearly returned. "Clever boy," he said in his wheezing voice. Then Ambrose was gone, consumed by the sunlight.

The orb's light faded, then faltered. Ganelon dropped the blackened crystal into the ashes. With trembling hands he tore into the duffel once more, searching for the silver knife. There might still be time to kill Azrael, to save Helain and everyone else from eternal slavery.

But Ganelon had already ensured their freedom. The poppy seeds he had secreted in the items Azrael used for the rite, the flesh and the greenery he had tossed into the vat, were not enough to kill the werebadger. They were, however, sufficient to taint the drink, to force his body to reject it.

Even as the roiling mass of darkness threatened to burst the dwarf like an overfull wineskin, he vomited it up.

The captured shadows poured from Azrael, bleeding from his nose and mouth, seeping from his eyes and ears. They filled the Black Chapel, each one echoing the dwarf's tortured scream. Ganelon felt himself lifted by that sea of darkness. It bore him along the tunnel and up the mine's main shaft.

Dazed, still clutching the shabby duffel that contained everything he owned in the world, Ganelon found himself lying in the ruins of Veidrava's Engine House. How much time had passed he wasn't certain. A geyser of shadow still rose up from the pit. The darkness was amassing in the sky high overhead, merging with the shadows spewed up from the Great Chasm a hundred miles to the west.

The last of the darkness rose into the heavens. For a time, the gathered shadows hung motionless, their bulk blotting out the triple moons that shone in the twilight sky. Finally, the ebon mass shuddered and began to fall.

To Ganelon, it resembled nothing so much as a mountain hurled from the stars.

* * * * *

Nedragaard Keep was burning.

Screams sounded from the tower's upper floors. The clash of steel in the bailey had been replaced by the shriek and thud of blazing bodies plummeting from the battlements. It was little consolation, but the corpses met their shadows as they struck the ground.

The mountain of darkness had burst apart upon impact, hurtling the individual shadows back to their originators. It was the unstable nature of the massed darkness that prevented it from doing even more damage to the Sithican countryside. Still, the spectral mountain had laid low the Land of Spectres, and it would be years before it recovered fully.

Through it all, Soth and Isolde stood silent at the center of Nedragaard's main hall. They regarded each other with eyes that saw through the centuries, to a time when they had been the still point at the center of another cataclysm. Like

Azrael's foiled scheme, that disaster, too, had been within Soth's power to prevent, but his rage had mastered his mind and his heart, just as it had on the outskirts of Veidrava.

"I think it's time for you to run along, little girl," the Whispering Beast said to Inza. He slid down into the throne, caressed the Vistana's thigh with one stinking, outstretched foot. "Too bad, too. We could have had fun." He playfully nibbled one of the severed ears hanging at his chest.

"She has other playmates waiting for her," the Bloody Cobbler said. He thrust Inza off the dais. She landed in a fighting crouch, dagger already plucked from her boot. "You'll want to save that for outside," noted the Cobbler. "They're waiting."

"They know what you've done," the Beast added, "to the giant, the Wanderers, your mother, all of it."

"Everyone will know," chimed the Cobbler. "For ever and ever. Sithicus is going to be like that soon."

A tremor shook the tower, and a rain of stone and dust showered the main hall. The Cobbler held his hand out as if testing for rain. The Beast leaped from the throne. He crouched in a fighting stance mimicking Inza's. "Off with you," he growled, slapping his misshapen hands on the stone.

Inza turned and ran. Soth started after her, but Isolde laid a restraining hand on his arm. "No, Loren," she said softly. "Other powers control her fate."

The Vistana emerged into the chaos of the

courtyard. The dead and wounded covered the ground. Soth's thirteen skeletal warriors marched among the bodies, methodically hacking anything that moved or wept or bled too much. Overhead, the thirteen banshees wove frenzied patterns around the keep in their wyvern-drawn chariots of bone. The light of the blaze and of the new red moon, shining full and bright over Nedragaard, made the usually pallid spirits appear drenched in gore.

Inza passed through the carnage untouched, as if surrounded by an invisible shield. She reached the courtyard's edge. There, the gaping rift in the outer curtain opened onto the isthmus and freedom. Only, the isthmus was gone. The section of the earthen bridge closest to the keep had collapsed into the Great Chasm. On the opposite side of the gap stood the hapless giant Inza had crippled, with the three remaining Wanderers crowded at his strangely booted feet.

Nabon started to back up, as if he intended to leap the gap. Inza could see Alexi, ever-practical Alexi, trying to make the giant reconsider. Piotr and Nikolas, on the other hand, cheered him on. It was obvious that the giant would make it. His anger and his hatred would vault him over the entire chasm itself if necessary. Inza knew Nabon would tear her limb from limb for what she'd done to him.

Nabon started forward. His footfalls shook the fragile banks of the remaining isthmus, sending chunks of rock into the eternal murk of the Great

Chasm. Inza met the giant's charge with a smile of defiance on her face and her storied ancestor's dagger in her hand. But before Nabon could leap, Inza Magdova Kulchevich threw herself from the cliff.

They watched her fall, the giant she had tortured and the adoptive kin she had betrayed. That insolent smile remained on her lips—until she felt the darkness cradling her, slowing her descent. As vile hands lowered her into the chasm's lightless depths and the gloom closed over her like a shroud, Inza finally screamed.

Within Nedragaard's main hall, the White Rose nodded again to Soth. "There," she said. "The sound of justice."

The Beast lowered his necklace of ears, which he had raised in a mocking posture, as if they might amplify the Vistana's shriek of horror. "Come now, what does *he* know of justice?" he rumbled. With one grimy hand he indicated Soth. "I swear he could not define the word."

"You must know something to pervert it," the Cobbler offered. He walked slowly around the death knight, regarding him carefully. "Just as you must recognize the path of the righteous to choose not to tread upon it."

"Respect," Isolde chided. "Regardless of what he is, you must show your father respect."

Though his face was hidden by his helm, Soth's voice made his horror clear. "These monsters are not mine, woman."

"We are," the Cobbler said, "and we are not alone. This entire land was built around you,

Father. Why should you wonder that you are the sire of its nightmares, too?"

"We are monsters only to the likes of you," the Beast snarled, "to men who swear oaths and break them."

"To those who recognize, but squander the gifts the gods have given them," the Cobbler added. "They afforded you the capacity for valor, for honor, and the strength of arm to protect the innocent. But you wasted their munificence."

"Honor is an illusion," Soth replied. "You can be no progeny of mine if you do not know that."

Isolde stepped forward, gently lowering her cowl as she came. Her flesh was charred from the fire that had claimed her life, a blaze much like the one burning above them in Nedragaard's upper floors. "This place has made you forget. That is its nature."

"I forget nothing," Soth said as he, too, unmasked.

Like Isolde's, the death knight's flesh was blasted, withered. But around this never-changing, ever-corrupt core a phantom hovered, a ghostly reflection of the honorable man he'd once been. Had Soth cared to look, he would have recognized his own deep-set eyes in the Cobbler's handsome face. Even the Beast, beneath the outward filth and seeming armor of corruption, resembled his sire.

Smoke had begun to fill the hall, and Isolde swayed, more from remembered pain than any actual discomfort. The Beast and the Cobbler were at her side in an instant. They stood to either hand, steadied her, as she faced Soth. "The curse I laid upon you at my death is strong, Husband, strong enough to send me here to ensure you do not escape its sting. Before I can be released, I must be certain you are ready to feel its barb once more...."

Isolde drew her hands together. As she did, the Beast and the Cobbler melted into mist. The pale fog flowed into the White Rose's outstretched arms, reformed as a whimpering, skeletal infant swaddled in a fire-blackened bunting.

The blaze had burned down to the main floor at last. The ceiling groaned under the weight of the toppled stone and timber pressed down upon it. Isolde held out the mewling child, poor slain Peradur, and said, "Please, my lord, he is your flesh."

Soth placed his helmet back onto his head. He stared for a moment at the monstrous thing in Isolde's grasp. Even as he recognized the spectral child as his own, his spirit rebelled at the thought of accepting it. To do so would overturn the final action that had brought Isolde's curse upon him and made him what he was. To do so would be admitting he'd been wrong.

The ceiling collapsed. Burning wood and blackened stone rained down upon the hall. Indifferent to the havoc, Lord Soth turned away from Isolde and Peradur, just as he had a world away and several lifetimes ago in Dargaard Keep.

With that decision, the death knight's scarred and patched memory finally healed. He looked inward and found that the last missing fragments of his past had been replaced. His history unfurled before him, a grim pageant that he had scripted, he had directed.

As he looked out upon all his deeds, both glorious and infamous, the Knight of the Black Rose felt that same history enfold him in its cold embrace.

EPILOGUE

Through the perpetual twilight of Nightlund they came, the undead and the undying, the things of darkness that made that cursed realm the sorrow of all the peaceful lands surrounding it. The air shivered with the tread of monstrosities. The blasted fields stirred to the unsettling susurrus of lost souls wending over the earth. They put aside their quarrels, those beasts that lived for bloodshed alone. If only for one night, they recognized a unity of purpose.

They came to pay homage.

They came to prove for themselves that the tales were true.

When those foul creatures saw the light burning within the ruins of Dargaard Keep and glimpsed the armored figure standing atop the fire-blasted battlements, they quailed and cursed, even as their corrupt hearts rejoiced. The Knight of the Black Rose had returned.

Unquiet dreams plagued the peoples of Krynn that night. From the deepest tunnels of

Thorbardin to the most isolated, moonlit glade in the Silvanesti Forest, the sleeping minds of men and elves and dwarves alike were overwhelmed by a similar vision. A black rose had taken root in the garden of Ansalon. Its petals slowly opened until, immense and festering with corruption, the bloom engulfed the entire world.

The denizens of Sithicus, too, dreamed of the tainted rose, but in the nightmares of those luckless, terror-ridden people, the flower that had so long loomed over their land shriveled and fell away. Lord Soth was gone, and with him the plague and the White Rose, the Whispering Beast and the Bloody Cobbler. Nedragaard Keep had toppled. Its ruins sat upon a spike of stone in the Great Chasm, cut off from the cliffs, surrounded on all sides by a sea of hungry shadow.

A single moon shone down upon that rubble and all the other destruction wrought by the shadow mountain's impact. Some claimed the pattern on the orb formed a rosette with petals of white and black and crimson. Others saw things more ominous than a rose in the pattern, though they were reluctant to describe just what it was they recognized there. The only thing upon which all could agree was the strangeness of the moon's triple-hued light. Such weird illumination befitted the curious land Sithicus had always been.

If Inza Magdova Kulchevich ever saw the light of that strange moon, she kept her thoughts to herself. The Vistana hadn't been seen since the Hour of Screaming Shadows, as the Sithicans had come to call that terrible afternoon. Still, the brave souls who ventured close to the Great Chasm often told of a woman's mocking laughter from the depths. Those who tarried at the brink had also heard grim murmurings in Patterna, the Vistani dialect pilfered from a hundred other tongues. Wisely, they never lingered long enough to make out just what ghastly confidences the murmuring revealed.

Nabon knew the truth of those tales. He knew, too, the dark things Inza whispered deep within the shadow-choked scar. With Alexi and Piotr and Nikolas, the remnants of Magda's caravan of outcasts, the giant walked a ceaseless patrol around the chasm. Wanderers all, they shared stories of Inza's perfidy and waited for the traitor to show herself. When they met again, the fragment of Gard they had recovered from Magda's grave would be their gift to her, a stake destined for her black, loveless heart.

Two last wayfarers made their way through the strange light of the triple-hued moon. One brought hope to the farmers and miners and villagers of Sithicus, the other dread.

Few were the men or elves who did not recognize the soft *clank* of Ganelon's leg brace as he made his way through the countryside. The road he traveled was lonely, but he never failed to pause long enough to offer aid and comfort to those in need. Through the severed ear left him by the Beast, he cultivated reason in minds overgrown with madness. With the Cobbler's blood-spattered silver knife, he cut away sickness and despair from the innocent, life itself from the hopelessly corrupt.

The blade could not exorcise his own suffering, though. For all that he longed to see Helain again, Ganelon knew that her life was forfeit should they meet. If his resolve ever weakened, he needed only to recall the deaths of Ambrose and Kern and Ogier in the Black Chapel to remind him of the power of Inza's curse. So he drifted through the Sithican night, hoping for and dreading a reunion that should never be.

Fewer still were those who did not recognize the ear-splitting howls of Azrael as he raged through the Fumewood and the Iron Hills, or the clatter of his carriage, still armored with the teeth of his fallen enemies, as it raced along the Merchants' Slash. To meet the dwarf in the flesh was to meet death. The tenuous strands of restraint and rationality that had kept his wildness in check had withered at the Hour of Screaming Shadows. If he was not mad, he was as close to that abyss as any sane creature ventured.

It was not just the defeat of his grand scheme that so unhinged the dwarf. All his life, he had trusted the dark, and the dark had lied to him. He could not think about that betrayal without a greater, more awful question pressing to the fore of his troubled mind: If this much of what he had believed was a lie, how much else was a lie, too? The answer was there, but he did not want to hear it.

The dwarf's was a common enough problem in Sithicus in the wake of its old master's departure. The nature of the domain had changed with the death knight's passing, transformed by the White Rose's magic and the nature of Soth's original curse. The place that had fostered so many half-truths and deceptions, lost histories and corrupted memories, revealed its new nature in a hundred horrible ways. To those, like Azrael, who had armored themselves in illusions for so long, the transformation of Sithicus was the most harrowing.

Like everywhere in the domains of dread, grim things lurked in the Sithican shadows. They preyed upon the minds of the weak, whispered tales that opened the portals of madness.

But in Sithicus, those things in the darkness now spoke the truth.

DRAGONLANCE

THE SOULFORGE
MARGARET WEIS

The long-awaited prequel to the bestselling Chronicles Trilogy by the author who brought Raistlin to life!

Raistlin Majere is six years old when he is introduced to the archmage who enrolls him in a school for the study of magic. There the gifted and talented but tormented boy comes to see magic as his salvation. Mages in the magical Tower of High Sorcery watch him in secret, for they see shadows darkening over Raistlin even as the same shadows lengthen over all Ansalon.

Finally, Raistlin draws near his goal of becoming a wizard. But first he must take the Test in the Tower of High Sorcery—or die trying.

THE CHRONICLES TRILOGY
MARGARET WEIS AND TRACY HICKMAN

Fifteen years after publication and with more than three million copies in print, the story of the worldwide best-selling trilogy is as compelling as ever. Dragons have returned to Krynn with a vengeance. An unlikely band of heroes embarks on a perilous quest for the legendary DRAGONLANCE!

DRAGONLANCE is a registered trademark of TSR, Inc.

DRAGONS OF SUMMER FLAME
Margaret Weis and Tracy Hickman

The best-selling conclusion to the stories told in the Chronicles and Legends Trilogies. The War of the Lance is long over. The seasons come and go. The pendulum of the world swings. Now it is summer. A hot, parched summer such as no one on Krynn has ever known before.

Distraught by a grievous loss, the young mage Palin Majere seeks to enter the Abyss in search of his lost uncle, the infamous archmage Raistlin.

The Dark Queen has found new champions. Devoted followers, loyal to the death, the Knights of Takhisis follow the Vision to victory. A dark paladin, Steel Brightblade, rides to attack the High Clerist's Tower, the fortress his father died defending.

On a small island, the mysterious Irda capture an ancient artifact and use it to ensure their own safety. Usha, child of the Irda, arrives in Palanthas claiming that she is Raistlin's daughter.

The summer will be deadly. Perhaps it will be the last summer Ansalon will ever know.

THE CHAOS WAR
Margaret Weis and Don Perrin

This series brings to life the background stories and events of the conflagration known as The Chaos War, as told in the *New York Times* best-selling novel *Dragons of Summer Flame*.

DRAGONLANCE is a registered trademark of TSR. Inc.